DATE DUE		

The Autobiography of
Joseph Stalin

The Autobiography of

JOSEPH STALIN

Also by Richard Lourie

Fiction

Zero Gravity

First Loyalty

Sagittarius in Warsaw

Nonfiction

Hunting the Devil: The Pursuit, Capture, and Confession of the Most Savage Serial Killer in History

Russia Speaks: An Oral History from the Revolution to the Present

Predicting Russia's Future: How 1,000 Years of History Are Shaping the 1990s

Letters to the Future: An Approach to Sinyavsky-Tertz

Selected Translations

Memoirs by Andrei Sakharov

Visions from San Francisco Bay by Czeslaw Milosz

Goodnight! by Abram Tertz (Andrei Sinyavsky)

The Autobiography of JOSEPH STALIN

a novel

RICHARD LOURIE

COUNTERPOINT
WASHINGTON, D.C.

Excerpts from Trotsky's biography of Stalin are from *Stalin: An Appraisal of the Man and his Influence*, by Leon Trotsky (New York: Harper & Brothers, 1946).

Library of Congress Cataloging-in-Publication Data
Lourie, Richard, 1940–
The autobiography of Joseph Stalin : a novel / Richard Lourie.
p. cm.
ISBN 1-58243-004-7 (alk. paper)
1. Stalin, Joseph, 1879–1953—Fiction. 2. Trotsky, Leon, 1879–1940—Assassination—Fiction. I. Title.
PS3562.O833A95 1999
813'.54—dc21 99-11195
CIP

Printed in the United States of America on acid-free paper that meets the American National Standards Institute Z39-48 Standard.

COUNTERPOINT
P.O. Box 65793
Washington, D.C. 20035-5793
Counterpoint is a member of the Perseus Books Group.

10 9 8 7 6 5 4 3 2

To whatever spirit possessed me to write this book,
may it be gone forever now

A bad will is the cause of bad actions, but nothing is the cause of a bad will. For when the will abandons what is above itself and turns to what is lower, it becomes evil—not because that is evil to which it turns, but because the turning itself is wicked.

Saint Augustine
The City of God

The death agony was horrible. He literally choked to death as we watched. At what seemed the very last moment he suddenly opened his eyes and cast a glance over everyone in the room. It was a terrible glance, insane or perhaps angry and full of the fear of death. . . . Then something incomprehensible and awesome happened that to this day I can't forget and don't understand. He suddenly lifted his left hand as though he were pointing to something above and bringing down a curse on us all. The gesture was incomprehensible and full of menace.

Stalin's Death as Described by
His Daughter, Svetlana

So, after perestroika and all that, they published Svetlana's book, *Twenty Letters to a Friend,* and since I'd been in charge of maintenance at Stalin's dacha and knew the Boss pretty well myself, I thought I'd read the book and see what she said about her papa. And when I read the part about the Boss dying, I thought to myself, maybe he was just pointing up at the ceiling. To make a long story short, I used my old connections to get into the dacha and then went up to the crawl space. And what did I find there?—Stalin's own autobiography. First I said to myself maybe it's a forgery, but after I read it, I said, no, only the Boss could've written this one.

Interview with Ivan N.,
Former KGB Maintenance Man

PART

I

1

Leon Trotsky is trying to kill me.

He has every right and reason. By hook or by crook, I defeated him in the power struggle after Lenin's death in '24. I expelled him from the Party. I banished him from Moscow. I exiled him from Russia. I hounded him across Europe and drove him to seek refuge in Mexico earlier this year.

I am destroying his organization, annihilating his followers. In his opinion, I have "betrayed" the Revolution and fouled its honor with unspeakable crimes.

As a communist, it is Trotsky's mission to rescue Soviet Russia from me. He knows he is the only man in the world capable of the task. Hitler could invade Russia and burn Moscow to the ground, but Hitler could never take my place in the Kremlin. But Trotsky could. And believes he should.

The past demands that he kill me. The future demands that he kill me. In a word, history demands that he kill me. And history is our element, our god.

But exactly how will Leon Trotsky try to kill me? That's the question. He'd be a fool to pin his hopes on a single method. As the former leader of the Red Army, Trotsky knows that victory in combat results from using all possible means at the proper time and in the proper sequence—artillery, cavalry, infantry. So, to get at me, he'll do anything and everything—infiltrate the secret police, subvert the army, rile up the working class, corrupt my guards, enlist my cooks and food tasters, my doctors and dentists. And I would be twice a fool if I did not operate from the assumption that Trotsky will strike at me in all these different ways.

But now Trotsky has hit upon yet another way to destroy me and, though he may not have fully realized it yet himself, it is the surest way of all. Trotsky is writing my biography.

Yes, the Russians attribute great significance to literature, even exiling and executing writers, but isn't this a bit much, the great Stalin afraid of a book? No, it is not a bit much at all.

Though he's barely begun work, it's already clear that Trotsky's book about me will be both character assassination and indictment. I can be a touchy man, but I am able to bear his attacks on my person. And nearly all the crimes he will accuse me of are already a matter of public record—that I do not fear. In fact, certain crimes must be known if they are to have their proper effect, though I have always taken pains to shroud my own responsibility in ambiguity. It wasn't Stalin's fault, the secret police were too zealous, that sort of thing.

But there are also crimes that must remain forever unknown. In my case there is one crime that must remain forever unknown. Instinctively, Trotsky, in the writing of my biography, has to be searching for *that,* the one crime whose revelation would destroy the mystique of authority by which I rule. After all, what is authority but a trance of obedience? Certainly, power does not reside in physical strength. I am as easy to kill as anyone else. A touch under five feet four, I may be even easier than most. One strong man could throttle me in the night. One cook could slip enough poison into my stew to stop my heart. Why hasn't that happened yet? Because no word has yet been spoken to break the spell.

Since the very logic of his being and situation compel Trotsky to kill me, every time he puts pen to paper he is searching for the words that can break that spell and bring me down.

So, even though the year '37 has brought immense problems—orchestrating the terror, running the country, dealing with the threat of Adolf Hitler—nothing in all the world is of greater concern to me than what Leon Trotsky is writing about me.

Through comrades loyal to my person, I regularly read snippets of Trotsky's biography of me, entitled with appropriate simplicity: STALIN.

One of his housekeepers in Mexico, a peasant woman urbanized, proletarianized, and radicalized by coming to the city, is as good at microfilming as at dusting. I can just see Trotsky looking up from his desk as she comes in to empty the wastebaskets. He doesn't really see her. She's not important, she's not attractive. Maybe he smiles, maybe he nods, but then he goes right back to his writing. Once again, Trotsky is making the same fatal mistake he made at our first meeting thirty years ago in London in 1907 when, done talking with Lenin, he brushed right by me as if I were no more than a coatrack.

And he's still doing it. Because I can see into that room in Mexico City through the eyes of that woman. I am still in the room with him and he still doesn't see me.

My suspicions of hostile intent quickly prove well founded. No sooner does Trotsky claim that he will be "objective" and overlook no fact "redounding" to the hero of his book than he begins attacking that hero. Great leaders are masters of the "living word," says Trotsky, who puts Lenin and Hitler in that category. But Stalin?

"In this respect Stalin represents a phenomenon utterly exceptional. He is neither a thinker, a writer, nor an orator."

When Trotsky says Stalin is no thinker, what he really means is that Trotsky is by far the more brilliant. No matter what they say, egotists are always talking about themselves.

Now if thinking means comparing what one German philosopher said about another German philosopher and coming up with your own independent opinion, then I concede the point, Trotsky is the better thinker. But if thinking means using your mind to get what you want, then Stalin is a better thinker than Trotsky. We both wanted the same thing, the only thing worth wanting in Russia—the Kremlin. I've got it and Trotsky's raising rabbits in Mexico City.

And when Trotsky claims that Stalin is no orator, he is really only wondering how it could possibly have happened that he, famed as a great speaker, could have been hurled so far from Russia that his voice is not even a whisper here.

In the first place, he was not that great a speaker. I admit that during the Revolution and Civil War he was able to stir workers to revolt and soldiers to attack. But there were many people with that gift and the workers were ready to rise, the soldiers to fight. Otherwise there would have been no revolution. As a Marxist, Trotsky knows that.

And even if the workers and soldiers were ready for revolution, there would have been no successful revolution if the Communist Party had not been prepared to lead it, as demonstrated by the failure of previous revolts and revolutions. The critical element was the Communist Party, and the true test of any speaker was his ability to influence that critical element.

And Trotsky was not a great success with the comrades.

He had the too-perfect Russian of a Jew and spoke for hours on end, spraying saliva when excited, wagging his index finger when instructing. And after four hours of brilliant oratory, what would Trotsky do? He'd walk off the stage and disappear. Like an angel from heaven who delivers a message and then is gone. Angels don't stay and hang around with the people, ask after their parents' health, share a smoke.

The comrades didn't like that. The comrades don't believe in angels.

Trotsky has the intellectual's wit and irony but he couldn't joke. And the boys always like a little joking.

In the days when it was not yet so vital to win my favor, many of the comrades told me they much preferred my ability to sum things up in a few sharp words that stuck in your mind. Trotsky made speeches; I made allies.

And so then, who was the "living word" with?

The "living word" was with Stalin.

And Trotsky is also wrong about being a more important writer than me.

As a communist, Trotsky knows that the significance of literature is determined exclusively by how well it serves the cause. His own writing must be of no significance because, so far at least, his own cause is lost. But the fact that Trotsky is alone in exile surrounded by a mere handful of devoted followers does not reassure me in the least. Lenin too was alone in exile surrounded by a mere handful of devoted followers and he overturned all Russia.

Impact is what counts. And, by that standard, all of Trotsky's tomes are dwarfed by four lines of poetry I wrote in my youth:

> Know this, he who fell to earth like ashes,
> and was so very long oppressed,
> will rise higher than great mountains
> on the wings of shining hope.

These lines capture the spirit of that Georgian youth who would rise from poverty and obscurity to rule all Russia. The power of that young man's aspiration! Who in all the world had ever dared hope that much? It would even be no exaggeration for scholars to say that in his youth Stalin was a "Poet of Hope."

Certainly no other poem, nothing by Homer, Shakespeare, Pushkin, has ever played a role in human events like those four lines. At one of the great low points of my life, when I was lost in doubt and despair, those lines gave me the heart to commit the one crime that Trotsky must never live to uncover.

2

So, in my youth I wrote poetry.

Then, seeking adventure, I turned to crime.

Finally, I became a revolutionary because that alone united poetry and crime.

That's the dialectic of my life. The rest is just detail. But Trotsky uses those details as bullets against me in his attempt at character assassination. More important, he sifts through them searching for clues to my crimes in my character. And, who knows, some obscure fact of my childhood could ultimately lead him to *that*.

Like any detective, Trotsky asks the usual questions: Name? Date of birth? Place of birth?

But you don't have to be a detective to find out that I was born Joseph Dzhugashvili on December 21, 1879, in the part of the Tsar's empire known as Georgia, in the town of Gori, high in the Caucasus Mountains, which Trotsky calls a "gigantic ethnographic museum" of Turkish, Armenian, and Persian culture. But what Trotsky seems not to have found out is the old Persian superstition that male children born on December 21, the day of the longest night, should be killed at birth; when I learned of this at the age of eight or nine, it sent a shiver of terror and pleasure right through me. A sign.

Trotsky proceeds to peel off the layers of disguise that he says I have built up over the years—Stalin pretends to be a Russian though he is really a Georgian. But, no, he is not even really a Georgian!

Though Trotsky claims to be wary of straying "too far afield into the unprofitable region of national metaphysics," he in fact devotes whole paragraphs to the question of the Georgian character: "trusting, impressionable, quick-tempered . . . ," a people marked by "gaiety, sociability, and forthrightness. . . ." Therefore, I cannot be a Georgian.

Trotsky quotes various "authorities" to prove that either my mother or my father was an Ossete, that is, of a people who are "coarse, uncouth." This is the same legend to which the poet Mandelstam, another Jew with no sense of proportion, referred in his lines about me that, when he recited them in a small circle of trusted friends, resulted in his arrest:

> And every killing is a treat
> For the broad-chested Ossete.

But really, as far as Trotsky is concerned, all these ethnic niceties are beside the point. What he wants to prove is that I am an "Asiatic," a "Genghis Khan." He spells it out: "The frequent bloody raids into the Caucasus by Genghis Khan and Tamerlane . . . left their traces . . . on the character of Stalin."

In Russia even ancient history can be dangerous. It is true that for us growing up in the Caucasus, Genghis Khan was hardly ancient history. Many valleys still contained tall, beautiful stone towers built for people to take shelter in, to fight from, and, on top, to send signals with bonfires warning others of invasions by the Golden Horde. Genghis Khan has a unique distinction—he is the only invader ever to conquer Russia, proof that Russia, the great prize that eluded Napoleon, could be had by someone coming out of the dust of Asia. Though Genghis Khan was more tolerant than the Romans when it came to local religions, to a pince-nezed, goateed "European" intellectual like Trotsky, Genghis Khan is above all a symbol of utter ruthlessness. Genghis Khan was capable of anything. Stalin is like Genghis Khan. Therefore Stalin is capable of anything, even *that.* Though what "*that*" means, Trotsky still has no clue.

Trotsky goes on to say of Stalin: "Even in his physical type he hardly represents a happy example of his people, who are known to be the handsomest in the Caucasus." I find that in bad taste. Trotsky takes an entirely unhealthy pleasure in describing my body—the traces of smallpox, the withering of my left arm, and the two webbed toes on the left foot. Speaking of my numerous arrests by the Tsarist police, he writes: "In the enumeration of Stalin's distinctive marks by Tsarist gendarmes, a withered arm was not listed, but the adhering toes were recorded once, in 1903."

The withered arm was from one terrible illness, blood poisoning. I lay in bed listening to my heart, excited by the poison, pumping poison faster and faster through my system. By breathing slowly and counting backward, I tried to slow my heart down, but nothing helped. Poison could even turn your own heart into your enemy.

As I lay there in my sweaty bed, I could smell onions being fried. I wanted to tell my mother that the smell was making me feel worse but I couldn't make my lips form words, even when she was right beside my bed. Seeing me try to speak, she fell to her knees, kissed the cross around her neck, and prayed over me: "Please, God, spare my only son, Joseph, whom I named after the earthly father of Your only Son, and I will give my son to Your church as a priest to praise Your Holy Name."

My mother and I were close, if only because my father was rarely home. I played alone and spent a lot of time looking at the mountains. As soon as I stepped out my front door I could see those mountains, dark and mighty, flanking the town on every side. On the slope of one mountain was a ruined castle. I couldn't wait until I was big enough and strong enough to climb up to where the great lord had once lived. I would make up stories about what would happen when I reached the castle, most of them based on the folktales my mother taught me. I had a head full of legends.

Some days I forgot the mountains and the castle and only watched for mountain eagles soaring with their supreme confidence above the mountains, higher than the most high.

I would come out in the morning with a piece of flat bread and some tea. Smelling of soap and steam, my mother would stop doing the laundry she took in to make ends meet, come out onto the porch, and put her hands on my shoulders. I could tell just by the way she touched me what she was feeling. If she was remembering her three children who had been born before me and all died, her fingers would tighten on my shoulders. Or if she was being proud of me and wanting me to think of God who made the sky and mountains, she'd hold me firmly. But if she was just there for the morning air, her hands would rest as easily on me as they would on the porch rail.

Sometimes she'd sing. Not loudly, just to me, but with voice.

Her fingers always tightened when she heard the sound of the hoofbeats. We lived at Number 10 Cathedral Street in the part of town known as the Russian Quarter because of the Tsarist troops garrisoned there. I would run from her to watch them thunder by on their horses, a blur of boots, swords, mustaches.

They had the power to kill anyone the Tsar wanted killed. The Tsar lived in a great castle called the Kremlin. But castles can be ruined—as I saw every day, stepping from my front door into the cool mountain air.

After watching the last soldier pass, I'd run back to the house. My mother would be distant, offended. I'd sweep the floor so she would love me again.

But these childhood memories have been spoiled for me. Now, over the mountains appears the gigantic face of Trotsky peering down at me through a magnifying glass, snooping for hints of the murderer-to-be.

But I am glad to see Trotsky overlook one important clue. Perhaps the most important clue to my childhood and character, and the one pertaining most directly to *that.* Speaking of our family, in which I was both the last and only child, he says: "The first three children died in infancy." Then he goes on to something else without even pausing to wonder what effect that might have had on a child. Trotsky lacks insight, just as he lacks humor and poetry, because he is too far from his own childhood, if he ever even really had one and was not born a small adult.

But a child who hears his mother lament about her three children dead in infancy has to think certain thoughts. He says to himself—if all three had lived I would be the fourth child, barely noticed, neglected. And if two had lived I would be the third child who sometimes does well but never goes far. And if even one had lived, I would forever be the little brother, but since they all died I am the one and only. Another sign.

Sometimes my mother lamented for her dead children in a singsong voice as if she were just talking to herself. But other times she'd suddenly remember what she was really singsonging about and begin sobbing, her face contorted by suffering and sorrow. Maybe it was the clownish distortions of her face, the tearful hiccups, but, though one slap taught me to hide it, the sight and sound of grief has, ever since childhood, always made me laugh.

But I had grief of my own and at that I could never laugh. I was six the first time that it happened. My mother had fed me and put me to bed, making the sign of the cross over me. I did not even have the strength to beg for a story, I was so tired from a day of running the slopes and building dams in streams.

I was in a sleep deeper than dreams when the devil's hands reached inside my soul and yanked me awake so I could see his bloodshot eyes and smell his reek of wine and leather. My father was home.

My mother was in the doorway on her knees, weeping.

"Let's see your fat little face, the face I slave to feed," he said.

His hands under my armpits, he was holding me up in the air. I hung there limply, afraid he would bite my face. But he only hurled me against the wall like a cat.

The next thing I knew it was light and my mother was wiping my face with a damp cloth. And *he* was gone.

A shoemaker, poor and bitter, my father did not just vent his rage with life on me, no. He hated me in particular. He hated me because he knew I would escape his fate, that I would be better. Not only that, I already was better and he knew it and he hated that. I was singled out—by the webbed toes and by the death of his three children who preceded me. In his drunken rages, he blamed me for those deaths. And I could never think him completely wrong.

Trotsky quotes the reminiscences of one of my childhood friends who says that the beatings Stalin's father gave him drove "out of his heart the love of God and people. . . . Undeserved, frightful beatings made the boy as grim and heartless as his father."

That's not so. My father wanted to beat the superiority out of me so that I would be a failure like him, a broken, angry man. But he failed at that as well.

And it was not my father who drove the love of God and people from my heart. That, step by step, I did myself.

But the fact that Trotsky does not understand this is not important. What is important is the picture he is assembling of me in his own mind—a deformed Asiatic monster, a Genghis Khan, a son beaten mercilessly by his father, a man without love in his heart for God or people. My childhood becomes his assumption. And that assumption closes off no possibilities. In fact, it points him in exactly the right direction.

3

As I suppose is true of many people, sometimes when I wake up in the morning there's a moment when I don't know where I am. Or even who.

Then I remember: I am in the Kremlin. I am Stalin.

But who was I in that interval between waking and remembering?

Some foreign commentators have remarked that I will at times refer to myself in the third person as Stalin and this they consider a symptom of megalomania. A natural mistake on their part. They just can't imagine what it's like to actually "be" Stalin. It's not the same as being anybody else.

But I am not and was not always Stalin. Once I was simply Joseph Dzhugashvili, nicknamed Soso as a boy and Koba as a youth. And of course, since I was constantly sought by the Tsar's police, I had any number of aliases. Of all of them, I chose to become "Stalin." Stalin is a destination, an achievement, and yet in a way also something finished and ready that was always waiting for me.

And still waits. If Stalin is the person who avenges every insult and enemy, I can never truly be Stalin as long as Trotsky is alive. Like everyone else, I fail my best self.

But I can only give a few seconds to the riddle of who I was between waking and remembering.

Then I get right on my feet and do my morning calisthenics unless my little daughter, Svetlana, who thinks her daddy works too hard, has snuck into my room and stolen my alarm clock and it's later than I thought. Still, I do try never to miss my calisthenics. They clear the blood and tone the nerves.

Stripped to the waist, I splash my face and body with cold water after I shave. I don't read at breakfast and I don't like to talk first thing in the morning. I usually have some bouillon or a light meat dish, tea, and a glass of milk, preferably goat's milk, which in Georgia is believed to promote longevity, a subject in which I have more than a passing interest.

Then I have my first cigarette or pipe, depending on how I feel; sometimes I crumble a Herzegovina flor cigarette into a pipe, sometimes I smoke it straight. The first smoke of the day is important for setting your mood. If a pipe draws hard or leaves bitter juices in the bowl, if a cigarette is harsh and sears your windpipe, it can get you started wrong.

To some this might seem egotistical absorption in my own minutiae, which it would be if those minutiae did not affect so many other people. After a good smoke, if I am brought a list of Enemies of the People scheduled for execution and spot a familiar name, I might easily write, in my own hand, that the person in question is to be sent to the camps, whereas if a bad pipe has soured my mood, I'll sign the list without even looking.

Those and other papers are brought by Poskryobyshev, the only man allowed to enter my office unannounced. Chances are that he will be forgotten by history and yet in some ways he is a remarkable man—after all he has my complete trust, a rare achievement. He even has blanks signed with my name.

Bald and dumpy, he looks terrible in a military tunic. But it is his characteristics that matter, the soul of the man. He is like a perfect waiter who has refilled your glass before your thirst has even surfaced. You can have a conversation with someone in his presence and feel you are alone. By nature loyal as a dog, he seems to have no capacity for resentment, though in time that too will have to be tested. But most important is that he is completely satisfied with his position in life. He could imagine nothing more perfect than what he does and would not jeopardize it for anything in the world. In choosing him, I chose well. Personnel is everything.

This morning, Poskryobyshev has set three files on my desk: the list of those sentenced to the Highest Measure of Punishment; a specially prepared information bulletin marked World and Domestic Situation, April 2, 1937; and a report on Trotsky's latest activities, his writings included.

Breakfast was good and the pipe drew well. So, on the list of those to be executed, next to the name of Yuri Grishin, who always knew the latest jokes, I write: "Ten years."

This I do as an allusion to a joke:

A new prisoner comes into a cell and is asked, What sentence did they give you?

Fifteen years, he says.

For what? they ask.

For nothing! he says.

Couldn't be, they say, for nothing they give ten.

I hope Grishin will appreciate the allusion, along with being spared his life.

I make sure I hear the latest jokes because I know how important they are in gauging the national mood. And I get nervous when suddenly, as sometimes happens, there are no new jokes. In Russia jokes are the only rebellions.

Still, it's no joking matter to see the names of so many men I was once close to on the list of Trotskyite traitors. I am filled with disappointment. If they were incapable of loyalty, they should at least have been intelligent enough to know the future lay with me. The thought sours my mood and I am tempted to scratch out the change of sentence in the margin, but, since it is written, let it stand. I hand the list to Poskryobyshev in such a way as to dismiss him at the same time. Then he's gone as if he'd never been here, another of his attractive features.

Whether I look east or west from the Kremlin, I see only one thing on the horizon—war. There is no question that Trotsky sees the same from Mexico. There is no question that Trotsky realizes that his chances of destroying me will increase dramatically in the event of war. Trotsky knows that in Russia wars have a way of leading to the downfall of rulers—that's what happened to Tsar Nickie of late memory. And so there can be no question that war will give Trotsky yet another opportunity to destroy me. Trotsky and I are at war, and war will be the weapon of that war.

But which war? Who with? The war in Spain has proved a disappointment. At first, I operated on the principle, If there's going to be a war, let it be as far from here as possible. I hoped Spain would be the next Balkans, that the situation there would flare up into a world war; the imperialists, fascists, and always hard-to-control foreign communists would all just devour each other and that'd be that.

That's not how it turned out. Hitler and Mussolini helped Franco plenty but the Americans, English, and French didn't lift a finger to aid the Republicans. It became fashionable for the Western intelligentsia to go fight in Spain—Hemingway went, that sort—but it never became fashionable for their governments. Spain would be a double loss—not only would there be no great war far from Russia but the Fascists will win the day.

I had to get something out of it. So I've turned the Spanish Civil War into a little civil war of my own. Needless to say, the best and bravest of the Trotskyites abroad flocked to Spain to fight. And that must be viewed as a bit of luck—your enemies willfully congregating in a place where it will be relatively easy to dispose of them. In the midst of a war with bullets flying everywhere, God only knows what can happen.

So I can confidently predict that the winners in Spain's double civil war will be—Franco and Stalin.

In his effort to defeat me, Trotsky will have to look elsewhere for partners. The capitalists are in a depression and not in the mood to fight another war with people whose names they can't even pronounce. So who does that leave?

The Second Moscow Trial proved beyond any shadow of a doubt that Trotsky has struck a formal alliance with Hitler and the Emperor of Japan. Trotsky had agreed to work with these monsters for the military defeat of the USSR and, after its defeat, to cede the Ukraine to Hitler. In addition, specific cases of sabotage toward achieving those greater aims were documented and all the needed confessions were obtained.

Nevertheless, there were some problems. It was essential to the prosecution that one of the main defendants had held a secret meeting with Trotsky in Oslo in December 1935. But two days after the trial started, the Norwegian press reported that no civilian aircraft had landed in Oslo's Kjeller Airfield at any time in the month of December. Sloppy work. And in time it will cost the current head of the secret police, Yagoda, his job. Though I have other and better reasons for ridding myself of him.

Otherwise, the Second Moscow Trial was a bit dull. There were no major figures in the dock, no memorable lines as there'd been in the first trial, in which Lenin's comrade-in-arms Zinoviev had confessed in a statement that managed to be both concise and slobbering: "My defective Bolshevism became transformed into anti-Bolshevism and through Trotskyism I arrived at fascism."

And Zinoviev's death was hilarious. When he was being led out to the execution cellars, Zinoviev had dragged his feet and moaned, his eyes wild with fear. At one point he fell to his knees, embraced a guard's boot, and cried: "For the love of God, will you please call Stalin!" Then, seeing all hope was lost, the old Bolshevik began praying: "Hear, O Israel, the Lord our God, the Lord is One." Then, his terror at its zenith, Zinoviev even switched to Hebrew: "*Shema Yisrael Adonai Eluhenu Adonai Ehud.*" When I was told this story at a banquet by the head of the guards I laughed so hard my ribs hurt. Again, I said, tell it again. From the start to the *Shema.* Priceless.

Still, on the whole, the Second Moscow Trial must be counted a success. All the defendants were found guilty as charged and sentenced to death. Trotsky was sentenced to death in absentia. His two sons were also implicated in his treacheries, both Lyova, the son who runs his affairs in Paris, and the son he left behind in the USSR who had attempted a mass poisoning of factory workers. As a father myself, I cannot understand how Trotsky could possibly leave a son behind in Stalin's Russia.

Needless to say, Trotsky was incensed at being sentenced to death in absentia, which has for the time being at least diverted him from any further research into my life. He's been too busy convoking an international commission headed by an American professor of philosophy by the name of John Dewey to look into the question of his guilt. Trotsky has also released a public statement:

> I am ready to appear before a public and impartial Commission of Inquiry with documents, facts, testimonies . . . and to disclose the truth to the very end. I declare: If this Commission decides that I am guilty in the slightest degree of the crimes that Stalin imputes to me, I pledge in advance to place myself voluntarily in the hands of Stalin's executioners. . . . But, if the Commission establishes . . . that the Moscow trials are a conscious and premeditated frame-up, I will not ask my accusers to place themselves voluntarily before a firing squad. No, the eternal disgrace in the memory of the human generations will be sufficient for them! Do the accusers in the Kremlin hear me? I throw my defiance in their faces, and I await their reply!

We hear you. And we're laughing out loud. Nineteenth-century Russian provincial theater at its worst—"I will deliver myself voluntarily into the hands. . . . Eternal disgrace!"

But Trotsky's inhuman purity won't play well with the public, even over there. The intelligentsia in the West is used to a balanced, moderate point of view, and so will think that no one is as evil as Trotsky paints Stalin.

No less a person than George Bernard Shaw has written to the Secretary of the British Committee for the Defence of Leon Trotsky: "The strength of Trotsky's case was the incredibility of the accusations against him. . . . But Trotsky spoils it all by making the same sort of attacks on Stalin. Now I have spent nearly three hours in Stalin's presence and observed him with a keen curiosity, and I find it just as hard to believe that he is a vulgar gangster as that Trotsky is an assassin."

Of course, there's a terrible flaw in the logic of people like Shaw. They see that the accusations made against Trotsky are wild and grotesque. Therefore, they can't possibly be true. So far, correct. Then they see that the accusations made by Trotsky against Stalin are also wild and grotesque. Logic dictates that Trotsky's accusations against Stalin must also be way off the mark. No longer correct. What I have already done and what I am now doing far exceeds anything their imagination's capable of. They just don't have the range.

So I am pleased that the Second Moscow Trial has forced Trotsky into spasms of theatrical rhetoric and wasted days of self-defense. But I can't rest easy. I can't help but think, Could the very wildness of my accusations have caused Trotsky's mind to start moving toward the wildest accusation of them all?

4

God was the Tsar of the Universe who ruled from the Kremlin of Heaven.

As a boy, I would look up from the mountains to the million stars and sometimes for a second I could even feel God squinting back down at me. As if to say, What's that down there?

I did not believe God was all-merciful and neither did the priests, nor anyone else for that matter except a few old ladies. The sweetness in the priests' voices when they talked about God the All-Merciful could not have been more synthetic.

But I believed in God the Almighty. Especially during lightning storms and earthquakes. That God was stern and wrathful and had His own ways, His own justice. He alone was free. All the people on earth were His serfs. But God had His representatives on earth—the Tsar, the little father, and the big father, your own.

I didn't need the synthetic sweetness of the priests to know that God was not all-merciful—no mercy was reaching me. I was older now and heavier. It was not so easy for my father to hurl me against the wall like a pesky cat and so he had taken to beating me with fists and belts.

I looked like my father. The red-black hair, the complexion both swarthy and ruddy. He was of medium height, wiry, dangerously strong. Black mustache and beard, dark bloodshot eyes. He smelled of leather and cheap tobacco.

One day he was sitting on the front steps smoking and he patted the space beside him for me to come over and sit down. I was always watchful of his moods but didn't think there was anything to fear this time.

"It would be wrong," he said, "if you never heard anything about your great-grandfather Zaza. He was a serf, like everybody else after the Russians took over. One day there was some new ruling that was of course good for the Russians and nothing but another insult to us. So your great-grandfather Zaza led a revolt. For miles around everybody rose up in rebellion. Throats were cut, Joseph," he said, lifting his chin and drawing a finger across his own throat. "But the Russians never caught him. Zaza gave them the dodge."

Then I understood why he hated me. Because the blood of Zaza had only passed through him to me. He had a miserable life with a weak-wombed churchy woman who had given him three dead sons before delivering me. He could not have helped hating me; his outbursts of violence were only natural. In his position, I am sure anyone would have done the same.

In fact, he had another good reason for hating me. Not only did I act superior, I *was* superior. I was outstanding as a boy. The best swimmer, the best wrestler, the best student. People looked smilingly on me the way they always do when they think a boy is destined to go places. My father saw that. No one had ever looked at him that way as a child because they could see that he wasn't going anywhere and would end up as the kind of miserable drunken cobbler who beats his wife and son.

Still, I am grateful to my father because he taught me that people hate it when you flaunt your superiority. That he knocked out of me, once and for all. Nothing could be more valuable. Trotsky should have had a father like that.

When I was five, my father left home to live and work in Tiflis at the Adelkhanov shoe factory on Erevan Square, the same square where many years later I would stage the most successful bank robbery in Russian history. My father would come home from time to time—to rest, to drink, to beat us—but mostly I spent those years with my mother, who was always singing. Sometimes she would invite me to sing along. I sang in the choir as long as I was in school.

When I had fallen ill, my mother had prayed over me, making her deal with God. God kept His half of the bargain. And my mother did everything in her power to keep her half. She was constantly lecturing me on the greatness of the priesthood, that there was nothing higher than to serve the Lord. But I had Zaza's blood in my veins and deep down I did not want to serve any lord.

Still, I did not argue when she insisted I attend the Gori Theological Elementary School, which could lead on to the Tiflis Theological Seminary.

Trotsky thinks in Marxist categories and, as a Jew, he has no feel for the allure of the priesthood.

"The dream itself," says Trotsky, "to see her son in priestly robes, indicates how little the family . . . was permeated with the 'proletarian spirit.' A better future was conceived, not in consequence of the class struggle but as the result of breaking with one's own class."

Trotsky is always accusing me of falsifying history, but here that's exactly what he's demanding I do. Nobody's family was imbued with a "proletarian spirit" in those days. Not mine, not Trotsky's, whose own father engaged in the un-Jewish profession of farmer and exploited the labor of hired hands.

What does he want—some socialist realist novel by Gorky with the mother sending her son off to defend the working class against the capitalists and the bourgeoisie?

That's not how it was. She wanted me to be a priest and would do anything to make that dream come true, even if it meant working her fingers to the bone sewing and sweeping at the Gori Theological

Elementary School, where she enrolled me on September 1, 1888, four months shy of my ninth birthday.

Trotsky's problem is that he was always too much of a communist. He seems to have been militantly atheistic from birth. But the truth is that the question of God never really interested him. He was too interested in other things—politics, literature, himself.

For me the question of God was very real and very important. I thought of God often. I used to make up conundrums about God—Could He create a stone that was too heavy for He Himself to lift? If there was a God, why did He let my father beat my face?

And I struggled with those questions mightily. These are the heaviest of weights, the tons of God, and you gain strength every time you try to budge them.

Trotsky never deigned to. He slighted God as well as Stalin.

* * *

Now, like a pervert, Trotsky is prowling the schoolyard looking for me among the mass of other black-haired boys.

School is always the same, school is eternal. There is always the fat boy, the smart boy, the bad boy.

In school there are always groups. A few boys go their own way, but usually only after failing to be taken into one group or another. Children will make it clear if they want you and if they don't.

There can be no group without a leader. A group may begin to form without one but in the end can only take shape around a leader.

At that age, when everything you do is sincere and instinctive, I knew I had to be the leader. Otherwise the shame would have been too great.

When one boy sees another, the first thing he thinks is, Can I take him in a fight?

How you act and talk is important, but sooner or later the point is proved with fists.

One of the boys in the neighborhood who had the same nickname as me, Soso, challenged me when our group was just forming. I could tell just by the way the talk started that he wasn't going to back down. And when the talk is like that, the other boys come running.

I sized him up again. He was a strong kid. By then I had already suffered from smallpox and blood poisoning. If I wasn't careful, I could start to doubt my own strength.

Then the shoving started, the shouting. All the boys crowded around, but making sure to give us room to fight. They were peering for any sign of weakness—every blink, every gulp.

There was plenty of noise. Some cheered for me, some cheered for him, some cheered for the sake of cheering.

Then the shoving stopped and the first punch was thrown. The first few punches and counterpunches mean a lot, but they don't mean everything. Even if you lose the exchange and the crowd is now cheering for your opponent, you can still win if you don't lose heart and presence of mind.

I was glad to lose the first flurry. It got my anger up and hot and that always helps. And in the next exchange my punches were sharp and fast, and his punches didn't slow me down. Now the crowd was cheering for me.

They were cheering for us by last name since we had the same nickname, though of course there were a couple of idiots shouting, "Come on, Soso," but they were really just there for the fight.

The third exchange was more even. By some unspoken agreement, we had now switched from body blows to face punches. The boys loved it: blood could be drawn, a tooth knocked out, even an eye.

I remember how the black hair over the other Soso's forehead bobbed up and down. I looked right into his eyes, answering their determination with mine. You can lose a fight with your eyes before you lose it with your fists.

The last exchange was quick. I faked a left to his face and with a right to the solar plexus I knocked Soso to the ground, so he was out of breath for a second.

But he was going to come back quickly, I saw. I circled around in back of him so that it looked like I was only pacing while waiting for him to get up.

Usually, how you're fighting—clean or dirty—has to be declared right from the start. But there is no law against switching if that's what you want and if you're willing to pay the price.

The other Soso was on one knee and dusting himself off when I rabbit-punched him at the back of his neck under the ear. He went down, shocked and dazed by the treachery. I kicked his head, aiming for the corner of his eye with the tip of my shoe. I didn't stop kicking the first time he shouted, "I give up!" It wasn't loud enough for everyone to hear.

Then I stood back up and faced the crowd. Some of them were booing but their voices faded when my eyes fell on them. There were a few more catcalls but no one stepped forward.

The other Soso looked up and in that moment everything was clear between us. He would submit.

I looked from him back out to the boys to see if they had seen. They had.

If the British are right about the playing fields of Eton, then the fate of a dozen nations was decided that day.

5

I WAS THE BEST NOT ONLY IN THE SCHOOLYARD BUT IN THE schoolroom as well.

This irritates Trotsky no end. He quotes a classmate of mine: "During the first years, in the preparatory grades, Joseph studied superbly, and with time . . . he became one of the best pupils." Then Trotsky goes on to say: "The circumspect expression 'one of the best' indicates too obviously that Joseph was not the best, was not superior to the entire class, was not an extraordinary pupil. Identical in nature are the recollections of another schoolmate, who says Joseph 'was one of the most . . . gifted.' In other words, not the most gifted."

No doubt Leon Trotsky, or Leon Bronstein as he was known then, was the best, most extraordinary, and most gifted pupil in his school. Even this late in the game it's important for Trotsky to prove that he was a better student than Stalin! But this is all to the good. The more Trotsky's blinded by his own vanity, the less he'll see of the real Stalin.

Whether Trotsky likes it or not, the facts are on record. I received straight A's in all my years at Gori Theological Elementary and graduated at the head of my class.

I have a phenomenal memory. Throughout my life people have commented on it. I can memorize instantly. That wasn't a skill shared by our neighbors, the Charkviani brothers, who couldn't learn anything unless they shouted it out loud. They'd go outside their house and holler out the day's readings. I'd stand by our door and listen; when they were done I'd be ready for tomorrow's lesson. But one time they misread something and when I was called on the next day it was one of the rare occasions when I gave the wrong answer. I could have killed them.

Trotsky quotes several of my teachers and classmates as to my "phenomenal" memory, but feels compelled to add: "As a matter of fact, Stalin's memory—at least, his memory for theories—is quite mediocre." Isn't there even a whiff of heresy here, since for Marxists there is only one theory that needs remembering?

"He was always poring over a book," says one classmate. True. I was and remain a great reader.

Three books influenced me most: a novel, a history book, and a work of science. In that order. And that order has a certain logic of its own.

The novel was called *The Parricide.* The hero, Koba, is an outlaw Georgian who revolts against the Russians and avenges the wrongs done to his people. Koba is a swordsman, a dead shot, dashing, tragic, brave; that was something to be, not a priest, not a cobbler.

I made all the boys call me "Koba," and they were all smart enough to do it. Besides, they had all read the book too and liked the idea of having their own Koba, and who else could it be but me? I was good at reading books but even better at reading the boys: The type who wants to follow, glad not to have to think of what to do, glad to leave that up to me. The type who wants my friendship and protection. The type I could bully into anything. The type who loves praise. And the type who bears me secret hatred, thinking himself better.

But just seeing who each one is isn't enough. You also have to learn how to play on them and to play them off against each other. You must experiment with combinations, see what happens. But in this sort of thing science can only hone an instinct you've either got or you don't. It's a gift.

I was always practical. And my idea of reading was, What good is a book if it can't help you in life? And so it wasn't long before I put the inspiration I got from the novel about Koba to the test. In 1890, two years after I entered school, Russian was made the official language of instruction and Georgian was given two hours a week as a foreign language. That hurt our pride. Of course we were all touchy patriots, as red-blooded boys always are, especially if it's an excuse to cause trouble.

So, one day after school, I told a couple of the boys to round up the others. Some are good at rounding up, but there's also the sort you send out and they get involved in something else and never come back. The boys liked it that I always picked right. A leader has to keep earning his slot.

When they were all rounded up, I told them: "Tomorrow at lunch, we all stand up and start shouting—Georgian is our language, Georgian is our language. First we shout it in Georgian, then in Russian."

I told them I'd go first and made each of them agree in front of the others to jump up after me.

The next day when we sat down at the dark brown benches, I could feel all their eyes on me. I had maybe ten seconds. Monks were scurrying around, slapping boys for misbehavior. The walls suddenly seemed especially thick. Even the air felt heavy, pinning me to my bench.

It was one of those very clear moments. With my will I whipped myself to my feet, shouting with excitement and hatred: "Georgian is our language!"

Some of the boys were faster to their feet than others, but it wasn't long before they were all up and shouting. The first tin mug went flying through the air.

I was punished but not expelled.

Koba also inspired me in my war with my father. No sooner had I begun to excel in school and prove a natural leader than he decided I must follow in his footsteps as a cobbler.

Perhaps he was affected by the rumors that I was not in fact his son but that my mother had been up to no good with a priest or a prince, depending on who you listened to. Three times he had failed to father a son who lived, and so she went looking elsewhere.

I don't buy it. She wasn't that kind. The blood of Zaza Dzhugashvili flows in my veins. That son of a bitch was my father.

So he dragged me off with him to Tiflis to work alongside him in the Adelkhanov shoe factory.

That was my first time in the capital or any big city. And what a city Tiflis was! Palaces, cathedrals, stores, banks—including the main one that I was later to rob—camels, street magicians, women of fashion, booksellers, parrots, dervishes from Turkey, Armenian merchants, sacks of pistachio nuts, honey, halvah.

And I saw who my father was to the other men at work. Nobody special. A few other losers liked him. Some were afraid of his temper—and a drunken cobbler always has plenty of sharp tools at hand in the event of an altercation. But most of them grinned at him, a grin of toleration and contempt.

He was mostly sober then and, when sober, he was a good worker. Though I resented it at the time, he did instill good work habits in me.

And so I learned a little bit about the shoe business: the smell of glue and leather, the rattle of the stitching machines, the dizziness that comes from breathing factory fumes all day. It was valuable experience—it gave me a taste of working-class life. But I was a quick study; after a couple of weeks I knew I'd rather die than do that kind of work.

Zaza would never be a cobbler, Koba would never be a cobbler, and neither would I. I knew that if I did not rise against my father's will, I would never return to school, would never have the life that was supposed to be mine.

The simplest solution would be if my father just died. The problem would disappear along with him. I had wished him dead in the past but never as I wished it now. Now he was not just going to beat me with his knuckles, now he was going to steal my life.

I prayed: God, please let my father be run over by horses, let him fall drunk in front of a train, let him suffer from blood poisoning as I had but let the poison take his life.

I even tried to kill him myself.

He and my mother were arguing. For once in her life, my mother stood up to him. For her son Joseph's soul and for her dream of the priesthood she would fight.

"So he's too good to do the same work his father does to feed him and feed you!"

"All his teachers say he's smart enough to get a scholarship to the seminary in Tiflis. They never said that of you."

"How the hell do you know what they said about me in my youth? And who says a priest is any better than a shoemaker? A shoemaker at least does something, makes something."

"Both are good, both are good. I'm not saying that. All I'm saying is that I promised God that if He'd make Joseph well when he was so sick that I would do everything in my power to make him a priest."

"But nobody asked me about that."

"You were away when he was sick."

"That's right, I was away, earning a living, that's what a man does. And what a man does is run his family. And it's not going to be run by any woman."

He slapped her face. He stank of wine, but this time it wasn't just the wine. It was something else. It was everything.

My mother had been cutting bread when he came in and the knife was still on the table.

At first, I picked up the knife thinking only to get it out of his sight, afraid he might use it on her, on us.

But he saw me. "What are you doing, you fucking mama's boy!"

I threw the knife right at him. It went over his shoulder and into the wall, where it hung for a moment before falling on the bed.

In those few seconds, time came to a complete stop, then he lunged for me. I raced by him and out the door, never once looking back. I hid with neighbors for a few days until I heard that he had left again.

After that, there was no more talk about my working in a shoe factory. In a day or two I was back in school.

I never knew what had really happened. My mother probably pulled some strings with the local authorities—church, gendarmes, school. The church doesn't give up its best student without a fight. Especially to a drunken cobbler with no power, except the power to beat women and children.

And then as if the whole thing—the shoe factory, the knife, hiding—had been just another nightmare, I was back where I belonged, in school, poring over books. Of course, sometimes I'd lift my head and think of my father. Then it was the school and the book that seemed like a dream.

Maybe it was because I had now ridden on a train and seen the great city of Tiflis that my interest turned to history. The next great book in my life was *The History of Russia.* In fact I devoured several histories of Russia, Russia, only Russia. I did not care about foreigners and foreign lands. I only wanted to know what had happened in Russia, where the most unbelievable events constantly took place.

My view of Russian history was childish, extremely simple, and, ultimately, correct.

Every schoolchild learns the myth of the origin of the Russian state. The Vikings are *invited* to assume control of Russia. A chronicle of the time has the Russians saying: "Our whole land is great and rich, but there is no order in it. Come to rule and reign over us."

I was embarrassed for Russia for not having the pride and sense to suppress the record of this shameful event.

I liked Grand Prince Vladimir of Kiev, who forced the Russians to accept Christianity and ordered the pagan idols smashed, burned, and hurled into the river.

And I admired Genghis Khan's Mongols, who arrived in 1240. Then Russia had a taste of the whip for more than two centuries. They wanted to be ruled, they'd be ruled.

The Mongols took no interest in the religion and internal politics of their subjects. All they wanted was money and obedience, and for 250 years they got what they wanted. Then their empire fell apart from within and the Mongols withdrew.

Then came my hero, my model, my rival—Ivan the Terrible. Ivan's task was to reunite Russia, shattered into a hundred petty principalities by the Mongols. The only problem was that the princes were in no hurry to surrender their power.

But Ivan understood the great secret: Cruelty is the cutting edge of history. The deciding factor is always the greatest degree of cruelty most intelligently applied.

So Ivan created the first secret police. Six thousand of them. Dressed in black, riding black horses. Their saddles emblazoned with iron emblems of a dog's head and a broom, symbolizing their mission to sniff out treason and sweep it away.

Ivan had invented Terror. He even took a very modern and "scientific" interest in it. Ivan was often accompanied by his son to the mass tortures and executions. They did what they could with the technology of the time—traitors were whipped, castrated, slit open, roasted on slow fires, then thrown under the ice of rivers, axes waiting for anyone who bobbed up to the surface.

For Ivan these were also practical experiments under conditions of unique extremity and control. Exactly how long does dignity endure? Exactly how many minutes can courage last?

In my boyish fantasies sometimes I was Ivan, sometimes Ivan's son. But that changed when I learned that Ivan, suspecting his son of treason, had struck him in the head with the sharp iron staff he always carried. The son died in Ivan's arms, saying, "I die as your devoted son and the most submissive of your subjects." Ivan went mad with grief and guilt, going from one monastery to another, beseeching God for forgiveness. After all, hadn't God let His own Son die on the cross?

The Ivan I preferred to remember was the one with the poetic audacity to blind the architect whom he commissioned to build St. Basil's Church on Red Square, so that the man could never create anything so beautiful for anyone else.

But I did not learn history only from books. I witnessed it in the town square of Gori, where a gallows was built over the course of a few days, and finally the Russians hanged two Georgians for all to see.

Standing toward the back of the crowd, I spoke directly to God, issuing my first challenge: If You want me to believe You exist, make one rope snap.

Needless to say, nothing of the sort happened. The two men kicked and twitched for a few minutes, then it was over.

But I'd be lying if I said my faith died there on the spot. No, if anything, that was only the sharpening of the struggle.

I was eleven when my father was murdered in a barroom brawl. I wasn't surprised. My father was a very murderable man. Even his own son had thrown a knife at him.

Now the great philosophical questions, what Dostoevsky calls the "accursed questions," became pointed and vivid for me.

Where was my father now? Was he in Heaven? Or Hell? Someplace where he could still see what was happening in this life?

If there truly was a God, there'd truly be an afterlife. If there was truly an afterlife, my father was somewhere in it. And from there he could see into his son's heart.

And in my heart was the certainty that there was a line, a straight, magic line, between my own desire for my father's death and his murder by a stranger in a brawl. It was not that I felt guilt. Not at all. I felt wonder.

And fear that my father could somehow strike back at me, even from there.

But if there was no God, there was no afterlife, and my father would be nothing.

So now my greatest wish was that there be no God.

To look up into empty sky.

I had declared war on God and I waited for Him to strike me down as any enemy should be struck down. But He did not strike me down. And the more of His power over me I shed, the better I felt, the lighter, the freer.

My new faith in myself was growing, but God was my doubt.

When I sang in the choir at services, I looked around at the faces of the other boys and of the priests for signs of faith, while mocking God in my thoughts and singing like an angel.

To have those kinds of thoughts and feelings is one thing, but to bring them to a head is another. One afternoon I went for a long walk alone in the mountains, up past the ruined castle. It was a clear day. Eagles were flying. I sat down by a tree on some pine needles the color of iodine.

I looked up and, using the high-flown language I'd learned from the priests and my mother, I said to God: Right now, right here, I offer up myself to You and if You are there to take me as I've been taught, then You will take a soul sincerely offered. If You exist, it isn't worth being myself, and so I will die in You and be what my mother has always wanted me to be, Your servant and Your priest. Take me, Lord!

And I was untaken by the Lord.

Just as I had hoped.

I had tricked God.

Into revealing his nothingness.

Yet there was something lacking.

Compelling corroboration.

And I found it.

In my third great book.

Darwin.

I looked at the pictures of monkeys' hands and human hands. Everything was clear. People weren't created by God. They came from the apes. Science said that God wasn't necessary. And what could be more unnecessary than an unnecessary God?

My joy was boundless, I bubbled over. I ran to tell everyone. Trotsky quotes one of my classmates who remembers me saying: "You know, they're deceiving us. There is no God . . . it's all proved in Darwin . . . read it right away."

Here Trotsky makes a double error. He says: "A thirteen-year-old boy in a backward town could hardly have read Darwin and derived atheistic convictions from him."

Gori was not a backward town. By the end of the nineteenth century, it had sidewalks, streetlights, a telegraph office, and was directly connected with Tiflis by rail. There was nothing to prevent a volume of Darwin from arriving by train. Not only that, in Gori there was a bookseller by the name of Arsen Kalandadze who took pleasure in feeding young minds with various sorts of incendiary literature.

". . . could hardly have read Darwin and derived atheistic convictions from him." Not *could* but *did.* What other kind could you derive?

As I later learned from passing the time of day with comrades from the working class, many of them had read Darwin around that same age and it had exactly the same effect on them as it did on me. Didn't matter what their religion was before—Christian, Jew, Moslem. They had seen the monkeys' hands.

Reading Darwin had an enormous impact on me. It corroborated my defiance of God and inspired me to systematically break all the Ten Commandments, which I now realized were only chains. Though I had stolen and lied before, I now stole and lied with a higher purpose—freedom of self. And the effects on my political philosophy were equally lasting. Historians of the future may even conclude that Darwinism + Leninism = Stalinism.

Trotsky hates the idea of the young Stalin reading Darwin, and not only reading him but understanding him more profoundly than Trotsky ever could. For Trotsky, Darwin had not been part of any inner struggle but just another important theory. And Trotsky of course did not have a "mediocre" memory for theories.

Trotsky had never wrestled with God—he'd snubbed him just as he had snubbed me that day in London in 1907. And he ignored both at his peril.

If he had struggled more with God instead of just spitting on his Judaism and walking away, Trotsky would have been a better man. And what Trotsky of course can never admit to himself is that I am his superior in spiritual depth. You do not become Joseph Stalin without first settling accounts with God.

6

Hitler has just done me a nice favor: his latest speech has so inflamed Trotsky that he again set aside his research into my life to fire off his own reply.

I too read all of Hitler's speeches, and agree with him on certain points. The harmfulness of Jews, for example. But he focuses too narrowly on that. There are always many harmful influences at work and it pays to keep your eye on all of them. Still, the Jews are particularly harmful.

I know from possessing the state archives that the anti-Semitic tract *The Protocols of the Elders of Zion* was a Tsarist secret police forgery. Hitler believes in the *Protocols* because his enemies don't and because he wants them to be real.

But just because the *Protocols* were a forgery doesn't mean that the most brilliant Jews don't meet somewhere in secret and plot their strategy. To people like Hitler and me who came up through secret organizations that dreamed of seizing power, there is nothing unusual or exotic about such an idea. If the Bolsheviks and the Nazis were smart enough to have a secret organization, why shouldn't the Jews?

The number of Jews is so insignificant that their presence should almost not even be felt. But what do we see? Jews everywhere. Statistically speaking, there shouldn't have been a single Jew in the inner circle of the Revolution, but there were several, Trotsky chief among them.

The Jews are great insisters. They insist on their survival, they insist on being heard. And Trotsky continues to insist that he is the rightful leader of Soviet Russia and the world communist movement. And so, if he is a man of his word, a man of integrity, Trotsky must bend his every effort to a single goal—my downfall, my death.

Apart from unmasking my one secret crime, Trotsky has two other main routes to my undoing: he could strike at my person by infiltrating my entourage or strike massively at my rule by gaining political control of the army.

I have infiltrated his entourage; why shouldn't he try to infiltrate mine? For the time being I have only a cleaning woman and, of late, a secretary (Maria de la Sierra, code name: Africa) in his household. Who could he have in mine? The smartest move would be to enlist my cooks and food tasters. A little poison goes a long way.

But that's not Trotsky's style. He likes the big stage, the grand gesture. He feels out of his element in the back corridors of intrigue.

No, Trotsky as the "creator" of the Red Army would have to reason like this: I created that army and the army remembers me because the army is a traditional organization with a living sense of its past. Officers aren't fools. They've had a chance to see what Stalin is like, and now they know. They control the army, the weapons, they have the *means* to seize power.

The officers and Trotsky may not have realized this yet, but sooner or later they will, simply because it is so.

And for that reason it would be suicidal on my part not to act while I still have the jump.

I call in Poskryobyshev. His expression is both impassive and alert. He displays no curiosity, but I know he always enjoys learning what the next thunderbolt will be. By the tone I choose I let him know how he is to react to my instructions. With what speed. With what degree of security. The level of satisfaction required.

So, letting him know that this is still preliminary, yet of the utmost secrecy, I say: "If Trotsky wanted to move against me with the army, what generals could he enlist? And if some generals would have no part in it, then exactly why not?"

Poskryobyshev leaves at once as he knows he is supposed to. The whole thing couldn't have been clearer to him—Stalin will decimate the leadership of the Red Army. And I could sense his approval, though he did not allow it to surface.

And I value his response. He has sense and taste in these matters—he had a hand in the assassination of the royal family. I wouldn't have taken it as a good sign if I couldn't sense his approval as he shuffled out the door.

It will be all to the good. The army will cease to be a potential weapon for Trotsky, and the new generals will owe their loyalty to me. There should also be a relatively light comb-out of the lower officers and the ranks. The generals should be held for a decent interval, tried in secret, then executed at once.

This will of course be made public. Russia will know. Hitler will know. The whole world will know.

Could there be any more positive proof that Stalin is interested only in peace than the fact that he has beheaded his own army? It is only Trotsky who can benefit from war, not Stalin. Trotsky is the real threat to international peace.

It is never advisable to fight a war on two fronts, and Stalin is already engaged in a war on the domestic front. Stalin has unleashed a terror that makes the excesses of Ivan the Terrible seem antiquated. Russia has never known nor will ever know again a year like the year '37. Truncheons. Confessions. Trials. Cattle cars by the tens of thousands haul prisoners to Siberia. The brick execution cellars reverberate with gunfire night and day.

Engineering all this, coordinating it, manipulating all the levers and pedals and pulleys, is an enormous task.

Stalin needs peace for terror.

7

Two turns for the worse. Trotsky is back on my case, and my mother died yesterday, July 9, 1937.

She had three wishes in this life: that her son become a priest, that her son attend her funeral, and that a cross be placed over her grave.

Stalin will not attend the funeral.

Stalin would not be Stalin if he attended. Dialectically speaking, his absence is his presence.

On her eightieth birthday, the one occasion when I returned to Gori, my mother gave me a frank look as only Georgians can, then said: "I still would've rathered you became a priest."

I burst out laughing, I couldn't help it. That angered her a bit but the anger didn't last long either.

I was, in the end, a disappointment to her. I didn't live out her dream for me.

For a time, it looked like her wish for me would come true, which must have made it even harder for her later on. In September 1894, I, the fourteen-year-old atheist, was enrolled—with a full scholarship—in the Tiflis Theological Seminary.

And that scholarship must have been her doing; she pulled every string she had for her Straight-A's Joseph.

The seminary smelled of candle wax and mice, and had that same strange combination of dankness and dryness that I would later experience in a dozen prisons. And essentially we were prisoners, let out free only two hours a day, from three to five.

Trotsky now zeroes in on the true training I received in the seminary—duplicity, not theology: "His every step was taken before the eyes of monks. In order to endure this regime for seven years or even five, extraordinary cautiousness and an exceptional aptitude for dissimulation were needed. . . . His hostility was reserved, underhanded, watchful."

But duplicity was in fact a healthy response. It was the only way to keep something of yourself alive in that regimented world of classes, services, prayer, meager meals, sudden inspections for worldly literature or nationalist propaganda, which they were also afraid of. That of course only made those authors and subjects more attractive. I devoured novels—Hugo, Dostoevsky, Gogol. The nationalist propaganda didn't attract me as much as the novels. Partly that was because I was in my "literary" phase and partly because I could see that even if Georgia became free again, it would never be more than a little kingdom of vineyards and vendettas. Russia was the land of greatness. That was clear from its literature. Pushkin, Dostoevsky, Tolstoy, the names went off like cannons.

It was in those years at the seminary that I tried my hand at poetry. Naturally, I dreamed only of becoming a great poet. The problem was that even though I was fluent in Russian, it was still easier for me to write in my native language. But to be a great Georgian poet was small potatoes. I'd have to truly master Russian to write great poetry in it. I applied myself to the task.

After a time, I made an appointment to see Arkady Volsky, the literary editor of the local Russian-language newspaper, having dropped off my poems a few days earlier, during the three-to-five break.

When I got to the door of the building, which was in the Renaissance style favored by the Russian ruling class and had a brass plate with the paper's name engraved in script, I was suddenly paralyzed and couldn't bring myself to go in. But after talking to myself, I finally regained my self-control and walked up the smooth stone stairs to his office.

"Ah, the seminarian," said Volsky, who was heavy and thick-boned but had a nimble mind. "Sit down. Tea?"

I shook my head.

"So you want the verdict right away. Fine. I have a better chance of becoming a famous ballerina than you do of writing deathless verse in Russian. Period."

I was heartbroken, furious.

I withdrew into myself for days, weeks. I would never be a great poet in a great literature. Period.

But then I saw that I didn't really want to be a poet anyway. Most of them had miserable lives—if they weren't exiled by the Tsar, they were killed in frivolous duels or died penniless. That was no life.

And, oddly enough, I realized this while reading a poem. It was a translation of Whitman—"We are alive. Our blood boils with the fire of unexpended strength."

That was it! To live! To really live! Poetry had done its job and pointed me back to life.

And, for me at that time, life meant the great city of Tiflis, a name the Russian Tsar had imposed and which I would later change back to its true name of Tbilisi.

Trotsky has dug up a good traveler's account of the city from the year 1901, though he uses it to stress my Asiatic background as much as to provide some local color:

> Alongside of streets that bear a contemporary European character nests a labyrinth of narrow, crooked, and dirty, purely Asiatic lanes, squarelets and bazaars, framed by open stalls of the Eastern type, by stands, coffee houses, barber shops, and filled with a clamorous throng of porters, water carriers, errand boys, horsemen, lines of pack mules and donkeys, caravans of camels, and the like.

I did enjoy wandering the side streets and rubbing shoulders with an amazing array of humanity—Georgians, Russians, Armenians, Persians, Greeks, and Jews—to loiter at markets that sold melons and old carpets, to talk with camel drivers who were forever complaining about the nastiness of camels, especially when they're in heat.

The Armenians I liked, the Jews I didn't. The Armenians were good at business because they kept their greed under control. With the Jews you always had the feeling you were being taken.

What seems like a digression on Trotsky's part into the labyrinth of back lanes in fact proves a direct avenue to my life of crime.

Hanging around the backstreets of Tiflis, it was inevitable that I'd get into trouble. First with the crooks, then with the communists.

Crooks isn't quite the right word; back then in Tiflis they were called *kintos,* and in fact Trotsky is now sketching out a chapter on me called "Kinto in Power."

For him *kinto* is a term of abuse, for me it's one of nostalgia and praise. But that's not what matters. What matters is that Trotsky has once again caught hold of a thread which, if he pulls at it carefully enough, could unravel everything I've woven together over the years. The tangled backstreets of Tiflis are where I was initiated into the craft of crime. It's one thing to call me a Genghis Khan, another to begin compiling a case file of my crimes, starting with the pettiest and leading inevitably to *that.*

Trotsky defines *kintos* as "heroes of the street, fast talkers, singers and hooligans. . . . From them Stalin acquired his crude ways and his virtuosity at swearing."

For Russians swearing is a sport and an art. Performed at the moment, on the spot. Instinctively, Russians rank each other on their ability to swear. Nothing is quite so pathetic as a man who can't get his swears right. I would rank Trotsky low as a swearer. He curses like an intellectual, satirically, always a little too aware of breaking a tabu. No art to it, not something you just stand and listen to for the sheer pleasure of seeing what comes next, one curse topping the other, shooting off into side curses but then roaring back to the main curse and blasting it with such ferocious inventions you can't help laughing out loud in sheer admiration.

Yes, it was from the kintos that I acquired my "virtuosity at swearing" and it was with the kintos that I learned the thrill of burglary. To be by stealth in someone else's apartment somehow makes you feel fantastically alive. Your hearing becomes ten times more sensitive. Every creak of a staircase, every bark of a yard dog, every cough. Almost unbearable sometimes.

Our leader was called "Monkey" because of his long, hairy arms that were covered with homemade green tattoos and because he could climb up anything. He'd shimmy up a drainpipe to a third-floor window, then let us all in the front door. We'd take money and small things that might not be missed right away. But if there was good food around we could never resist.

Once in a while we'd take something large—a candelabra, a silver box. And sometimes, if he felt like it, Monkey would shit on the floor.

There are three reasons why burglars do this. First, it's of course the ultimate contempt—I shit in your house. Second, it's an assertion of freedom—if I want, I'll even shit here. Third, it's a way of making light of the whole business—I took your shit and left you some of mine.

But the kintos had one fatal failing: in the end they really didn't give a shit about anything. The most they could imagine was a robbery they could live off of for the rest of their life.

They were small-time.

But how else could it be? If they cared about anything, they couldn't be kintos.

The communists at least thought big. They knew what they wanted—kill the Tsar, take power.

That was the third great idea of my life:

There is no God.

Man comes from the apes.

Kill the Tsar.

Then, for a time, I gave up burglary for the reading of revolutionary literature. Each day I would smuggle a pamphlet or two back into the seminary, taking satisfaction in passing a monk in the corridor and letting his fierce eye look right into mine and see only a chaste, sincere seminarian.

Revolutionary pamphlets were read by candlelight, discussed in whispers. It was inevitable that a group formed to discuss these ideas. Since the monks were always patrolling the corridors and listening in at doors, most of the discussions took place in the free period between three and five and were all the more intense for that.

At first, our group formed around Sergo, one of the older boys, who was best at explaining ideas like capital and the exploitation of the working class. Sergo was tall and lean and so excited by these new ideas that made sense of the world that he could barely sleep at night. For a time I was content to learn from Sergo.

But then I got restless. Even if I couldn't explain the ideas as well as Sergo, I'd understood them well enough; he had nothing left to teach me.

Within any group there are various degrees of loyalty to the leader. As with a woman whose faithfulness to her husband can be sensed at once, some were unshakable, but some were not. I found those. I spent time with them. Told them how I saw things. But I knew it wasn't my presentation of the ideas that mattered to them so much as a certain something else about me. Though I told absolutely no one about my escapades with the kintos, still all that had given me an aura of seriousness and experience.

I was instinctively experimenting with one of the principles that would guide my career—the art of forming the breakaway group.

One cool spring day, a bunch of us went walking in the park, away from people, where our discussion could not be overheard. I was waiting for Sergo to come up with the first point I could challenge him on. I wanted the showdown to come as early as possible during those two hours, but I didn't want to challenge him on just any point—it had to be one where I could inflict some real damage.

Finally, he said: "There are some actions a revolutionary must never take."

"Like what?" I said.

"Like . . . slaughtering the innocents."

"Wrong. Because the revolution's enemies have already proved a thousand times they are not afraid to slaughter the innocent. As long as that power is exclusively in their hands, they will always win!"

A great argument erupted. Everybody had something to say and nobody could wait. Everybody talked at once; some shoving even started.

At one point, saying nothing, I made my move. I turned my back and walked away. The message was clear—I was leaving the group and anybody who wanted to could follow me. A couple came right away, a few others only after we'd put some distance between ourselves and those who would stay with Sergo.

I had reached a new stage in my development—leader of a gang with an idea. I gave them all my time and energy. My marks took a nosedive. And now I kept being sent to the punishment cell for being found with subversive literature; I could no longer restrain myself. I was breaking the mask and the mold of seminarian.

To actually graduate, to actually become a priest, even for one second, was now anathema to me.

I had found a dream of my own stronger than my mother's dream for me. It was an act of tremendous faith in myself not to stay on until graduation. Of course, breaking with the seminary meant breaking my mother's heart. Only I had the power to make her dream come true. But only one dream can run a life, only one. I had to break her heart; what would I be if I hadn't?

Breaking with the seminary also meant great personal sacrifice. I had to give up my gang. But so the boys would stay bound to the cause and to me by suffering, I hid revolutionary literature under their mattresses, then had the authorities informed. I managed to implicate all the boys in my own group and in Sergo's, while at the same time "slaughtering" a few "innocents."

And then I was gone.

It was 1899, the last year of the century of railroads and factories, Darwin and Marx, when that young man set out on the path that would lead him to the Kremlin.

And here in the Kremlin today I met with the committee in charge of my mother's funeral, instructing them that, while she might be given a traditional Christian burial, no cross should ever mark her grave.

PART II

8

After leaving the seminary, I "kintoed" around for a while. Then, in 1900, at age twenty, I found a small job at the Tiflis Geophysical Observatory that provided room, board, and plenty of time for stirring up the masses, known then as "agitation." The underground was my natural element; I rose so fast that within four years I was disputing policy with Lenin in person.

Oddly enough, it is easier for Trotsky to track me through the twists and shadows of the underground than in my two decades "above ground." Now he can make use of police records, the recollections of my comrades, witnesses to my acts and nature.

Those earliest days, determining as they do the angle of my rise, are of particular interest to Trotsky. Noting that I was drawn to the "hard-line, violent" left, Trotsky says, referring to me by my childhood name: "Because of his early environment as well as his personal character, it was natural that Soso should instinctively incline toward the Left Wing. A plebeian democrat of the provincial type, armed with a rather primitive 'Marxist' doctrine—it was such that entered the revolutionary movement, and such in essence he remained to the very end despite the fantastic orbit of his personal fate."

Though that last sentence is mostly a sputter of insults, it does, however, end nicely. Trotsky's his own worst enemy. He lets his vision be clouded by envy and wounded pride. He is outraged that my fate went into a "fantastic orbit" while his took a fantastic decline. To have been bested by the "primitive" Stalin violates his sense of justice and meaning. That impels him to destroy me, yet it also throws him off the track. But he always gets back on.

My work in those years was straightforward. First you had to prove yourself in the field.

I was part of a small group of Social Democratic revolutionaries who worked the train yards in Tiflis. A good place to break into organizing. I was still young enough to enjoy watching the locomotives chug by, all black steel and rivets in clouds of steam. But there were good, hard reasons for working the yards. It was those thousands of miles of track that stitched huge Russia together. Pull out the stitches and she falls apart.

I sit in a shed with a half dozen workers drinking tea and smoking. I've posted a loyal worker, Danko, outside to keep an eye out for yard dicks. And inside, one of the workers keeps watch through a little window streaked with frost and coal dust.

I am wondering which of the six is a police informant, or has just about decided to become one.

It's time to start. The trick is always to find the right tone, the right lingo.

"Just go look how the bosses live compared to you, that's all you got to do," I say. "Go look at their fucking houses, their hospitals, their schools. Use your own eyes."

I pause to let that sink in and check for reactions. Did my language offend any good family men?

"The authorities don't care if you hit the bottle and beat your wife or go to church and pray, all they care about is that you slave for them fourteen hours a day and then at the end of the week you put out your hand for a few lousy rubles and bow your head in thanks to them."

"But they've got all the guns," says one worker, a man in his late thirties, railroad grime embedded in the creases on his face. I can tell he thinks I'm too young.

"Not all," I say, patting my shirt.

"Nearly all."

"But who's got those guns? The soldiers. And who are the soldiers? The soldiers are the sons of workers and peasants. And they are ruled by the officers just like you're ruled by your bosses.

"You know what the word *revolution* means? The word *revolution* means to turn something all the way around," I say, making an abrupt switching motion with my right hand. "If the soldiers turned their guns from the people to the officers, now that would be a revolution, wouldn't it?"

"You'll never convince the Cossacks," objects another, a dark-eyed man whose high cheekbones glisten with machine oil.

"Not even all Cossacks are stupid," I say, and they laugh.

"But we're not soldiers and you're asking us to take to the streets and protest when there'll be plenty of stupid Cossacks waiting for us."

"That's why we got to bring out big numbers. There's safety in numbers. Four hundred people going against a couple of hundred Cossacks is one thing but two, three thousand people is an avalanche."

"You mean you don't think the Cossacks will attack if the crowd is large enough?"

"It's not up to the Cossacks. It's a political decision. The Cossacks will just do what they're told. The officials making the political decision might decide that it's just better to wait out the demonstration until people are tired and go home. Or they may decide that you represent a serious force and sit down and negotiate. Or they might send in the Cossacks."

"In which case we lose some."

"That's true of any war," I say.

There was a moment of silence.

"You going to be there?" asks the man with the grimy creases.

"I'll be there."

Suddenly we all hear the clang of metal on metal. Everyone freezes; I paste on a grin. The man watching the window says, "It's nothing. Danko dropped a wrench."

I expected to be arrested at any moment, but couldn't let that show here. Every action I took was dictated by eluding arrest—how I slipped away through the boxcars at the end of the meeting, leaving the train yard so that I reentered Tiflis through the crooked lanes at the edge of town. My eyes were always scanning the street to see who was up ahead, but in some way my back was also able to sense hostile attention.

Certain bitter communists in Russia and abroad, and certain anti-communists in the West, claim that Stalin went to work for the Tsarist secret police in order to get money from them. They reason: In those years Stalin had no means of support. His few articles could have paid only a few kopecks at best. Stalin had no cover position like printer or railroad man that would have given him access to the working class while earning him a living. The Party had no money to pay organizers. The secret police, on the other hand, had plenty of money earmarked to recruit informers. Stalin had money, therefore it could only have come from the secret police.

The logic is flawed. Stalin had been trained in the one trade that eliminates all the steps between the need for money and the money itself. Stalin was a kinto, Stalin was a thief.

And so at that time I was in fact eluding arrest by the Tsar's secret police for organizing workers *and* by the regular police for theft. The odds were greater for being arrested as an organizer—more people involved. Which was unfortunate. Thieves were punished less severely. Stealing money was considered less important than stealing power.

I stole both. To me there was no difference. Both were attacks on society. The money I stole freed me to go on assaulting the existing order. A juster combination could not be imagined. At least not by a "primitive Marxist."

9

The demonstration took place, and I was there. On May Day, 1901, more than two thousand workers gathered in the Soldiers' Bazaar in the center of Tiflis.

It was an early spring day, cool, the sky blue gray. Some of the workers were solemn and wearing church clothes but most of them were cheerfully defiant and wore their work clothes so there could be no mistake about who they were. They were there to show how many of them there were and that they were conscious of themselves as a class. I noticed that some of them had hammers, knives, or lengths of chain tucked inside their jackets or shirts. I had instructed the ones marching in front to wear heavy clothing, two overcoats, since they'd have to act as "shock absorbers" if the Cossacks charged.

My job was to nip at the demonstrators' heels and get them into some sort of rank and order. But they didn't need too much nipping. Something magnetic was happening. Groupings formed naturally. Where there had been ten dark jackets, now there were forty. I looked like everyone else, just another mustached guy with a cap pulled low. I'd stay at the edges, pointing people to their friends: "There's Lalo and them, over there on the left, they were looking for you." Or: "If you want the guys from the lathe shop, they're up at the front."

That was my idea. I went around the train yards and asked everyone, Who're the toughest guys? A few said themselves of course, but most everyone else said the boys at the lathe shop. And who's the head guy there? I asked. Shosta, they said. So, I went to the lathe shop and found Shosta. I said, "Most everyone says that the guys at the lathe shop are the toughest. Want to prove it by walking up front?"

I darted to the front to make sure the lathe boys were still all together and hadn't drifted off into little groups around a bottle. There was some of that, but they were holding together well as a group. Shosta was out front, moving around, yelling. If anything, the lathe boys seemed impatient to get going.

I ran back, passing a few of the other organizers on the way. Sometimes we gave each other a quick nod, but usually we didn't. By then things were speeding up. Still, I'd take a second to watch the other organizers work, see if I could pick up a trick or if I was already better than them.

I saw Vano, one of the workers who, when I asked who was the toughest, said they were. I ran over to him.

"Have a smoke on me," I said, offering him some good cigarettes I had lifted from an apartment along with a gold medal that'd probably already been melted down and made into rings.

"Thanks," he said, always glad for a free smoke and a good one at that.

"Your guys all show?"

"Except for Nika."

"What's with him?"

"Got a new wife."

"If he does show, tell me, maybe I'll slip by his house."

He laughed and I faded back to the sidelines.

Then for a second something strange happened. I don't even know how to describe it. I just stood there and watched as all those dark jackets and dark caps began to merge until all the thousands had become a single living thing. A long, huge, dark creature that moved close to the ground. Suddenly everything I had been taught, everything I had read, everything I had preached, was there before my eyes, the word made flesh.

And I saw that it was true: strong, united, armed, the working class could bring down the regime of the Tsars. And that cool spring day they were united, by a song, the Marseillaise, which started up at the front and gradually spread back.

Even though I couldn't see the people in front from where I was, I could still feel them start moving; a sort of energy came crashing back through the crowd as it does through a freight train when the engine is coupled on.

People began shifting from foot to foot, waiting for the ones ahead of them to move so they could start walking.

Then suddenly dozens of red banners were unfurled, like fighting plumage.

The song was reverberating off the buildings. Everybody was moving now and that made us feel even stronger, to have all of us moving at once. I sang too.

We marched along a street lined with evergreens whose fresh aroma was bracing and gave us heart.

I ran to the front of the crowd, shaking a hand or two on the way, making sure people saw me.

I signaled to Shosta, the leader of the lathe boys, throwing him a quick salute. But I always kept moving in a way that said, You've got your job, I've got mine.

I wanted a taste of battle. I was young, I wanted to know what it would feel like, how I'd do. But I certainly didn't want my arm lopped off.

I had brought a small revolver with me. The trigger was light and quick. But I had only three bullets. Bullets were always hard to come by.

Nothing could be seen up ahead yet. Just empty street and the start of a long gray wall. But I'd been over the route and knew that a turn was coming up ahead. I stayed with the lathe boys. They were singing the Varshavianka now. Bottles were passing. I had one good nip of cold vodka.

The crowd was moving faster now, everybody wanted to see if they'd be there around the bend.

And there they were, still a good ways from us, blocking the street that led to the central square. A gray-brown cloud, two hundred Cossacks, mounted, their horses stomping and steaming.

I could feel the hair on my forearms stand up as the slowing of the men in front sent an electric signal back through the rest of the crowd. The Cossacks had been seen.

And we had been seen by the Cossacks.

The plan was simple. Show them we come in peaceful protest, but, if they charge, fight back.

We were moving slowly now. "Keep it slow!" I kept yelling.

The distance between us was evaporating. A breeze picked up, fluttering the banners. The air became very clear as it does just before it starts to snow.

They would have to charge in the next thirty seconds if they wanted their horses to build up a head. I kept working the crowd, telling people to go slow, at the same time making my way back. I tried to figure how many men it would take to absorb the first impact. But still I wanted to be right up there close enough to feel the shock of it pass through me.

And to fight. My right hand was inside my jacket, my fingers tightening by themselves on the handle of the revolver.

"They're charging!" shouted someone in the front, and a second later I could hear the clatter of hoofbeats on cobblestone. The singing turned to cursing, everyone working himself into a rage.

For one long moment the demonstrators hesitated, unsure whether to absorb the blow or to charge, but then a great cheer rose from the front and everyone rushed forward. I pulled out my revolver to urge on the men around me with the sight of it, letting a few more ranks past me.

Then it hit, two locomotives head-on. For maybe five seconds it was just pure clash, then you could feel us give as they broke through our outer membrane.

Now the air was slashed by hooves, whips, sabres, and crisscrossed by jets of blood.

The Cossacks were less than ten feet ahead of me now. I'd judged it right. The Cossacks were still surging but in several places they had been torn from their mounts to the ground, where they were beaten with wrenches and lead pipe. I leveled my gun and fired, stinging a Cossack on the side of his arm. Pure joy. But, jostled from behind, my second shot missed.

Excited as I was, I was still aware I had only one bullet left. The whips were close, one flicked my neck. A severed hand went skidding on a patch of ice. Everyone was howling. Time to get out of there. I'd done my job. Now history would have to play itself out.

I had been over the route several times and knew there was a side street a little off to the left. But for the moment the way was blocked by Cossack sabres threshing shoulders and heads.

Then I saw my chance—a few Cossacks had gotten bunched up together and were being attacked. I slipped in with the attackers but not too close, always moving toward the left. When I saw the street coming, I stumbled off doubled-over to the edge of the crowd and into the side street, cursing with the pain of the wounded but still able to notice three onlookers grab barrel staves and join in.

I didn't look back again until I'd covered a few hundred yards. I saw a Cossack on horseback chasing a man on foot who had a good start but one that wouldn't last long.

I ducked into a gateway.

Even from a distance I could make out the Cossack's face—a wedge of blond beard, light blue eyes like a pig's, and fleshy red lips that looked raw, as if the outer layer of skin had been peeled off. That mouth kept opening wide as he gave one Cossack war cry after another.

The worker and the Cossack were going to pass me at the same time and I pulled farther back into the gateway. All I saw was the worker and the side of the horse and the whip catching the back of his head and hurling him to the ground.

The Cossack's momentum carried him on and I knew he would have to slow, wheel, and turn. I moved to the front of the gateway. The worker was trying to get to his hands and knees but could barely manage that. Now the Cossack had wheeled and turned and was building up a charge, his mouth opening wide as he shouted, Oooooooraaaa!

Those raw red lips made a perfect target against the gray of his uniform and the blue gray of the sky. When he saw me aiming at him, he looked astonished, amused, angered. He charged harder and made the mistake of cheering even more loudly.

The bullet went out the back of his throat and he grabbed his own neck as if trying to strangle himself. He was stuck straight up in the stirrups and the horse kept charging up the street, back toward the crowd where it could still do some damage—innocent people trampled by dead Cossack on horseback, good propaganda.

I picked up the wounded worker and slung his arm over my shoulder. I didn't say anything to him until I had dragged him well into the crooked side streets of Tiflis. Letting him stop for breath, I wiped the blood off his face and told him what I'd been taught: "Head wounds bleed easy, they look worse than they are. Don't let the blood scare you."

Though still dazed, he was able to tell me where he lived.

There were practically no people on the streets. Everyone was either at the demonstration or locked up tight in their homes. We did pass an old woman with a donkey, the kind of old woman who doesn't even know what century it is; she looked at us with simple scared interest.

He lived on the second floor. By then he could just about walk up the stairs himself.

His wife opened the door and gasped.
"I'll be all right," he said in a soft voice.
She looked at me with eyes full of scorn and gratitude.
I told them my name, so credit would be given where credit's due.

10

After helping lead the demonstration and killing a Cossack, I had to vanish from Tiflis like steam into air. Yet I could not help but think that half of the apartments in the city were empty and all the police were down at the square.

So, with a pocketful of easy rubles, I fled back to my hometown of Gori, but not to my mother's, of course; she never knew I was there. I had places to stay until things died down a little, as they always do sooner or later.

I had plenty of time to reflect on what I'd seen, and wrote one of my best early articles. I hadn't studied the science of dialectics yet and didn't know about the laws that always cause things to turn into their exact opposite. But I must have been a born dialectician because even at that age I was able to see that the Cossack's whip was not a weapon *against* the revolution, but *for* it. The whip turned "curious onlookers" into rioters:

"The 'curious onlookers' no longer run away on hearing the swish of the whips; on the contrary, they draw nearer, and the whips can no longer distinguish between the 'curious onlookers' and the 'rioters.' Now, conforming to 'complete democratic equality,' the whips play on the backs of all, irrespective of sex, age, and even class. Thereby, the whiplash is rendering us a great service. . . ."

Mostly I stayed indoors, especially for the first couple of weeks. And yet I had never felt freer or happier. Now I truly was Koba, the rebel, the avenger. I had become what I imagined.

Then, after another week or ten days, word got around that if you wanted to make a move, you probably could but you'd still have to be on your toes.

I was ready to get going. Tiflis was out for two reasons. Number one, the police of course, but number two, my standing with certain party workers was low. They accused me of forming splinter groups, discourtesy in clashes. And I had also committed the heresy of speaking out against having workers on the party committee, saying that, politically, they were only half-conscious at best and who wants a half-awake engineer in the locomotive of history?

The high-minded ones hated this; they couldn't bear to say anything bad about the people and the workers, which of course made them fools to the people and the workers, who had a healthy contempt for themselves and everyone else.

The nearest place that made sense was Batum, a Black Sea town just a little north of the Turkish border. It had a population of about thirty thousand, more than a third of them workers. Most of them were employed at oil refineries where they put in a fourteen-hour day and never saw the sun. One of the refineries was owned by a Rothschild.

Back organizing, I told the workers: "Not only is your refinery owned by a Jew; he's not even one of our Rabinoviches, but a foreign one! You're killing yourself fourteen hours a day to make a rich foreign Jew even richer, could you think of anything worse?"

They ate it up. Even less sophisticated than the workers of Tiflis, the workers of Batum were angrier and easier to rile.

I also wrote some inflammatory proclamations. The operation couldn't have been simpler. I'd sit at a table with a pen and paper and when I was done with a sheet I'd hand it to the printers, who had a little handpress on their table. The print was kept in lettered matchboxes and inked with a shoe brush.

I organized at both refineries in Batum, but I always had the feeling that the Rothschild would go up the easiest if there was the right incident. And the spark came on February 25, 1902, when the Rothschild refinery posted a notice announcing the dismissal of 389 workers. Immediately there were strikes, clashes with the police, and arrests followed by protest demonstrations in front of the prison where the workers were being held. Finally on March 7, 1902, two thousand workers marched to the police barracks and demanded that the prisoners be released or that all two thousand of them be arrested. There were no Cossacks in Batum, so this time it wasn't the whip that proved the secret friend of revolution, but the rifle. First, the police tried to clear away the workers with their rifle butts, but when the workers began hurling cobblestones at them, the police turned their rifles around and opened fire, killing fifteen, wounding fifty-four.

My own role was pretty much the same as in Tiflis, except that I fired no shots and was in a good position to flee, as most people did when the shots rang out. These sorts of things never last long. Violence is quick.

But I wasn't.

A little more than a month later, on April 18, 1902, a date I will never forget, all the anticipation of arrest was dispelled by the fact.

I've since discussed the art and science of arrest with many professionals in the field and almost to a man they agree that the first arrest is like no other. The shock to a man's nervous system is so great that for a certain period of time he's in your control. It's like the work of a diamond cutter except that here the idea is to shatter the jewel.

I knew this instinctively back then. I was constantly engaged in a strange contradictory activity, doing everything I could to elude arrest while at the same time doing everything I could to prepare myself for it.

But in the end there's no eluding it and no preparing for it either.

It was a Friday. Some of the younger organizers had gotten together to drink a little Georgian red wine, smoke, and talk things over. The atmosphere was still heavy, the wounds of the slaughter still fresh. But those who agreed with me that whips and rifles were the friends of revolution were in good spirits.

Someone was just proposing a toast to the memory of the fifteen killed by police bullets, when the lookout suddenly shouted: "They've got the building surrounded!"

It had to come. And here it was.

My nerves were jangled, my blood speeded up. But I fought to keep a clear head. I told myself I was lucky they weren't snatching me alone off the street and that I had a last few moments to get ready for it. The only question now was whether they'd come in firing.

"The Tsar fucks his mother!" someone shouted.

"In the ass and in the ear," added someone else, and everyone roared.

We heard their boots in the hall, then their rifle butts at the door, which fell in front of them like a gangplank. They came in with rifles leveled, bayonets fixed.

I slowly raised my hands, dropping my cigarette on the way. They weren't going to shoot.

* * *

Then came my initiation into what in time would become an all too familiar procedure—booking.

Last name, first name, date and place of birth. Against the wall. Face to the side. Face front. Left thumb, right thumb, press hard.

They made you strip, looking for identifying marks—tattoos, scars, birthmarks. They noticed my webbed toes, but I'm not sure if they wrote it down that time or in '03 as Trotsky says. They talk about you like you're not even there, another one of their tricks.

Batum's prison stank of lye and diarrhea. I would be in more famous and more interesting prisons later on; their memories have blurred but my first prison remains fresh in my mind.

If you haven't experienced at least once that moment when you first stride into your cell and face your cellmates, then you haven't really lived. An electric moment, the nervous system can barely withstand the charge. The presence you generate in that instant determines your fate in the cell.

I came in strong, ready to clash.

There were no immediate challengers from among my three cellmates—Abdumanov, a worker, an Uzbek with pale golden skin and a black skullcap, in for taking part in the demonstration that turned bloody; Sasha, a party worker, a tall, light-haired Russian, picked up in the same sweep as me; and Benno, the only one to smile at me when I walked into the cell, and who was, as he put it, "suspected of counterfeiting."

Sasha the party worker and I took an instant dislike to each other. He was the pure party intellectual type. To him I was just a street organizer, a thug who'd read a few pamphlets. Abdumanov the worker was still stunned by his arrest and worried about his wife and children. Mostly I talked with Benno in the cell, not that we said much there, just for the company.

I immediately established a routine—calisthenics in the morning. Everyone respected the fact that a certain portion of the cell floor was mine at that time of the day. Benno was amused, Abdumanov indifferent, and Sasha was resentful, though he masked it with purposeful activity like communicating with other cells by means of the tapping code—he even played chess that way, using bits of bread for pieces, a sheet of paper for a board.

Exercise in prison is a science in itself. You want to keep your muscle tone, your spring, you want to feel your blood circulating. This keeps your strength and spirits up. But you don't want to feel too good either. The more vitality you have, the thicker the stone walls seem.

Prison was the seminary all over again. Gloom. Regimentation. Study. And the reading of inflammatory underground literature smuggled by visitors past lax guards.

I read some Marx but was more interested in the Russians who were adapting Marxist theory to revolutionary action. I kept reading all those different writers, trying to find the one book that said it best and clearest to me. And that one was *Russian State Capitalism* by V. Ilyin, whose mind soared like a mountain eagle.

I asked around about him. All I could find out was that Ilyin was the pen name of a Russian exile named Ulyanov, who some people said was the true leader of the revolution, or would be. I also learned that his brother had been hanged as a terrorist. It would be three years before I encountered the author himself, who by then was using the name Lenin.

And so my first bond with Lenin came from reading him in prison, a pure meeting of the minds.

"What is it with this Marxism shit?" said Benno the counterfeiter when we were out in the yard and they had us shuffle around in one long circle.

"You like the guys who put you here?" I said, answering a question with a question.

"No. But who says a bunch of plumbers and bookworms are going to be any better?"

I laughed, even slapped my leg. Benno liked that.

Then I said, "But at least we're more like you."

"You maybe," he said, "but not that other one in our cell."

"Sasha wants to make the world better so it'll be as good as him," I said and this time it was Benno's turn to laugh.

I always pictured counterfeiters as thin, but Benno was built like a bulldog. He kept his hair very short; his eyes seemed a little too close to his nose. His hands looked small in proportion to the rest of his body, but he had great fingers, so alive they were always moving around in the air when he talked.

"So what notes were your specialty?" I asked him.

"Except for value, my hundred was as good as the mint's."

"And what do you sell them for on the ruble?"

"Thirty kopecks on the ruble. You pull in thirty percent of what you print, minus expenses. Why do you ask? Interested?"

"Something to think about. The party always needs money. And as you and I both know, there are more ways than one to get money."

Benno grinned and made a little whisking gesture with his hand.

We were close after that.

Which made trouble for me. The strict party types had a tabu on associating with the professional criminals. Word got around that I was spending time with Benno in the yard and with other criminals I met through Benno. Some of the politicos now made a point of shunning me.

That scorn spread to Sasha. He still only showed it in small ways. He'd spend time with Abdumanov, trying to improve his class consciousness. Abdumanov was getting more bitter, harder. He was turning from a rioter into a revolutionary, just as I had said in my article.

Of course, Sasha could always say he was only doing what a good party organizer is supposed to do, but I knew this was really a challenge to my authority in the cell.

Now in the prison yard the strict party types made a point of walking together, to show their numbers. And I made a point of walking with Benno.

"Benno, look, one of these days I'm going to have it out with Sasha. And soon. You may not give a shit about the revolution, but what I'm asking is, when it comes down to it, are you going to be with me?"

"I'm a good neighbor, I'll lend a hand. You want a little noise, a couple of quick ones to the head, just give me the high sign. He's a boring fucker anyway."

But I also spent a little time walking with Abdumanov. "Sasha's all right," I said to him, "but he's really not one of us. Sure he'll go to prison, that's expected, but they spend most of their time arguing and writing books."

"That's true too," said Abdumanov.

"I'll tell you something. The working class can win. You've got the numbers. But you can only win if you've got the right people in charge. So the question is, Who do you want up front fighting for you, people with guns in their hands or books?"

"A good question," said Abdumanov.

A couple of days later, I was lying on my bunk, pretending to doze. Benno was doing push-ups on his fingertips. Sasha was conversing with Abdumanov in a fairly low voice. Maybe he wasn't just being polite, maybe he didn't want me to hear what he was saying.

"Yes," Sasha was saying, "there will be more demonstrations and more violence. There's no way around that. But that doesn't mean that the working class has to go to war against the system to get fair pay and social justice. Enough general strikes paralyzing the country and you'll get what you want."

"That's pure shit," I said, coming out from my bunk. "They're never going to give you anything. You'll squeeze them, they'll bullshit you, you'll go back to work only to wake up in a couple of months and have to start all over again. And then they'll throw in some extra Cossacks and slice up so many people that everybody loses his appetite for demonstrations for a good long time to come. That's what's going to happen."

"No, it isn't!" said Sasha. "The working class doesn't need to seize power. All it has to do is realize that it already has the power."

"I'll prove that's bullshit," I said to Abdumanov. "I'll prove it right now."

Benno finished his push-ups and was standing in the back dusting off his hands.

"Nobody gives up power without a struggle," I said. "If you want their power, you've got to take it from them. And that goes for anybody who tries to take power from me."

"That's perfectly typical of your criminal mentality to think I'm interested in taking power from you," said Sasha. "I'm interested in liberating the power in the working class, which doesn't seem to be your number-one concern. You'd rather talk with crooks and thieves in the yard. They probably all have adolescent nicknames from cheap novels like you, Koba."

"I didn't think intellectuals would stoop to personal insults in something so important as showing a representative of the working class the truth—that power must be seized by violence because it will always be defended by violence," I said, looking Sasha in the eye, then past him to Benno.

Benno shoved Sasha hard from in back, shouting, "Who the fuck are you giving shit to him!"

Sasha stumbled toward me. I kneed him in the stomach and he toppled to the floor like a dropped sack. Benno kicked him five times in the kidneys, shouting, "I'll crack your head you pull that again."

That was all. Sasha slouched off to his bunk.

I said to Abdumanov: "So there it is."

"Yes," he said.

A week later I turned twenty-three.

11

"It is surprising that the records of Koba's police interrogations pertaining to that first arrest . . . have not yet been published," says Trotsky, assuming the reason to be that I relied more on my own "cunning" than on the "standard behavior obligatory for all." A revolutionary was honor-bound to protest—I repudiate and deny the accusations against me; I refuse to give testimony or to take part in any secret investigation. That sort of thing.

I'm relieved by Trotsky's "surprise." It indicates that he has not found any other documents pertaining to my first interrogation, which took a few surprising twists of its own.

A few days after Benno and I had put Sasha in his place, a guard and a warder came to our cell. The warder had a list in his hand, the guard was carrying chains and irons.

My name was called. I rose.

"This one goes to Special Cell Six," said the warder to the guard, who began handcuffing me.

I didn't like the sound of it. I looked over at my cellmates. Sasha was smirking, Abdumanov looked scared, Beno shrugged. We had all heard about the special cells, but none of us had been there yet.

Shackles were placed on my feet and connected by chain to the handcuffs so that I was hunched over and had to take short, rapid steps.

The walk was long; we kept turning corner after corner; the corridors were dimly lit. I paid close attention to the route, as if that could have any meaning.

A few men who had gone mad were screaming in their cells. But I had gotten used to that, just one of the sounds of the place, like squealing brakes in the train yard.

The guard halted me by putting a meaty hand on my shoulder. I could feel that hand ready to strike my head if I hesitated in obeying.

But that hand couldn't have been more deferential when knocking on the door of Special Cell 6. The door looked the same as any other—timber and steel, a slot for food, a spy window covered with a metal shield that could be slid aside.

A voice from inside gave permission to enter.

The guard held the door open for me.

My eyes went first to the man at the desk. Maybe forty, brown hair brushed straight back, an open, affable face but the gray eyes were sharp and mean. I could see no instruments of torture in Cell 6. In fact, it was larger and more comfortable than most, with a real bed instead of a plank. I didn't get it—maybe the interrogators slept there whenever there were mass arrests and they had to work late and start early the next morning.

With a slight motion of his head, the man at the desk indicated the chair, where I sat down.

To the guard he said: "Remove the cuffs. Leave the shackles."

When the guard had left, he said: "I am your investigator, Major Boris Filippovich Antonov, and you are here to answer my questions. Last name?"

"Dzhugashvili."

"First name?"

"Joseph."

"Date of birth?"

"December 21, 1879."

"Profession?"

For a second I didn't know what to say. I couldn't say organizer, I couldn't say thief. And so I said, "Poet."

Antonov looked right into my eyes, defying me to hold his gaze. For a second it seemed he half believed me. Revolutionaries and poets did look alike in those days—long hair, beards, shabby clothes, a checked bandana around the neck.

"So," he said, holding his pen up in the air, "I should add poet to organizer and thief?"

For a second I had the uncanny feeling that he was inside of me, reading my mind. But then I realized of course they know I'm an organizer, and thief might just be thrown in for an insult or they might even have their suspicions, why not?

"Poet," I repeated.

He smiled, as if genuinely happy, then jotted something in my file.

"I like poetry myself," he said. "Especially Pushkin's poems about Petersburg, which, as you know, he calls 'stately and severe.' I'm from Petersburg and I hate it here. Too hot and sticky. No winter. I also like that poem where Pushkin tries to foresee his death, you know—'Whenever I wander the roaring streets, Or enter in a thronged cathedral, Or sit among the madcap young, I give myself to reverie. . . .' But a new Pushkin like yourself shouldn't be sitting in a stinking little cell thinking of death. A poet like yourself should be in a nice cell like this one, with a real bed and table, with pen and ink, books, hot tea."

I nodded to indicate I understood.

"So," he continued, "say a poet like yourself receives a sentence of three years' exile to Siberia. But where will he be exiled? To a village where you can live like a human being, or to some disease-ridden, godforsaken settlement above the Arctic Circle?"

Antonov sat back in his chair and spread his hands apart as if to say how could one even be weighed against the other?

But I weighed them. I didn't need the nice cell. I could take a year in prison. In a youthful, romantic way, I even wanted to be tested by tough conditions. And if they could get you into the Arctic Circle, then there was a way you could get out. The Party had people in every province. You learn that right away in Party work.

And what were those better conditions to be weighed against? The betrayal of my comrades, actively helping the Tsarist secret police.

"One of the nice things about poetry," I said, "is that you don't even need pen and paper. You can do it all in your head. And they say your favorite, Pushkin, did his best work in exile."

Antonov jerked slightly in his chair, then said sharply: "Pushkin was exiled to his estate, not to someplace where half the convicts starve to death every winter." Then his tone became heavier: "And don't forget people were killed in that riot. Capital crimes are involved. The leaders will hang. We haven't identified all the leaders yet, but you'd only expect them to act defiant when being questioned, now wouldn't you?"

Suddenly the chains on my feet felt very heavy. Antonov was a representative of a state that had the power to kill and I had just been reminded of that. If I really believed it was a choice between betraying my comrades and my own life, I wouldn't have any hesitation about saving my skin. But I didn't buy it.

"Having a few drinks on a Friday night still isn't a capital crime, not even in Russia."

"Listen closely, now, Mr. Poet, because I'm going to tell you something you didn't expect to hear. A lot of people have sat in front of me on the same chair you're sitting on. And there are just a few basic types—the weak ones who break easy, the true believers who are a lot of work, like your cellmate Sasha, who's apparently better at standing up to us than he is at standing up to you."

That stung me. Stunned me. He knew everything that had gone on in the cell. Who'd squealed? Sasha, to get back at me? Abdumanov, to get his sentence reduced? Or Benno, who was capable of anything?

I looked over at Antonov, who had a satisfied, indulgent look on his face as if he knew exactly what I was thinking.

"You might think it's just a matter of chance, who ends up in a cell with who," said Antonov. "And usually it is. But not always. Sometimes we perform little experiments. Throw a worker in with two politicos and see which one is the serious one, the real activist."

"There's a weakness in your experiment."

"What's that?"

"You're depending on reliable reports from a counterfeiter."

Antonov grinned, but didn't take the bait. "So," he continued, "there are those who break easy, the believers who are tougher, and then there are a few guys like you. Not weak but not true believers either. Up to something else. And what it is, they don't know themselves. Not yet, anyway. But they'll figure it out. They only want to be on top and what they're on top of comes in second. That's you, Mr. Poet, and that's the reason I'm certain that you and I speak the same language."

At that moment, I had the most unexpected feeling toward Antonov. Gratitude.

But that only lasted a second. He was still asking me to betray my comrades. Some had taught me things or sided with me. Others had made no secret of their scorn for me; Sasha was hardly the first. But I would not betray my comrades except to save my own life or for some other purpose that I considered just as important. But I could not see what that more important purpose might be.

Oddly, the flash of tactical insight came first. If I were to betray any comrades, it shouldn't just be those who had acted insultingly toward me, because someone might spot the pattern. Besides, anyone can destroy enemies. It takes a special freedom to destroy friends.

For a few seconds, I withdrew, absented myself from the room, no longer aware of Antonov.

Quick, what is it you want? I asked myself. To be head of the Georgian revolutionary organization.

Could the police aid me in this? They could certainly hinder me, that was clear. But if I was cooperating with them, they wouldn't arrest and exile me, at least not so often and not for so long. And of course there was nothing to prevent me from feeding them information selectively so that I got rid of precisely those people whose positions I wanted to fill or assume.

Yes, but only at the risk of my own life: death was the penalty when revolutionaries exposed a double agent.

At the very least it was an intriguing possibility—not that I work for the Tsar's secret police, but that they work for me.

Then I refocused my eyes on Antonov, who was rubbing his thumb against his fingers in impatience.

"I'm a little fish," I said.

"Fish grow."

12

Nosing around my old police records, Trotsky has discovered that I preferred to associate with criminals in prison, but all he can document is that some of my behavior wasn't exactly "heroic." That in itself doesn't bother me. What bothers me is that Trotsky is working on material concerning my criminal proclivities just as the Third Moscow Trial is about to begin. Scheduled to open in early March '38, the trial could well spark a whole series of unfortunate associations in Trotsky's mind. In a way, I too will be on trial, with Trotsky sitting in judgment on me.

So why not just kill Trotsky now? Who knows, maybe I should have done it when Trotsky was still in Russia, not far away in Mexico in a well-fortified compound.

But killing Trotsky in Russia would only have made a martyr of him. His grave could have become a symbol, a clandestine meeting place. Anyway, killing Trotsky before destroying his followers might result in his organization splitting into factions, all the more difficult to track and eliminate.

No, there's a certain logic and order to these things. Trotsky can be killed only after his followers and organization are gone. The first shall be last.

But that also means running a certain risk. What if Trotsky has already guessed something about *that*? For all I care, he can accuse me of cannibalizing children in the Kremlin, but without proof, hard evidence, it's just more of the shrill hysteria that so puts off Western intellectuals like Shaw.

But what if Trotsky has in fact begun gathering *evidence* about *that*?

There too I have a certain advantage.

From Paris, Trotsky's son Lyova runs the European wing of his father's affairs and publishes the *Bulletin of the Opposition*, in which I am consistently attacked. For the past four years, beginning sometime in 1934, Lyova's right-hand man has been Mark Zborowski, a charming Polish Jew who writes fiery articles for the *Bulletin* under the pen name of Etienne. He also writes very succinct reports that go straight to me.

Though Etienne puts his literary gifts in the service of Trotsky's organization, he does not disdain the humbler tasks like handling the mail, sorting the correspondence. Which means he has access to the letters that pass between Trotsky and his son.

Etienne's reports to me always include interesting excerpts from that correspondence, and I trust him to separate the wheat from the chaff.

Relations between father and son have been strained lately. Trotsky demands too much of the young man, requiring him to chase down every last document that could refute the charges brought against Trotsky in the Moscow trials. Recently he wrote to the poor boy: "After all the experiences of recent months, I must say that I have not yet had a day as black as this one, when I opened your envelope, confident I would find the affidavits in it and instead found only apologies and assurances. . . . It is difficult to say which are the worst blows, those that come from Moscow or those from Paris."

That is simply inaccurate and unjust.

Our security and intelligence people hold Lyova in higher esteem than his own father does. Our people are always saying, "The youngster is working well; without him the Old Man would find the going much tougher."

Feeling hurt by his father, Lyova has naturally grown closer to Etienne. Etienne himself is, however, still in Trotsky's good graces because of his success in assisting Trotsky in his work on Stalin's biography, digging up old newspaper articles, various documents, reminiscences. I therefore know which period of my life is of current interest to Trotsky even before he has the material to begin working on it.

But even though having Etienne inside Trotsky's Paris operation is a great advantage, it has its limits. While I can instruct Etienne to alert me if Trotsky begins requesting documents relating to the period in which the most sensitive events occurred, I cannot be any more specific with Etienne. He has no need to know. The other problem is that Trotsky may have secretly created a task force to research all the weightier issues relating to Stalin. He seems to have lost faith in his son and may not wish to entrust him with anything so crucial.

History can get devilishly complicated. You think you see what's happening, but then it turns out that something else was going on all the time.

Look at Sukhanov, who wrote a vivid account of the Revolution that he no doubt thought reflected reality. But the name of Joseph Stalin is scarcely mentioned in that tome. So then how did Stalin end up on top?

Oddly enough, the one who saw me coming in those hectic days was a naive young American, John Reed, who in his book *Ten Days That Shook the World* said of Stalin: "He's not an intellectual like the other people you will meet. He's not even particularly well informed, but he knows what he wants. He's got will power, and he's going to be on top of the pile someday."

On the other hand, Sukhanov, who saw me often, only remembered me as a "gray blur." Sukhanov, who was executed in '37, probably believed that my anger at this "insult" was behind all the formal charges against him. Not at all.

I was a "gray blur" by design. No one saw me coming. That's only logical. Given who I am, I could not show myself.

No one really saw Hitler coming either. Now it's too late. Now everyone's watching him, and he's starting to move. Just a few days ago, on February 4, 1938, Hitler named himself Supreme Commander of the German Armed Forces. There's nothing wrong with a grand title or two, but exercising power is always the point. So the only question is when and where he'll do it first. I made a ten-ruble bet with my foreign minister, Molotov. He thinks Hitler will annex the Sudetenland first because it's smaller and no one cares about it. And I said, "No, Hitler really believes all that *Volk* shit and will take Austria first." For a moment Molotov looked worried about winning a bet with me, but then got over it, shook my hand, and said: "All right, ten rubles."

"That way," I said, "even if there's a world war it won't be a total loss; one of us'll win a few rubles."

And yet another good reason for eliminating Trotsky is that he takes so much of my time when I should really be paying more attention to Hitler, who does after all have a real army of which he is now the Supreme Commander.

Just days after Hitler named himself commander, Etienne informed me directly from Paris that Trotsky's son Lyova was suffering from a severe attack of appendicitis. Lyova had been delaying treatment in order to carry out his father's unending demands, but now could do so no longer and would tomorrow check in to a Russian hospital in Paris. Etienne would personally oversee his treatment. I sent Etienne the necessary signal.

Etienne is very sensitive, an excellent operative; he never does anything himself but always knows just who to get, as he proved in his first successful venture, the theft of Trotsky's entire Paris archives two years ago. Still, I was very tense the next few days and smoked more than usual.

But that mood broke when I received Etienne's next report—concise, to the point, without a wasted word:

> Registered as Monsieur Martin, a French engineer, Lyova underwent surgery on Feb. 9 for appendicitis. The operation was a complete success. However, after three days of successful recuperation, the patient suddenly lapsed into delirium. Further surgery and transfusions failed to save him and he died on Feb. 16, 1938. His wife's demand for an autopsy—she suspects he was poisoned—yielded no evidence of foul play. The hospital's doctors maintain the cause of death to be intestinal occlusion, heart failure, and low powers of resistance. An eminent physician, a friend of the Trotsky family, accepts that opinion. Situation unclear and likely to remain so.

Who's to blame here? On the historical scale—Hitler, who injected tension into the international atmosphere by naming himself Supreme Commander of Germany's Armed Forces. That in turn made it necessary that Russia pay more attention to Hitler. But that couldn't be done while Trotsky was still alive. And Trotsky could not be killed until the last trial of Trotskyite traitors was held in Moscow and until his organization had been smashed both here at home and abroad.

And Lyova himself is to blame. He should have made a life for himself and not been his father's little helper. Not that it would have mattered much. What son would ever be good enough for Leon Trotsky?

And Lyova is also to blame for playing a game for which he had not the slightest talent. To cross swords with Stalin and then let him place Etienne at your right hand is simply shameful. But ultimately the heaviest load of blame must fall on Trotsky's own shoulders. He is the father, after all, and should know more than his earnest, sensitive thirty-two-year-old son. He should have seen that the boy was not cut out for this kind of life, this kind of work. He should have let him go, should have told him, Go do what makes you happy.

But, no, he preferred to exploit the boy's energy and talent in the name of a doomed cause. Trotsky himself shouldn't even be in the game. He's as taken in by Etienne as his son was.

And what Trotsky should have been doing was constantly testing security. It's almost insulting. I do it for him.

Trotsky should not have been working his son to the bone and accusing him of being worse than Moscow. He should have been constantly warning his son of Moscow, which always aims for your head and attacks your blind spot so that at most all you see coming is a sort of "gray blur."

13

Though Lyova Trotsky's appendicitis was a matter of pure chance, there was good reason to end his life in February 1938. I want Trotsky distracted by grief on the eve of the last great Moscow trial, which will commence in early March if all the defendants have been persuaded to cooperate. Of the twenty-one defendants, two are of special importance—Bukharin, the "darling of the party" as Lenin called him, everyone's favorite; and Yagoda, former head of the secret police, a man no one liked.

Even though Trotsky should immerse himself entirely in grieving for his son, he will still no doubt be paying close attention to the trial. Trotsky knows this must be the last of the great show trials for the simple reason that there's no one of any significance left. And he must also realize that, once Stalin has convicted these last important figures, he will be free to move against Trotsky himself.

My hope is that Trotsky's grief will distract him from the trial. But the trial might distract him from his grief. And the trial could give him *ideas.* And that could send him back to his research with fresh will. Especially since with the death of his son, Trotsky has yet another motive to destroy me.

In his obituary for Lyova, Trotsky wrote: "The first and natural assumption: he was poisoned. To gain access to Lyova, to his clothes, his food, presented no great difficulty for Stalin's agents. . . . The art of poisoning has been developed to an exceptional degree. . . . It is fully possible that there now exists a poison that cannot be traced after death, even by the most thorough analysis."

For someone who should be distracted by grief, the old man is thinking all too clearly.

The trial of the Twenty-One is also very important to me on the international front. The world will be watching. Foreigners will attend. I want no hesitations, no embarrassments.

I receive daily written reports, transcripts, copies of signed confessions. There are always some who confess, then recant. And there are even a few who seem so caught up in cycles of confessing and recanting that you can't be sure how they'll act at a public trial.

Interrogations of special interest to me are conducted in a room that is wired for sound and connected directly to my office in the Kremlin so that I can listen in, either by phone or by speaker.

In some ways this is the art of listening at its highest. You must be sensitive to every nuance of panic and contempt.

How sincere was that confession? Was it only to buy a respite from torture or had the man been broken?

The foreign press has been invited to the trial. Everything must be done right. With decorum.

If the defendants' crimes are properly presented, Western politicians and journalists will say, Of course, Stalin had enemies; how could a man like that not have enemies? And the fact that he dealt with them harshly isn't surprising, what do you expect, it's Russia, not Switzerland.

And the Russians will say, How did a Jew like Yagoda get to be head of the secret police in the first place? And there's something fishy about that Bukharin too, darling or no darling.

But that's only *if* their crimes are properly presented, without hesitations or embarrassments. And since this is so important to me, I don't confine myself to written reports and listening in. If need be, I conduct interrogations myself.

Logistically, it couldn't be simpler. Late at night it's less than a five-minute drive from the Kremlin to Lubyanka, which not only is security police headquarters and a prison for especially important suspects, but also has execution cellars and a small crematorium—everything under one roof.

Still, it's not just a matter of jumping in a car and driving over. Certain preparations are required.

Last night I listened in on the interrogation of Yagoda for about thirty minutes and was not in the least satisfied with the way it was going. After all, the man had been head of the secret police; he knew all the tricks and the dodges.

Yagoda could cause more trouble at a public trial than Bukharin could. Bukharin might appeal to Lenin and honor and the ideas of the Bolshevik cause. But Yagoda actually *knew* things.

Yagoda had of course taken a solemn oath of secrecy, but that will lose meaning for him when facing death. He is not a man of especially strong character.

He's also something of a fool. Shortly before his arrest, he was busy designing all sorts of fancy uniforms for himself and his men—gold braid, little naval swords, that sort of thing. But fools are dangerous too; who knows what they'll do next?

And who knows about the men interrogating Yagoda? Maybe they have some feeling left for their old boss. Or maybe they're asking themselves, If it can happen to him, why can't it happen to me? Though that should only make them work all the harder.

I called Lubyanka on a line only I can use. "I will interrogate Yagoda tomorrow night at two o'clock in the corner room."

"Yes, Comrade Stalin," said the duty officer, a salute in his voice.

But as the hour approached, I began to get nervous, superstitious. Yes, it's only a five-minute drive from the Kremlin to Lubyanka, and it's wintry, late February—there won't be anyone out. Yes, the car is armor-plated and bulletproof, yes, I will be well guarded. But a limo is not a tank. A sufficient explosive charge, especially from below, can tear a vehicle apart. The charge could be concealed under a manhole. Someone could reason, and reason correctly, that Stalin is very interested in the outcome of the Trial of the Twenty-One. Defendants as important as these would surely be held in Lubyanka. Given Stalin's nature, he might just take it into his head to go over to Lubyanka and crack the whip on the spot. And there are only so many possible routes from the Kremlin to Lubyanka.

If I could think that, why couldn't somebody else?

Besides, murdering leaders is a Russian tradition. We killed the Tsar. A woman tried to shoot Lenin. In all of Russia there still must be a few people as brave as that woman.

The logic of self-preservation dictates that I exert extra precaution at this time.

At around midnight, I buzz for the chief of the guards. "Summon Boss Two at once," I say.

Boss Two enters my office about thirty minutes later, still looking freshly woken and flushed by the frosty air. Otherwise, he couldn't look more like me, right down to the curl at the end of the mustache.

"You've been well?" I ask.

"Can't complain," he says.

I'm about to smile at this line, which is what he always says, but then I think, Why couldn't Kremlin intriguers loyal to Trotsky just quietly do me in and use one of my doubles for public appearances until the new power arrangements were made? Which meant that the man standing before me represented a serious potential threat. But then, on reflection, I considered that unlikely and so did smile a little.

"At twenty to two, you'll go over to Lubyanka. You'll wait there. The car will come back for me. You stay at Lubyanka until I'm ready to leave. Clear?"

"Couldn't be clearer."

"The wife, the family?"

"Everyone's fine."

Though I'm direct with them, I'm usually fairly polite to my doubles. There is an etiquette with doubles that's like nothing else. Sometimes they strike you as comical, sometimes they cause a flash of hate. But still there's a tendency to treat them a little better because they help you live your life and might even die your death for you.

"Call me on the direct line as soon as Boss Two is inside Lubyanka," I order the head of the guards.

I decide to have a pipe or two before leaving for the interrogation, but not to smoke there.

"Boss Two has arrived," came the call.

"Send the car."

The driver and bodyguard seemed in good humor, glad for some night action—driving Stalin to Lubyanka beats tea and talk.

It was either snowing lightly or a light wind was picking up the loose snow on the ground. As we drove across the cobblestones of Red Square, I could not help but glance over at St. Basil's, whose architect Ivan the Terrible had blinded, but this time the history I was remembering was my own. It was there in front of St. Basil's quite a few years ago that I'd reached the decision to proceed with *that* and to involve Yagoda.

The night was black and Moscow was deserted. But a few people were out even at this hour, the usual drunks, doctors, shift workers. But I do not like to glimpse even a single person when I'm on the way to Lubyanka.

We pull up. Gates open, salutes.

This is a high-security operation and the only people aware of it are the driver, the bodyguard, Boss Two, the officer I spoke to on the phone who greets me there, and the two guards who will bring the prisoner in to be interrogated. Anything further represents a breach of security.

"And where is Boss Two?" I ask the officer as he escorts me to the corner room.

"Alone. In a room. Reading."

"No one else saw him?"

"No one."

The corner room is of medium size, the bottom third of the light blue walls are painted dark blue. The room contains only a desk and two chairs, one behind the desk, one in front. Behind the desk are also two stands mounted with large spotlights and reflectors.

I sit down at the desk and test the buzzer. A guard is in the room with weapon drawn in two seconds. Not that I need to worry about Yagoda. After a man has been woken every ten minutes all night for a few weeks, the fight pretty much goes out of him.

Then we test the lights. One of the two guards is an expert at lighting. The officer plays Yagoda walking from the door to the chair, waiting to be told to sit, blinking all the while from the blinding light.

"I couldn't get a glimpse of who's behind the desk on the way from the door and I still can't," he says.

"All right, now start turning the lights down slowly," I say to the guard and then to the officer: "Tell me the second you see my face!"

"Now!"

"Good."

"Shall we bring the prisoner in?"

"You have mops and pails?"

"Outside the door."

"Get the prisoner."

Sometimes people ushered into my presence lose control of their bodily functions and though there is some tribute in this, I do like it cleaned up right away.

I heard them coming. The guard was tapping his keys against his belt buckle to alert other guards that the prisoner being escorted through the corridors was not to be seen.

Yagoda's face was a bit washed out, but otherwise he looked pretty much the same—the same hound-dog jowls, the same postage-stamp mustache, something I could never quite understand; if you're going to grow a mustache, then grow one.

I could see how painful that light must be to eyes just woken from sleep. He moved slowly, mechanically, as if by rote.

"You may sit down," said the guard who had escorted Yagoda and who remained behind him.

The other guard was at the control switch for the lights.

Yagoda's eyes could not blink fast enough. After a while, I gently touched the sleeve of the guard, who then slowly began dimming the lights.

I almost laughed at Yagoda's startled expression when he saw my face emerge from the darkness into the shrinking circle of light.

"You?" he said.

"Me."

"Why?"

"Aren't you flattered?"

"Is that the word?"

"Why not?"

"Look, I know the game. So what do I have left? Very little."

"Next to nothing."

"Yes. And so . . ."

"One moment," I said. "The guards are dismissed."

When the guards had left, I said: "And so?"

"And so there are some things I don't want heaped on my name."

"But your name is already ruined."

"All the more reason not to make it worse."

"And what makes it worse?"

"Having to say I did it all for Trotsky when I did it all for you."

"And you will say you did it all for Trotsky for me too."

"I know this organization can always get results," he said. "But I also know there's a fine line to be walked. It takes a while to get a prisoner back in shape after torture; you don't want me collapsing in the dock."

"Are you threatening to collapse?"

"Collapsing's the only thing I can threaten."

"Don't even threaten that."

"All right, but why couldn't I be a traitor for other reasons?"

"Let's say you could. Let's say you, a Jew, had been reached by Jewish capital and paid to assassinate me. How's that?"

"Better."

"Better? Better for who? Not for the Jews of Russia. And not for the Russian people either. Why should they have to suffer and worry that Jewish financiers had even infiltrated the Soviet security organs? What would that do to their sense of security when any fool knows the country is on the eve of war? To damage your country on the eve of war is the worst possible treason."

Yagoda slumped a little in his chair, but then a second later he sat back up and said: "But, look, let's you and I cut the crap—we both know that all this talk about Trotskyite saboteurs and traitors is blown way out of proportion. Yes, there's some, but you could shoot them all in a single night."

"Trotsky is not the enemy because he has so many followers. Trotsky is the enemy because he is the only man on earth who can take my place in the Kremlin. Hitler could invade and take Russia and take my life but he could never take my place in the Kremlin, my place as the leader of Soviet Russia. Trotsky will still be the enemy even when his organization is smashed and there's only Trotsky left. To refuse to say you served Trotsky in the past is to serve Trotsky in the present. Which is even worse."

Yagoda withdrew into himself. Prisoners under interrogation will do that. And you must let them. This is the moment when they come to some final decision. Sometimes it is followed by an emotional outburst, tears, wailing.

But prisoners undergoing interrogation must not be allowed to withdraw for too long either. They must not be allowed time to harden a position, they must always be kept off balance. It's a delicate art to know just when to break the spell with one sharp word.

"Yagoda!"

"Yes?"

"No sleeping."

"I wasn't . . ."

"No sleeping."

"What do you want, I've already signed the confession."

"I won't be happy until I am certain that you will perform well at the trial."

"Worried that I might say something I shouldn't? Worried that I might jump up and tell them about *that*?"

"No. Because how much could you say about *that* in the few seconds before the spectators shouted you down and the judge was banging his gavel so loud no one could hear you? So not only will you fail to make any startling revelations but if you so much as try, I promise you that, just as I am conducting your interrogation now, I'll personally conduct your torture. And I don't think you want that."

"But I always hated Trotsky."

"So now do him harm."

"Yes," he said, "I can see that."

But had he? He knew what to do. A person in that position knows what to do. Slowly Yagoda raised his eyes to mine so that I could look into them, into him. He had to open himself so that I could pace the floor of his soul and look into every corner.

But people are such liars, they can fake anything.

Still, he was probably sincere because the next moment, his eyes wide and his lips barely moving, he said, "I see. . . . You're the devil. . . ."

He had gone mad for a moment. That happens too.

"Yagoda!"

"Yes?"

"You're dreaming again."

"I was?"

"Yes, now listen to me. You will learn your lines and play your part. You will get up in the dock and say the lines you learned so that you can bring harm to the enemy and not bring more harm down on yourself. You will learn your lines and play your part. Say it!"

"I will learn my lines, I will play my part."

"And who did you work for unceasingly, day and night?"

"For Trotsky, for Trotsky, only for Trotsky."

"And not a word about *that*?"

"Not a word."

Then there was the question of what to do with Boss Two. I could send him ahead to the Kremlin or go first myself and have him brought after. But by then it was three-thirty in the morning and I figured there was no harm in both of us riding back together.

Though I wasn't really one hundred percent sure about Yagoda, I was still in good spirits. And so when I spotted a drunk reeling down the street, I couldn't resist telling the driver to slow down. The car pulled alongside the drunk, who slowed his pace at seeing the blue-black limousine. I lowered the window. I can't even begin to describe the expression on the drunk's face when he looked inside and saw—two Stalins!

"Drink a little less," I said, and we roared away.

14

Today, March 2, 1938, should have been a good day.

It started auspiciously. The trial of Yagoda, Bukharin, and the other defendants opened in Moscow's House of Columns, all marble and pillars, solemn and grand. And lighting effects were put to good use. Vyshinsky the prosecutor was spotlit in an otherwise darkened courtroom when he made his opening speech, and his voice lashed the defendants with indictment after indictment. Everything from plotting Lenin's death to acts of industrial sabotage like slipping ground glass into foodstuffs, particularly butter.

I attended. Great pains were taken to conceal my comings and goings—a corridor for my use only, a private box with dark tinted windows.

There was plenty else I could have been dealing with. Ten days ago, on February 20, 1938, Hitler had demanded self-determination for Germans in Austria and Czechoslovakia. First he names himself Supreme Commander, then he's demanding self-determination. The use of force can't be far behind.

I reminded Molotov of our bet.

But the trial was more important to me because, dead son or no dead son, Trotsky would be watching.

As the lights came back up, I switched my attention to the defendants, especially Bukharin and Yagoda. Bukharin was sitting up straight, but not defiantly straight. The good intellectual, he was paying attention. Though his eyes seemed to be darting, Yagoda was slumped a little in his chair. I couldn't read him. Was it exhaustion? Indifference? Or was he saving his strength for something?

The boys at Lubyanka like to say, Give us a man, we'll build a case. I approve of their optimism and readiness to work. But this is a more important matter than most. It's not enough that the crime fits the man. The man must rise to fit the crime.

Are the defendants guilty as charged? The answer is a no that dialectically becomes a yes.

In a certain highly literal sense of the word, most of these men are not guilty of most of these crimes. They may, however, be guilty of many other crimes, crimes for which the state has decided to spare itself the expenses of a trial but which would have cost them their head in any case.

Yagoda's a perfect example. A pharmacist before the Revolution, at Lubyanka he set up his own lab known as the "kamera" where he performed highly sophisticated experiments with poison. Many people died from those poisons. But let us say for the sake of argument that Maxim Gorky, the grand old man of Soviet literature, was not one of them. Let's say that Gorky died a natural death and Stalin wants to turn the failure of some heart valve into a political assassination.

Yagoda is already stained with the blood of ten thousand deaths. No justice could ever be adequate for a hyena like him. But if his confession can serve some higher cause, his life will be partially redeemed. But of course that's a type of argument that would appeal more to the "theoretician" Bukharin than to a former head of the secret police. Yagoda's much trickier to deal with. You can promise to spare his life, but he's told that same lie too many times himself. You can promise to spare his loved ones, but who does a man like that really love?

Things got off to a bumpy start. One of the minor defendants pleaded "not guilty." Court was adjourned. The next day the man acknowledged that he had pleaded "not guilty" by mistake.

Maybe the defendant simply shares my dialectical view of guilt and had just momentarily confused the literal with the real.

But I was displeased.

And I was even more displeased when Trotsky fired off his latest blast at me in his *Bulletin of the Opposition*, which Etienne was now editing. Of course he couldn't stop Trotsky from publishing; the best he could do was supply me with a copy of the text before the type was set.

It seems I'm not the only one who refers to himself in the third person. Trotsky writes:

> Trotsky has only to blink an eye for veterans of the revolution to become agents for Hitler and the Mikado. On Trotsky's "instructions" . . . the leaders of industry, agriculture, and transport destroy the country's productive resources. On the orders of "Public Enemy No. 1," whether from Norway or Mexico, the railwaymen destroy military transports in the Far East, while highly respected doctors poison their patients in the Kremlin. This is the amazing picture painted in the Moscow trials, but here a difficulty arises. Under a totalitarian regime it is the apparatus that implements the dictatorship. But if my hirelings are occupying all the key posts in the apparatus, how is it that Stalin is in the Kremlin and I'm in exile?

I read that bulletin on the very morning that Yagoda was scheduled to take the stand, and so was in ill humor when I arrived at my box.

And Yagoda's testimony did nothing to improve my mood.

Willing to admit to poisoning Gorky, which he did not do, all of a sudden he had scruples about admitting to murdering his predecessor at the secret police, Menzhinsky, which he did.

YAGODA: I did not bring about the death of Menzhinsky.

VYSHINSKY: But didn't you admit it in your deposition?

YAGODA: I did, but it is not true.

VYSHINSKY: Why did you make a false deposition?

YAGODA: Permit me not to answer this question.

Vyshinsky kept hammering away at him. Just as Yagoda seemed about to do something truly irrational, a rather dramatic little incident occurred.

Among the foreign guests whose reactions mattered to me was Sir Fitzroy Maclean of the British Embassy. In a cabled report that was intercepted, he reported the incident as follows: "At one moment during the trial a clumsily directed arc lamp clearly revealed to attentive members of the audience a drooping mustache and yellowish face peering out from behind the black glass of one of the private boxes that commanded a view of the courtroom."

The description is accurate enough, though my mustache is still bristly. And he's wrong about the arc lamp. Any clumsiness was solely apparent. The point was to remind Yagoda of our evening together in Lubyanka and of the promise I had made him. The same man who ran the lights during the interrogation was in charge of them in the courtroom.

But even that didn't seem to work.

Yagoda said, as if speaking to the prosecutor, but no doubt addressing me as well: "You can drive me, but not too far. I'll say what I want to say . . . but . . . do not drive me too far."

Yagoda kept playing it just right, admitting enough to prevent any further adjournments, but giving himself one last vain hour of freedom. And there wasn't a goddamn thing I could do about it but sit there and smoke one bitter cigarette after the other.

After Yagoda's testimony, I went out to Zubalovo, one of the two country houses where I spend most of my time. I ate lightly; the food gave me no pleasure and the wine no peace.

That night I dreamed I was in prison, a horrible dream. I kept pacing back and forth in the cell, panicked like a dog lurching at his chain. It was a very small cell, only three bunks. On one a man was sleeping with his face to the wall, on the other sat Yagoda wearing a uniform, fancy but dirty.

He kept yelling: "Stalin put the glass in Lenin's butter!"

Then the man on the bunk turned his face from the wall and I could see it was Trotsky's son. He said: "I was young."

15

Even though it looks like Hitler might invade Austria at any moment, I am still giving my full attention to the trial, at least while Bukharin is on the stand.

Though he did not know any great secrets like Yagoda, Bukharin was a problem too. He was not the type that would respond well to severe interrogation. He might easily go out of his mind. He has an artistic temperament, emotional, impetuous.

Bukharin was the sort everyone liked. But there was contempt behind that affection. Trotsky called Bukharin "semi-hysterical, semi-infantile, lachrymose." And Lenin, though terming Bukharin the "Party's most eminent and most valuable theoretician," also called him "soft wax."

And that soft wax might just melt away into nothing under the heat of torture. So a special three-pronged strategy was devised for Bukharin.

Bukharin, at forty-five, had recently fallen in love with a beautiful young woman and had a child with her. Needless to say, as is common in such cases, he was filled with tenderness, excitement, joy. Prong One: Promise that no harm will come to those he loves.

Prong Two: Promise that he will be imprisoned, not executed. To feed that false hope, he was given what investigators like to call a "rubber tit." A meeting was arranged in prison between Bukharin and a defendant in the First Moscow Trial whose death sentence had been commuted to ten years' imprisonment. Proof that a deal was a deal.

Prong Three: Work on the communist and theoretician in Bukharin, convince him that ultimately the charges against him served the only idea and cause that give his life meaning. For a man of his inner consistency not to render this last service would be spiritual suicide.

I had already tested Bukharin and knew how he would behave. Three years ago, I sent him to Western Europe to purchase some of the archives of Marx and Engels. All he had to do was stay there. He knew the risks of return. He said it himself: "We all rush into his jaws, knowing he'll devour us."

Returning to Russia was his first mistake. Why did he do it? He couldn't have a real life outside of Soviet Russia. It's one thing to be a Marxist emigré *before* the revolution, something else entirely *after* it. Trotsky could do it because he has the steam and self-importance, but Bukharin doesn't.

So even knowing that the risks were sky-high, Bukharin returned, which meant that at the most basic level he was ruled by his sense of Bolshevik loyalty.

But, dialectically, Bukharin's return to Stalin's Russia was also an implicit betrayal of Stalin's Russia. Bukharin did not return because he was loyal to Stalin's Russia, but to his own Bolshevik values, which by their very nature had to oppose Stalin. Bolshevik types like Bukharin could never work well with a Stalin. And a Stalin could certainly never work well with them. Those Bolsheviks could make a revolution but they could not keep it.

In any case, Bukharin's the last of Lenin's crew, the last of the old Bolsheviks. In recent months so many of the old guard have vanished, a new joke's even making the rounds:

Knock, knock.

Who's there?

Secret police.

You want the communists, one floor up.

Actually, the first mistake Bukharin made was not returning to Russia, but what he said of me while still in Europe: "Stalin is actually unhappy at not being able to convince everyone, including himself, that he is greater than everyone; this unhappiness of his may be his most human trait, indeed his only human trait, but what is no longer human, but something devilish, is that because of this unhappiness of his he can't help revenging himself on people, on everybody, but especially on those who are superior to him or better at something. If anyone speaks better than he does, he is doomed! Stalin will not let him live—since such a man would be an eternal reminder that Stalin is not supreme. If anyone writes better than he does, he's finished, because only Stalin, only *he* has the right to be the premier Russian writer."

It could be Trotsky speaking! That derision of me as a writer is another link between Bukharin and Trotsky. As men of intellect, they cannot help but feel superior to me. Yet they hate it when I act superior toward them. And cannot bear it when I prove superior.

And though Bukharin's return to Soviet Russia was for me almost a foregone conclusion—he could no more live without it than a polar bear could live in a desert—still, what a risk I ran. While out of the country, Bukharin could have linked up with Trotsky; the two of them together would have made for a formidable opponent. But if I couldn't read Bukharin, I couldn't read anyone.

So he came back. To reward him and make good use of his "theoretical" abilities, I made him principal architect of the 1936 Stalin Constitution.

He came back and now he's in the dock, not looking bad, his hair, goatee, and eyes still a dark brown, slightly resembling Lenin but without his vivid hardness.

Bukharin splits hairs, arguing every little point as he responds to the accusation concerning Trotsky's negotiations with Hitler to cede him the Soviet Ukraine.

Vyshinsky: Did you endorse these negotiations?

Bukharin: Or disavow? I did not disavow them: consequently I endorsed them.

Vyshinsky: I ask you, did you endorse them, or not?

Bukharin: I repeat, Citizen Prosecutor: since I did not disavow them, I consequently endorsed them.

Vyshinsky: Consequently you endorsed them?

Bukharin: If I did not disavow them, consequently I endorsed them.

Vyshinsky: But you say that you learned of the negotiations post factum.

Bukharin: Yes, the one does not contradict the other in the slightest.

You could scream.

And Bukharin also refuses to accept responsibility for plotting to assassinate Lenin, trying to wriggle out of it with subtleties and compliments:

"We rose up against the joy of new life, using highly criminal methods. I reject the accusation of having attempted to kill Lenin, but I led a band of counterrevolutionary accomplices who attempted to murder Lenin's work, carried forward with such tremendous success by Comrade Stalin."

But true to himself as a Bolshevik theoretician, in the end Bukharin, despite all his ironies and reservations, did say the one thing he had to say: "I plead guilty to being one of the outstanding leaders of the Trotskyite bloc. I plead guilty to what directly follows from this, the sum total of crimes committed by the counterrevolutionary organization, irrespective of whether or not I knew of, whether or not I took direct part in, any particular act."

This will all be much too fancy for the man in the street, who only wants to know: "Did Bukharin admit it or not?"

Bukharin sits down after his closing words, looking flushed, defenseless. Too tender for all this, he was wrong to have come back. He forgot Esenin's great line: To the brute is given joy, and to the tender—sorrow.

And Bukharin was wrong about my supposed one human trait of unhappiness. I am a happy man.

I'm happy to be sitting alone with a glass of wine now that the trial is over and all twenty-one defendants have confessed and been executed. I'm happy that all the Trotskyites in the camps—some of whom even had the nerve to organize strikes, demanding a shorter work day—are also being shot as fast as manpower permits. I'm happy to be free of all enemies in Russia.

And I am happy that, though it will take some time and some doing, nothing on earth can now prevent Trotsky's assassination, except for an accident or his own natural death. And so for that reason, here and now, I drink to your health, Leon Trotsky!

PART III

16

To SOMEONE LACKING FINESSE AND EXPERTISE, FALL 1938 might seem the perfect time to eliminate Trotsky. The Moscow trials are over. Yagoda, Bukharin, and all the rest of Trotsky's people have been tried in the dock and shot in the head. But I can't do it right now, for three reasons, one international, one domestic, one personal.

The international situation is getting hellishly complicated. In March '38 Hitler took Austria and I collected the ten rubles from Molotov. In August Hitler called up a million reserves, in October he grabbed the Sudetenland of Czechoslovakia.

I look at the West and cannot for the life of me figure out what's going on over there. England's Prime Minister Chamberlain visits Hitler, gives away the Sudeten in exchange for "peace in our time," then goes home to drink tea. The American aviation hero Charles Lindbergh is personally decorated by Hitler in Berlin with the German Service Cross. The French and the Germans are discussing a "Friendship Pact." The only thing I do know is that any deal is possible if only because every country will follow its own interests. America would line up with us if that served its interests, and, if with us, why not with Hitler?

The American press is full of propaganda against both Hitler and me. But lately the American press is writing a bit more favorably about us, especially since we introduced our new Constitution and began the wind-down of the Terror. The Western newspapers are owned by rich men—I never heard of a poor man who owned a newspaper. The rich men will support their country's policies and will order their newspapers to write well of us if need be. If Hitler becomes their enemy, I will be their enemy's enemy.

But if Trotsky were suddenly killed in Mexico, a scandal would erupt. There'd be no burying the story. Reaching into a sovereign nation and assassinating someone as prominent as Trotsky would produce all the wrong sorts of headlines.

For the time being, Trotsky's remaining alive serves the foreign policy interests of Soviet Russia until the political situation is clarified.

Then there's the domestic front. The Terror is winding down but there's still a lot of mopping up to do. But that's not the main thing. The main thing is that the secret police must be blamed for the excesses of the secret police. That means that the current team has got to go. And that means that I have to create my own secret organization within that secret organization so that at the proper moment they can do what I want done and be ready to take the places that will suddenly become vacant.

For that reason in July I appointed a new deputy chief of the security organs—Lavrenty Beria, a fellow Georgian and distant relative. There are some advantages to being able to speak with him in Georgian: no Russians ever bothered to learn our language, not even the revolutionaries, who as a matter of principle had been opposed to the Tsarist policy of stamping out Georgian and making us all speak Russian, which turned out to be one of the best things that ever happened to me.

Beria was well qualified for the job because of his skills, looks, and vices.

Of skill what can you say? Some hunters bring home more ducks than others. And Beria bagged quite a few.

He forged an effective security organization in Georgia, knew how to reward his men, win their loyalty and admiration, was, in a word, a true leader. This is both good and bad. Good because the security organs will need to feel they have an intelligent, capable, concerned leader—otherwise that important organization will take too long to recover from the purges now harrowing it. And bad because people with leadership abilities are by definition potential rivals.

A master in the use of the blackjack, Beria is also adept at what could be called the diplomacy of human relations. He took good care of my mother while she was alive and stood in for me at the funeral when she died. My children became close to Beria when they went to Georgia to visit their grandmother. And I remember that when I myself went to Georgia on the occasion of my mother's eightieth birthday, she was always referring to Beria as "our Lavrenty."

"Our Lavrenty" is also skilled in flattering me. He made sure no issue of any Georgian paper appeared without photographs of the "Great Stalin" or quotations from the "Great Stalin" or praise for the "Great Stalin." Beria commissioned and put his name as author to a book (later executing the ghostwriters) entitled *On the History of Bolshevik Organizations in Transcaucasia*, highlighting the central role of the "Great Stalin." In addition, he presided over the opening of a monument—the two-room brick hovel where I grew up was encased in a huge, magnificent marble structure resembling a Greek temple supported by four classical columns, which, as Beria said, stressed both the humble working-class origins and awe-inspiring achievements of the "Great Stalin."

Foreign commentators, including Trotsky, make the case that Stalin has an immense appetite for flattery and adulation. They say his likeness is sculpted into mountains and worn in lockets around widows' necks, and so on and so forth. Then some of them analyze this in psychological terms, at times making reference even to Freud, whose works I have both read and banned—they simply have nothing to do with real life as we know it, though some of his ideas like the death wish do seem to apply to some people.

I am only human and must admit that the sound of a million throats roaring my name with wild joy produces a certain pleasant effect. But, like everything else, you get used to it.

My critics are simply wrong in thinking that I have an unnatural appetite for praise. All the adulation and flattery does, however, serve two other purposes, both much more important to me than the gratifications of the personality. First and foremost, adulation is a sign, symbol, and measure of power. If your face and words are in people's minds and acts, if they feel more powerful identifying their will with yours, your power has extended as far inward as it can go, into the ganglia of the nervous system. Secondly, flattery is really a code revealing loyalties and intentions. Beria is a case in point. His style of flattery signals his eagerness to serve and his willingness to submit. The whole thing is more Darwinian than Freudian.

As far as looks are concerned, Beria resembles a professor, with his thinning black hair, high forehead, and owlish eyes; he even wears a pince-nez. He reads books in a few languages, has good taste, lives in a cultured home with his charming, beautiful wife and well-mannered children. Quite the opposite of the current head of the secret police, Yezhov, a stunted, brutal man, hated by all and called the "bloody dwarf" behind his back. It is on Yezhov that all the excesses of the Terror must be blamed. And what better symbol that the worst is behind us than a man with good manners and even a pince-nez?

Beria's vices also qualified him. He likes to be driven around Moscow in his limousine with its dark tinted windows, through which he scans the streets for schoolgirls who catch his eye. The driver brings the schoolgirl to the car and Beria rapes her. The greater her horror, the greater his excitement.

Personally, I don't approve. From time to time, by sheer chance, Beria selects the daughter of some influential person and a small scandal results. This is bad for the prestige of the secret police, whose lost luster he is supposed to restore. But it seems like a small price to pay—it keeps him happy in the meantime and can always be used against him later. And besides, I do not like people who are too pure.

I do, however, hate the cologne Beria wears; it's sweet and rank at the same time, like flowers at a funeral.

So it's not so much that the Terror is over but that it is now raging within the ranks of the secret police itself and is, for that reason, largely invisible.

Simply on the manpower level, this means my best and most trusted people are too busy to deal with Trotsky.

Of course, we have always kept a close eye on Trotsky ever since he was marched onto a ship in Odessa and exiled from Soviet Russia in '29. And we now have several operatives surveilling Trotsky and his compound in the Mexico City suburb of Coyoacán.

The cleaning woman has provided us with a much more detailed layout of the house than the one we obtained from the municipal records commission, which only showed the floor plan. She supplied all sorts of valuable details—which corridors were clogged with crates and trunks and would take longer for any help to come down. In addition, we have in our possession many photographs of the exterior of the house and of the surrounding streets and houses. We have good maps of the area. There are also of course the press reports and photos—Trotsky wearing whites while taking tea or in his blue French peasant's jacket feeding his rabbits with a special mixture that he has "scientifically" devised himself.

Attempts are being made to learn more about Trotsky's bodyguards, their background, politics, personal weaknesses.

And of course we continue to read Trotsky's correspondence with Etienne.

The file grows a little thicker every day.

Trotsky seems less far away. I can picture the house, the corridor, the study where he works. I recognize the faces of the guards when new photos arrive. Even the rabbits are starting to look familiar.

The third and last reason not to eliminate Trotsky at once is more subjective, personal. In fact, Trotsky himself has already found evidence of it. He writes that when speaking with Kamenev and Dzerzhinsky, Stalin "confessed over a bottle of wine one summer night on the balcony of a summer resort that his highest delight was to keep a keen eye on an enemy, prepare everything painstakingly, mercilessly revenge himself, and then go to sleep." I remember how shocked Dzerzhinsky looked, him, the founder of the secret police, able to empty a Mauser into the head of anyone even suspected of counterrevolutionary tendencies. But they were all the same in that—any act was justified if it served the Revolution, but God forbid you enjoyed it, God forbid it did you any good. So there will only be one night when I will go to sleep knowing that I will wake the next day to a world in which there is no Leon Trotsky, and I can hardly be blamed for wanting to choose that moment with enough care that it provides me the "highest delight."

But if I have any grounds for believing that Trotsky is about to come forward with documented proof concerning *that,* then it's to hell with the international situation, to hell with the domestic situation, and to hell with Stalin's delights.

17

Apparently, the trial of Yagoda and Bukharin did not give Trotsky any "ideas." But ideas are funny things. They can come in an instant or take a year, arriving when you least expect them—stepping out of a car or taking a leak. But, logically, if Trotsky had made any unwarranted associations, his first move would be to begin gathering proof, evidence, documents. Yet his most recent communications with Etienne in Paris have all been requests for additional material connected with the distant past, my first arrest, interrogation, exile.

After refusing to cooperate with my investigator, Major Antonov, I was transferred to Kutais Prison in preparation for exile to Siberia. It was a period of extensive study. I learned some Esperanto, the "language of hope." And I spent hours trying to master German because it was considered necessary to read *Das Kapital* in the original if you wanted to be considered anything more than a "practico." But by the time I'd find the goddamned verb, I'd have forgotten what the sentence was about.

But Kutais Prison was also a great "university," in Gorky's sense of the word, giving new lessons in people and life.

One evening, word went around that there would be an execution the next day, a hanging at dawn. The whole prison was up before daylight and, except for the few clangs inevitable in prison, all the cells were silent. A very different silence from the silence of the prison at night when everyone is sleeping. This was a silence tense with the expectation of suffering.

For the first time in my life I heard a man being taken out to execution. When the silence became unbearable, the prisoner screamed. It wasn't the horror in his voice that struck me. It was the loneliness.

I had received an administrative sentence—meaning by the police, not by the court—of three years of exile in the Siberian settlement of Novaya Uda. But the Russian authorities like to take their time. From the moment of my arrest in April 1902 until I was finally loaded on the train to Siberia in late 1903, twenty-one months had passed.

And three years was a fairly standard sentence. The only break I got was the place, one of the better parts of Siberia, not the Arctic Circle. Maybe Major Antonov had done me a little favor, given me a little something to remember him by.

Exile to Siberia was done "in stages," as they used to say in those days. All that meant was that trainloads of prisoners would travel to one city and wait there, a day, a week, a month, to be joined by another trainload until a full contingent was formed. Then once you reach the terminal in Siberia, you travel by horse-drawn sleigh to the village, where you're assigned to a hut with a few other exiles. You report to the police once a month; otherwise you're pretty much on your own, free to hunt, even with rifles, as well as to fish and trap to supplement the meager allocation for rations that you're issued.

Escaping from prison was just about impossible. Escaping from the train was doable, but it was asking for a bullet in the back if the guards on the roofs of the train cars spotted you against the snow. But escaping from Siberia was fairly easy. As even Trotsky says: "By the beginning of 1904 the exile system had become a sieve. In most cases it was not difficult to escape; each province had its own secret 'centers,' which provided forged passports, money, addresses."

I had never been anywhere but the mountains of Georgia and the port cities of the Black Sea. I had never seen the Great Russian

North. It took some getting used to. But I liked Siberia, its immensity, its severity.

I decided not to waste a minute. After nearly two years in prison, I could barely control the urge to act. But I didn't act until I had first reported to the police, so as to buy myself thirty days. But the fat, sleepy men in blue uniforms weren't the real authority—Siberia was its own guard.

Halfway on the eleven-mile walk to the safe house where documents and transportation could be had, a blizzard sprang out of nowhere, obliterating the road, which was only rut marks in the snow anyway.

Millions of flakes in the air, stinging like salt. The wind was howling and wolves joined in. My boots kept crunching through the snow as if they knew where they were taking me. I had a general sense of where to go, not that it was of much use in the blizzard. Some force must have been guiding me. Maybe it was the spirit of history. Right at that time, in early 1904, stupid Tsar Nickie decided to take on Japan, hoping to teach the "yellow monkeys" a lesson and win himself back some glory and prestige in a "short victorious war," to use expressions of the day. But it was the yellow monkeys—who had gone from samurai swords to dreadnoughts in half a century—that did the teaching. And the lesson was that, mighty as it appeared, Russia was a hollow giant. A lesson that wasn't wasted on the workers and revolutionaries, who began striking and assassinating as never before.

Or maybe I was guided by the spirit of love, for no sooner did I return from Siberia than I found my "destiny," as the Russians say.

I had one perfect marriage, one more than most men get.

Her name was Ekaterina Svanidze. I met her through her brother, Alexander, who had been at the seminary with me and had also become a revolutionary. But there wasn't an atom of revolt in her. Her nature and deepest instinct was to submit and adore. I saw that the second I met her.

I saw it in the outline of her body as she turned from the stove with a teakettle in hand. The kitchen was dimly lit, but her body was outlined by white winter light coming through the window. It was in the way her shoulders hung, the way she moved as if ready to apologize.

And then I saw it in her eyes when I went into the kitchen for tea, her brother saying he would join us in a moment. Her dark brown eyes, set deep in sockets where shadow gathered, could not withstand my gaze for even a second.

Without saying a word, simply by the way I stood and waited, I let her know that I wanted her to raise her eyes to mine, and it was only a second or two later that she held them up to me—bright, absolutely without guile, scared to death.

Her lips were soft, wide, full. Her face was oval and open, startled looking.

She could still only take it for a few seconds and she turned away to the sink, but not before I saw her making a little quick sign of the cross over herself.

I liked looking at her from behind, and I liked her knowing I was looking. Even though she wore loose, modest house clothes, I knew that she'd look good enough naked on the bed, burning with shame because she didn't have enough hands to cover all her parts.

Just then her brother came in, saying with surprise and indignation: "No tea for the guest?"

Referring to me by my underground alias, Trotsky says:

> Not without astonishment do we learn . . . that Koba, who had repudiated religion at thirteen, was married to a naively and profoundly religious wife. That might seem quite an ordinary case in a stable bourgeois environment in which the husband regards himself as an agnostic or amuses himself with Masonic rites. . . . But among Russian revolutionists such matters were immeasurably more important. There was no anemic agnosticism at the core of their revolutionary philosophy, but militant atheism. How could they have any personal tolerance toward re-

> ligion, which was inextricably linked to everything against which they fought at constant risk to themselves?

What Trotsky means is that my tendency to "betray" the Revolution was evident early and showed itself even in my choice of a wife.

He's right, I didn't marry because of ideology. I married Ekaterina Svanidze because I loved her. And I loved her because she was made to order for me.

Like Bukharin, Trotsky hates the idea that I can be happy—the final injustice. But I was. Trotsky quotes a friend from that time of my life who says of me: "His marriage was a happy one because his wife . . . regarded him as a demigod and because, being a Georgian woman, she was brought up in the sacrosanct tradition that obligates the woman to serve. . . ." And he adds that when I was away on Party work or in prison she passed "countless nights in ardent prayer."

But not only when I was away.

"Pray," I said to her, and she looked at me with those eyes.

"Pray!"

She fell to her knees.

"Pray aloud."

Head down, eyes closed, she began ardently whispering formal prayers for help from God.

"Pray from your heart, pray for what you want right now."

"O Jesus God, let my husband walk the path of righteousness and not be led into temptation . . ."

Then very gently I placed my knee under her chin and very gently tilted her head up toward me, which she knew meant to open her eyes and look up into mine. Her voice would break, gasp. My eyes streamed down into hers. Her wide soft lips were still moving but now the prayer was only the sound of prayer.

"Loud, pray loud."

"O God, let my husband be loosening his belt because he wishes to chastise me for my transgressions and for no other reason . . ."

Sometimes God would grant her half that prayer, the first half.

Nothing was ever quite so wonderful as taking her by the back of her full, thick hair and, still looking down into her eyes, slowly filling her mouth with me until the name of God was only a choked sob in her throat.

18

Trotsky is getting smarter. He's realized that the blanks in my record can tell him more than the few facts it contains. He's already discovered that the official record shows very little significant activity on my part during the Revolution of 1905. Stalin, Stalin, where is Stalin? In material I received only this morning, Trotsky writes: "Yet the question 'What did Stalin really do in 1905?' remains unanswered."

Trotsky is right in saying that I disliked the tumult of revolution, and 1905 was indeed tumultuous, every month a salvo.

January. St. Petersburg. On a Sunday, a priest, Father Gapon, leads a huge procession of workers to the Winter Palace to peacefully petition the Tsar for better conditions. They sing, they pray, they carry icons. The Tsar's not in the palace; the troops open fire. Dozens are killed. Word of "Bloody Sunday" crosses all of Russia in a matter of days by that strange grapevine that moves the news and rumors with astonishing speed.

What no one knew then was that Father Gapon was working with the Tsarist secret police, not to subvert the revolution but to co-opt it. The secret police, paid to be realistic, saw that the revolution was a serious force and gaining control of it a better idea than suppressing it. Or, to be even more precise, the best policy was to supress it where you could and co-opt it where you couldn't. In any case, strictly speaking, Gapon was not an out-and-out traitor, but that didn't save him from retribution a few years later by a revolutionary assassination squad. I had nothing to do with the demonstration or the subsequent execution of the priest.

FEBRUARY. Grand Duke Sergei, Governor General of Moscow and a hated reactionary, is gunned down. Again, zero involvement on my part.

The regime plays a new card, the Black Hundreds. Nongovernmental, purely "patriotic organizations"—though with ample government funding and legal protections—the Black Hundreds were composed of savage, drunken anti-Semites and xenophobes. First it was the Armenians in Baku who were looted, raped, and slaughtered, then of course the Black Hundreds moved against the real enemy, the Jews. Their motto, admirably terse, was Kill Kikes, Save Russia.

MARCH. The peasants revolt, beginning with a trick they've been using for centuries and which they call "letting out the red rooster"—burning down the master's house, preferably with the master in it. This was all spontaneous; neither I nor any other Bolshevik instigated it.

APRIL. Lenin dominates Third Social Democrat Party Congress. Though our meeting of the minds took place in prison, I still hadn't realized my dream of seeing the man with my own eyes.

MAY. The Japanese sink the Russian fleet in the Straits of Tsushima between Japan and Korea. That emboldens people.

JUNE. The first "soviets" are formed in St. Petersburg. These "councils" of revolutionary workers or soldiers are the backbone of the uprising.

Mutiny on the battleship *Potemkin*. Again, spontaneous.

JULY. The "soviets" spread. In some factories and regiments, they are really running things, but not where I was, in Georgia.

AUGUST. Stupid Tsar Nickie makes a concession—he offers a purely deliberative parliament whose delegates would include very few peasants and no workers at all. Uproar. Still, it was a sign of weakness.

SEPTEMBER. And Nickie looks even weaker in Portsmouth, New Hampshire, where the American President Theodore Roosevelt brokers a peace that seals Russia's humiliation—400,000 dead, a billion and a half gold rubles squandered, the fleet at the bottom of the ocean, big territorial concessions to Japan.

OCTOBER. By the end of the month, all the railroads in all Russia are on strike, Georgia's included. There I play my usual role. A general strike in Moscow; the whole city's out.

NOVEMBER. By now the soviets feel so confident they declare the eight-hour workday. Power seems close, there for the taking. All that remains is armed insurrection. Lenin is back in Russia.

DECEMBER. Armed insurrection. From one end of Russia to the other, Petersburg to Vladivostok. Soldiers come over to us; this time it's guns against guns. Now for a change our side is doing some killing.

Late December. As the pitched battles rage, Lenin calls an emergency conference of his Bolshevik faction in Tammerfors, Finland. As someone who has proved himself as a Bolshevik in the oil fields of Batum and the train yards of Tiflis, I am invited as a delegate, one of only forty-one, a great honor.

Trotsky, of course, was nothing less than leader of the St. Petersburg Soviet, while all the record shows me doing in the great year '05 is some strike work, a couple of pamphlets, a political funeral oration that gained some small renown, and a stint as editor of *Caucasus Workers' News Sheet.* What the record doesn't show is the drab day-to-day work on committees and subcommittees, the forging of little friendships and alliances that would pay off long down the road. I was an apprentice, learning to master the gears and levers of the Party machine. And it paid off. Lenin had noticed me.

Personally, I was fascinated by the hydrodynamics of power—how power flowed and shifted—sometimes it was enough for the person speaking to pause for thought to lose the momentum, which would be grabbed away. And the Russian revolutionaries were great arguers. They disputed everything. Each one proud of his own opinion and ready to clash. Every one a little dictator seeking to impose his will by force of passion and overwhelming logic. Which of course made them all impatient to speak. But I was patient, I could wait. When everyone was done and I could see the lay of the land, I would come in with a moderate position that would attract people from both sides. I was not seen as a leader, but a catalyst, a moderating influence, an excellent cover for jockeying toward control of the committee. I wasn't looking to make any big impression. As Trotsky rightly remarks about me at the time: "No one noticed his absence and no one noticed his return."

But I wasn't going to meet Lenin and not make myself be noticed. It was freezing cold in the north of Russia and in Finland. My little trek to Siberia wasn't enough; I still hadn't mastered the Russian cold. Not that it mattered to me. All that I cared about was that I, the delegate from Georgia traveling under the alias of Ivanovich, was about to be in the same room as my leader.

Several weeks ago Etienne informed me that Trotsky had requested the original publication of my first impressions of Lenin. I got out a copy of my collected works and reread that article myself:

> I was hoping to see the mountain eagle of our Party, the great man, great not only politically, but, if you will, physically, because in my imagination I pictured Lenin as a giant, stately and imposing. What, then, was my disappointment to see a most ordinary looking man, below average height, in no way, literally, in no way, distinguishable from ordinary mortals. . . .
>
> It is accepted as the usual thing for a "great man" to come late to meetings so that the assembly might await his presence with bated breath; and then, just before the great man enters, the warning goes up: "Shhh! . . . Silence! . . . He's coming." This rit-

> ual did not seem to me superfluous, because it creates an impression, inspires respect. What, then, was my disappointment to learn that Lenin had arrived at the Conference before the delegates, had settled himself somewhere in a corner, and was unassumingly carrying on a conversation, a most ordinary conversation with the most ordinary delegates at the Conference. . . . This seemed to me to be rather a violation of certain essential rules.

What strikes me as odd is that so far Trotsky has not quoted a single line of those first impressions, not even to lambaste my ham-handed style as he usually does. But how could it be that Stalin's first impressions of Lenin are of no interest to Trotsky? If our positions were reversed, I would be combing such material for clues to character, ambition, intent.

But Trotsky fixes his attention on another point, my clash with Lenin over the agrarian question, who gets the land. Trotsky says: "The very fact that a young Caucasian who did not know Russia at all dared to come out so uncompromisingly against the leader of his faction on the agrarian question, in which field Lenin's authority was considered particularly formidable, cannot but evoke surprise."

"The delegate should identify himself," said Lenin. He was five feet three at most but so solidly planted on the floor that he made you feel the smaller man. As the Hungarians say, his forehead reached to his ass, but his baldness was dynamic, not pathetic—as if intense thought had sent the hairs flying from his scalp. He wore a three-piece suit and had the lawyer's habit of hooking his thumbs inside his vest.

"Ivanovich," I said, using my current alias out of habit, then added: "Dzhugashvili."

"The delegate is from Georgia?" he asked.

"Yes."

"Is my information correct that many of the Georgian revolutionaries were educated in seminaries?"

"It is."

"And do you happen to be one of them, Delegate Ivanovich?"

"I do."

"Then I'll remind you of what you must have been taught there: we all sin but the worst thing is to persist in error."

Lenin and I shared a laugh over the heads of the other delegates, who also enjoyed the remark. Then, without missing a beat, Lenin launched into another tirade of logic that proved his position on the agrarian question to be the only right Bolshevik approach, the Bolsheviks then still only a faction, not a party, of course.

My own position on the agrarian question was that the land should be given to the peasants, not nationalized, but I don't think it was very important to me even at the time. I wanted to clash with Lenin, but over something that was not absolutely central and could be modified later. Why did I want to clash with Lenin? To test his strength of course, but maybe I was also influenced by the old Georgian custom of slapping a child's face when a prince visits the house so the child won't ever forget the day. But who was the prince here and who got slapped? Maybe both of us.

My other exchange with Lenin was less formal. Between meetings, the delegates received instruction on firing Mausers, Brownings, and Winchesters. We were either shouting or shooting. As soon as the conference was over, we were to rush to the barricades, weapons in hand, and join our brothers and sisters in Moscow where, latest reports indicated, things weren't going well at all.

I was firing a Mauser on a little homemade firing range—beer bottles with red circles on their labels lined up on a crooked slat fence in the snow. When I handed the gun to the next man waiting his turn, I saw Lenin standing right there, taking my measure with those squinting eyes of his, merry and suspicious at the same time, eyes that could not be looked into.

"Not the first gun you ever fired," said Lenin.

"And not the last either."

His turn to laugh. And that was it. Someone came running up with more bad news from Moscow. Hundreds killed. Mass surrenders. Lenin decided to cut the conference short. But the fighting was basically all over by then.

A dark time was coming. Years and years under the sign of the noose.

But Lenin had given me a great deal at the conference to tide me through those years. He had given me recognition and acknowledgment. He had given me inspiration—we Bolsheviks had a great leader. He had given me confidence in our methods and our cause. But, oddly enough, of all the gifts he gave me, the one that proved of most lasting value was that initial sense of disappointment.

19

During my first encounters with Lenin in 1905, both when we clashed and when we joshed at the firing range, I was aware of him taking my measure. A good leader is always looking for the right people to fill slots. Lenin knew the party had Russians, Jews, Poles, but very few people from the oil-rich Caucasus. And the few there were were mostly soft-line Mensheviks. And here was a hard-line Bolshevik organizer fresh from the train yards and the oil fields. Lenin the practical had to think, I can use him.

And the more use I was to him, the higher I would rise. So I tried to be of use to Lenin. I took his line. I fought for his line. But, of course, human nature being what it is, I had to inject a little of myself into the process.

And, as usual, that caused trouble.

The problem was that more than ever I wanted to be the leader of the Georgian revolutionaries and felt I deserved to be, which meant that I lived in a constant state of irritability. Some of that showed. I was young and was still learning the actor's art of masking feelings.

I had come back from meeting Lenin in Finland in a cocky mood. But it was more than my attitude; it was some of the actions I took that alienated the Menshevik majority of the Georgian Social Democrat Party with which we Bolsheviks were supposed to cooperate, especially now that the Tsar was crushing out the last sparks of the '05 Revolution.

I was brought before a three-man Party Disciplinary Committee.

"Comrade Koba," said the man leading the proceedings, "it is the common sentiment of this Party that you have violated the norms befitting a true revolutionary. You have advocated criminal violence, robbery, when you know this Party limits itself to revolutionary violence only. You give all your time to committee work and neglect entirely both the study of Marxist theory and practical work in the field, which at least you used to do. And the reason you give so much time to committee work is so that you can build up your own little entourage within the Party. How do you plead?"

"Guilty."

They were surprised.

"Guilty of every charge," I said. "I am guilty of the first charge—of advocating robbery—which I do believe in—but I now see my mistake was not having sufficient discipline to restrain myself. And I am guilty of neglecting theoretical and field work. And though I am not so sure that the many hours I spend in committee work are only for building up my own 'entourage,' I am willing to plead guilty to that charge as well—to show you here and now that though I have been guilty of incorrect behavior in the past, I am willing to submit to Party discipline."

It was wonderful to see the confusion and conflict on their faces. On the one hand, they disliked and distrusted me and wanted me expelled or punished. On the other hand, their Party psychology inclined them toward any comrade who had realized the errors of his ways, and of course every soldier was needed in the great unequal battle with the Tsar. Party psychology predominated over feeling, as I had figured—after all, what kind of revolutionaries would they be if it hadn't?

But I was no fool; I knew that those feelings wouldn't go away and sooner or later would rise to the surface, if only because sooner or later I would provoke them.

At the moment, however, I didn't want any trouble with the Party. A Party Congress was going to be held in Stockholm in April 1906. Lenin would be there. And I didn't want anything or anyone to prevent me from attending.

I asked the Disciplinary Committee for a couple of days to think everything over, and they obliged.

I traveled at once to Batum, but this time not to agitate in the oil refineries. Instead, I loitered in front of the pale yellow and white building with the stout classical columns where the Tsar's secret police were headquartered. The Tsar's secret police were only secretive about their actions, not about their presence, which they very much wished to make known. Even at the time, this struck me as a sound principle.

On the second day, around six in the evening, I saw the person I wanted and began following him as soon as he came down the front steps. I hung back, noticing that he was careful about looking around him; the Revolution may have been crushed, but assassinations were on the upswing.

Though Batum is semitropical, it was still a little cool that day. I turned my collar up and rubbed my hands. I followed the man for several blocks, the crowds thinning as the residential streets began. He was clearly on his way home.

When he turned the corner onto a quiet street, I waited a second, lit a cigarette, then came up quickly behind him. Hearing fast footsteps, he wheeled around, terror on his face. First a general terror at seeing any rough-looking man coming up quick behind him and then a specific terror as he remembered me.

Holding my cigarette up in one hand and raising the other to show I meant him no harm, I said: "Major Antonov, we need to talk."

"My house is just over there, you could . . ."

"Not your house."

"There is a safe house . . ."

"And no safe house either."

"Then where?"

"Tomorrow, at ten in the morning, I'll be in the Phoenix Café."

"Yes?"

"Arrest me there."

"You've gotten smarter."

"Fish grow."

I was on my second coffee by the time they came for me; Russians are never on time.

Though Antonov was polite to me when receiving me in his office, I could see that he also was angry at me from yesterday, for causing him fear, and, worse, for having seen it on his face. That made him a little gruff. At the same time he knew he had to treat me well because I must have brought him something valuable, otherwise why would I risk coming up to him on the street, let alone ask to be arrested?

He invited me to be seated, asked if I wanted tea.

I took the seat but refused the tea.

"And so what are we going to discuss today, Dzhugashvili—poetry?"

"Close. Publishing. Somewhere in the Caucasus, there's a printing operation that's driving you people crazy. The press turns out proclamations by the tens of thousands and counterfeit passports by the dozens. There have been raids from Tiflis to Batum, but nobody's found a thing, not even the special investigators they recently sent down from St. Petersburg. True?"

"Could well be."

"I don't know how your system works, but I'd think the person who broke that one would get a nice promotion and could maybe even put in for a transfer back to Petersburg."

"A just Tsar rewards good service."

"I'll give you that press, the whole operation."

"In exchange for what?"

"I don't want anything from you."

"I don't believe in deals where the other person doesn't want anything for himself. How do I know it's not a trap, a chance to butcher a raiding party? People don't get promotions for that."

"You couldn't do me a bigger favor than smashing that group."

"And why is that?"

"Because it's my ambition to be the head of the Georgian revolutionary party."

He burst out laughing. I was furious.

"This conversation is over!" I said.

"No, wait, you misunderstand me. I only laughed because, well, of your modesty."

"My modesty?"

"Yes, any man who can come up to me in the street and ask to be arrested so he can have his organization smashed will never be satisfied with running the party of a little province like Georgia."

For a second I could not speak because I knew he was right. Antonov had done it again. That really wasn't my ambition anymore. Not since I'd returned from that first meeting with Lenin. Or, to be even more precise, I still wanted the leadership of the Georgian party but now only because of where that could take me, though I still couldn't quite have said where that might be.

"Maybe," I said, "I will have a little tea."

* * *

They never would have found the printing press. It was located in a specially ventilated room at the bottom of a fifty-foot shaft on the outskirts of Tiflis. The area was mostly deserted—railroad tracks, sheds, warehouses, and a barracks for people with contagious diseases. In the heady days of the 1905 Revolution, this press, underground in every sense, turned out more than 275,000 copies of illegal newspapers and leaflets in three languages—Russian, Armenian, and

Georgian. Passports were also counterfeited in the same work space, and there was a small separate laboratory for making explosives.

I had never been there. I wasn't even supposed to know the exact location of the press, first because I had no need to know, and second because the Georgian Mensheviks weren't about to confide in me. But I found out. Secrets give power. Power feeds vanity—for some people at least, what good is power if nobody knows about it, if it can't at least be hinted at? So I found out a little from a lot of different people so that none of them would have the feeling that he'd actually told me anything I didn't already know.

The raid occurred on April 15, 1906. But by April 10, I was in Stockholm, Sweden, attending the Fourth Congress of the Social Democratic Workers Party. I had the best alibi in the world—Lenin.

If I had some disappointment on first seeing Lenin in what seemed an hour of triumph, I had nothing but admiration for the man in what was without question an hour of defeat. The 1905 Revolution had been crushed and Lenin had lost control of the party to the Mensheviks. But there wasn't an ounce of hangdog in him. On the contrary, he fought harder than ever. No matter what, there's always a fight going on and, no matter what, you must always win it.

There were two main issues fought over at the Congress, the same two topics revolutionaries always debate—what to do when in power and how to get there in the first place.

To me at least there was something vaguely comical about that small group of shabby bearded Russians fulminating over what they should do when they overthrew the Tsar, when they would have to borrow rubles from each other for the train fare home. What interested me more was the subject of financing the revolution. Once again the ruling Mensheviks came out against what they called "criminal violence," meaning holdups. Lenin was in favor of them. And he debated with great force, his sarcasm more wounding, his chin raised and bobbing like a fist. Lenin argued that robbing a bank was only expropriating what had been expropriated. That was a good formulation for intellectuals but too much of a mouthful for the people who would actually bring them off and who always referred to such expropriations as "exes." But that was still down the road, because the Mensheviks had the majority and their motion against forcible expropriation of funds passed handily, sixty-four to four, with twenty abstaining.

Though we expected this, it still came as a blow to morale for some of the comrades. But not to Lenin. He kept fighting, if only for the morale of a handful of followers. After the Congress, the Bolshevik delegates gathered in a small circle around Lenin, asking him for advice. In some of their voices, you could detect a tone of weariness, despondency. To them Lenin replied sharply, through clenched teeth: "No sniveling, comrades, it's certain that we shall win; we're right."

That was Lenin—hatred for sniveling intellectuals, confidence in his own strength, confidence in victory—and that's what made Lenin able to rally around himself an army that was faithful to the last.

I was in that group, toward the rear, but there were few enough of us in those days. At one moment, Lenin looked directly at me. I smiled at him, my leader, my alibi. He could see that my spirits were up and didn't need any lifting. This pleased him and though his head didn't move I could still sense a nod of acknowledgment coming from him.

After the little group broke up, Lenin strode right over to me and wasted no time in small talk. "What are your thoughts on losing that point about expropriations to the Mensheviks?"

"I hate to lose anything to them."

"That goes without saying. What are your *thoughts*?"

For a second I was taken aback. He was the older man, the leader, and he had put it right to me. "My thoughts are . . . simple. If you've got a few kopecks in your pocket, you can go into a restaurant and get some tea and a sandwich. But, no kopecks, no tea."

Lenin grinned. "I like that," he said. "No kopecks, no tea."

20

The bond with Lenin was crime, with Trotsky insult, and they both happened in the same place: London, 1907.

So far, Trotsky has found no traces of my collaboration with the Tsarist secret police, but for some reason he quickly zeroes in on the crime that bound me to Lenin.

The Fifth Social Democrat Party Congress in London was a large one. There were three hundred and two voting delegates, each one representing five hundred Party members. I was not a voting delegate but only what was called a "deliberative participant." That sets off Trotsky's suspicions.

"Why did Koba come at all to London? He could not raise his arm as a voting delegate. He proved unnecessary as a speaker. He obviously played no role whatever at the closed sessions of the Bolshevik faction. It is inconceivable that he should have come out of mere curiosity—to listen and look around. He must have had other tasks. Just what were they?"

There were two.

One task I had given myself—whenever possible to watch Lenin in action. Lenin was a great teacher. He showed you how to act, how to be. At the Congress in London, the Bolsheviks had the upper hand. Victory can turn the heads of some leaders; it makes them proud, boastful. But Lenin was not in the least like such leaders. On the contrary, it was precisely after victory that he became particularly vigilant. "The first thing," said Lenin, "is not to be carried away by victory; the second thing is to consolidate the victory; the third thing is to crush your opponent, because he is only defeated but far from being crushed yet."

And there was a second task, which Trotsky guesses. He knows that I met with Lenin one-on-one in Berlin before the Congress in London, and he is right on target when he says "it was not for the sake of *theoretical* 'conversations' . . . and almost undoubtedly was devoted to the impending expropriation. . . . There was no way to continue financing the Revolution except by securing the wherewithal by force. The initiative, as almost always, came from below."

I was that "below."

Lenin sent his wife out on some Party business. He and I drank tea on a balcony looking down on green leaves and the street traffic of Berlin.

He seemed friendly, cordial, and unbearably intense, all at the same time. A blue vein pulsed at his temple, his cup rattled in its saucer.

It wasn't that he was afraid. But he knew he was about to cross a line, the line between revolutionary violence and criminal violence. There was high political risk, especially if we failed.

I was still a little ill at ease myself in his presence, the way the younger man always is with the older man, no matter how much he prepares and rehearses. Not that that kept me from starting to notice some of his little weaknesses. His mind was too much the chess player's. It lacked the poetry of suspicion. The kintos would have respected him, though that would not have prevented them from picking his pocket.

"All right," said Lenin, "let's hear it."

"The Imperial Bank on Erevan Square in Tiflis."

"When?"

"This spring."

"And how much could it bring?"

"Hundreds of thousands."

He paused over that. Everyone likes the big numbers. "And what are the odds?"

"Good enough."

"And if it doesn't work?"

"Our story is that we broke from you because you refused to condone violence."

"You're coming to London?"

"Yes."

"I'll give you my answer there. As soon as the Congress is over. Right now I want a few days to think about it. And about you."

So, of course, that Congress in London meant a great deal to me. Lenin would either entrust me or not entrust me, bind himself to me or not bind himself to me. Though I paid close attention to the discussions, I had no interest in taking part in any of them. The words would not have come to me. I wouldn't have cared enough. And I did not care about the voting and the closed sessions. All I cared about was whether Lenin would vote for me in the closed session of our own.

Still, I could not help but notice Trotsky. He spoke often and long, with the too-perfect Russian of a Jew; saliva sprayed from his mouth when he was excited and his index finger was forever wagging. It was the first time that he aired his famous idea of "permanent revolution." He had fantastic notions that the average man would eventually reach the heights of a Goethe, an Aristotle. It was a strange situation. The Revolution of 1905 had been crushed, the screws were on tighter than ever, the hangmen working overtime. Workers and intellectuals were deserting the cause in droves, the workers because they were tired of getting hit in the head and the intellectuals because they now found erotic mysticism more interesting. Yet the Party itself was bigger than ever and Trotsky was prophesying permanent revolution. The Party may have been bigger than ever, but it was also broker than ever. I knew for a fact that if some English liberal hadn't come up with the money, we wouldn't have been meeting in that Brotherhood Church, or anywhere else for that matter. My hope lay in that fact.

At an earlier conference I had clashed with Lenin, but really in the same way a boy will crash into another boy in the schoolyard just to see how solid that other boy is. But Trotsky attacked Lenin, dueled with him, in no way accepted his leadership. He even lectured Lenin, on tactics, on Marxism. Trotsky was displaying himself to the other delegates so they could see there was competition for the leadership, competition for their loyalty.

I saw that Lenin was trying to win Trotsky over to his side. It didn't surprise me that he wanted that big gun firing from his side, not at it. Objectively that was no problem, but subjectively there was something about the way Lenin went about winning Trotsky that didn't sit right with me. It made Lenin too happy when he and Trotsky agreed.

I could see that Lenin thought he needed Trotsky; what I couldn't see was whether Lenin thought he needed me.

I passed Lenin a few times, and usually we exchanged a nod. I could read nothing on his face. And would have felt bad for him if I could.

Which didn't mean I didn't want to know. I can be the most patient of men, but time had gone faster in some of the jails I'd been in than it did in that Brotherhood Church, which may have been in London but had a distinctive Russian smell—damp overcoats, stale sweat, bad tobacco.

Sometimes I could make myself deaf to the delegates and attempt to anticipate Lenin's questions, objections. I had to know those answers. I wasn't like Trotsky; I had to win Lenin.

Or did I? What if Lenin says—No, bad idea. I'd still have a choice: obey or defy. If it doesn't work out and I'm caught, it means ten years in the Arctic Circle and by then Lenin would have forgotten about it. Or, if I pulled it off, how was he going to refuse rubles by the hundreds of thousands when it costs serious money to run a revolution and he can't even rent a church?

Knowing I had that choice gave me strength for going into that meeting with Lenin.

Time slowed down again as the Congress ended—concluding remarks, parting shots. Some people left right away, but, as usual, a good many stayed around, forming groups, arguing, discussing, haranguing. I stood at the edge of one of the larger groups, both so I wouldn't seem to be just waiting and so that Lenin could spot me. At one point Trotsky came over to that group to see what people were discussing. I watched how he listened. He listened badly. He is one of those people who do not really listen but are only waiting their chance to speak. You can feel the talk machine revving in him; at best he is barely able to restrain it. And when he was no longer able to, the words came bursting out as if the air had only been created for Trotsky to fill it with speech.

I also watched how people reacted. A few were mesmerized, but most had already heard enough from him during the Congress and weren't afraid to interrupt. Disgusted, Trotsky moved away, looking for another group to dominate and instruct, wagging that index finger of his.

It was just then that Lenin emerged from within a small group and began striding in my direction. I looked over at him as casually as I could to see if this was the moment and he would be trying to catch my eye. It was. The gleam in his eye was aimed directly at me. I could see right away how he wanted to do it—quickly, naturally, without breaking stride.

"Comrade Ivanovich," he said, "you barely spoke."

"I came to listen."

"All right then, listen . . ."

Suddenly, Trotsky was blocking our way.

"You're wrong," said Trotsky to Lenin, "to insist that expropriations are justified. The road to permanent revolution must be the high road." While speaking, Trotsky had looked at me for a second and I thought I felt a touch of his saliva spray onto my cheek. Again facing Lenin, he said: "If we don't maintain the distinction between revolutionary acts like assassination and criminal acts like theft, the primitive Russian people will see the Revolution as an invitation to plunder and murder."

Lenin smiled indulgently, too indulgently. "Allow me to introduce Comrade Ivanovich from the Caucasus . . ."

Trotsky looked at me, his face cringing the way cultured Russians will wince when hearing their language murdered by a foreign accent, even though I had not spoken.

I was just about to offer my hand when Trotsky shifted his cold blue eyes back to Lenin and said: "I cannot side with anyone who does not share that fundamental view."

Then he walked away, right past me, even brushing insultingly close.

"A hot head, but brilliant," said Lenin.

The moment was spoiled. I was almost indifferent now to whatever Lenin would say.

If he gave his approval to my idea, it would be forever tarnished by Trotsky's spray of saliva and squint of distaste. And if Lenin denied me his approval, the association would be no less permanent.

"Don't worry," said Lenin, "I'll introduce you another time. Maybe the three of us will sit down and drink some tea, maybe even have a bite to eat. We should be able to afford it by then, shouldn't we, Comrade Ivanovich?"

I understood. I nodded. I even managed something like a grateful smile. Then someone took Lenin by the arm and pulled him off to the side. Not that it mattered. Our business was done.

I immediately walked out of the Brotherhood Church into a London of drizzle and Tsarist police spies lounging too casually by streetlights, probably holding the same newspapers they'd been holding for all three weeks of the Congress—why waste money on newspapers you could barely read?

21

It's official. Today, March 11, 1939, in the late evening hours, the operation to eliminate Leon Trotsky was put into effect.

I began my workday by reviewing the file on Pavel Sudoplatov, the man Beria has selected to head up the task force. On paper Sudoplatov looked good. Born in the Ukraine of a Ukrainian father and Russian mother in 1907. I liked that touch—he was born in the same year that Trotsky insulted me in London.

At twelve Sudoplatov ran away from home and joined the Red Army. Fought well during the Civil War. By the time he was fourteen, he had joined the security forces, worked as a telephone operator and cipher clerk. Married to a Jew, also in the security forces. It's his whole life. Brave, energetic, resourceful.

Of course, in a case like this I would not make any decision based on the file alone, but as the Russians say, Information is the mother of intuition.

And then I remembered that of course I had met Sudoplatov before, two years ago, right after the celebration of the Revolution in '37, when the purges were at their most intense. Sudoplatov, thirty at the time, had been overwhelmed in my presence, and could not report coherently. I'd said to him: "Young man, don't be so excited. Report the essential facts. We have only twenty minutes."

I liked his response. "Comrade Stalin, for a rank-and-file Party member to meet with you is a great event in life. I understand I am summoned for business. In a minute I will control my emotions and report the essential facts to you."

And he had.

Those facts concerned a Ukrainian nationalist by the name of Konovalets who lived abroad and who had been sentenced to death in absentia for crimes against the Ukrainian proletariat. It was Sudoplatov's assignment to carry out that sentence.

I asked him if Konovalets had any personal tastes we could exploit.

"He's very fond of chocolates," said Sudoplatov.

"Maybe that's your answer," I suggested.

And it was. Sudoplatov blew the man up in a restaurant in Rotterdam with a box of explosives designed to look like Ukrainian chocolates. A sweet tooth was the man's undoing.

In any case, Beria will be staking his reputation on Sudoplatov. If Beria is right about him, Beria will rise even higher; if not, he will fall low. That is the rule of court, any court.

Somehow I had twisted my knee during my morning calisthenics and it gave me twinges of pain on and off the whole day. I didn't want it distracting me during my meeting with Beria and Sudoplatov, but still I was reluctant to take an aspirin. I dislike swallowing any pill, no matter how many seals there are on the bottle. I'd rather take the pain than take a pill that might have been prescribed by Dr. Trotsky.

I called the meeting for the Kremlin, though I would have preferred to have met Sudoplatov and Beria at my dacha. But I had other business in the Kremlin. Hitler had seized Prague. And there were armed clashes on our eastern flank with Japan.

At my desk, I filled a fresh pipe, but did not light it.

Poskryobyshev was engaged in a little meaningless dust flicking and chair straightening. Even though his back was turned to me, he was alert to any signal or gesture by me. And I was aware that he, though once again without showing it in the least, was happy that the operation was about to go into high gear. Something in his nature approved of the stateliness of it. That it hadn't been rushed, that it was going to be launched in the Kremlin and in the year in which I would turn sixty, a serious age.

No doubt Poskryobyshev had glanced at his watch while centering the chairs and knew as well as I that it was time for the appointment, which of course meant that our guests had already arrived. Beria had already told me by phone that he would summon Sudoplatov, berate him for inactivity in the last few months, then instruct him to accompany him to a meeting without telling him where he was going or who he was going to meet. Of course, by now it would be clear to him, but the idea was to throw him off a little, always a good way to see what a man's made of.

But I decided to keep Beria waiting a few minutes, and for the same reason.

Then I made a little sideways movement of my head and Poskryobyshev started toward the door. I waited at my desk until Poskryobyshev had opened the door for Sudoplatov and Beria. Beria let Sudoplatov in first, both as a sign of courtesy and to let me have an unobstructed first glance at him. Dark hair, bushy eyebrows, full features, looking more like a Greek than a Russian. And no fool. He knew just how to look at me and just how to let himself be seen. He smiled as if to say, I'm not the tongue-tied eager young man I was when you saw me two years ago, though my respect for you, if anything, has grown. Just right.

I came out from behind my desk and shook his hand. That was good too. He knew how to shake Stalin's hand.

Beria, his forehead lightly beaded with sweat, was staying in the background, aware that my initial impression had been positive. I motioned them to a table covered in green baize. For a second I caught Sudoplatov glancing quickly about, his eyes going from the portrait of Lenin behind my desk to those of Marx and Engels on the adjacent wall, as if trying to memorize my office before we got down to business.

Beria knew that I would speak last and that of course Sudoplatov, as the most junior man in the room, could not think of speaking first, and so Beria needed only the smallest of nods from me to start.

It was just then that I caught a whiff of that hideous cologne that Beria favored, the cologne of an unctuous headwaiter, the cologne of a rapist. It occurred to me that Beria must be more worked up about this meeting than he was letting show, and would probably go off on one of his expeditions after the meeting to bring himself some relief.

"In a matter of months, war will break out in Europe," said Beria. "Everybody's jockeying for position. We want to have as many agents of influence in place as possible in European business and political circles, trade unions, and the press. We want to influence Western opinion and decisions. By definition, the people who can serve as our agents of influence are left-wing sympathizers. The problem is that many of these people lean toward Trotsky."

A twinge of pain went through my knee. I rubbed it and stood up and began walking to shake it.

"Not many people," I said, "but some."

I paused to light my pipe, looking through the smoke at Beria to see how he would react to being corrected, chastened.

"Even some is too many," he said.

I smiled. I liked the line, the pipe was drawing well, and the pain had almost subsided. When I resumed pacing, Beria continued: "I propose that Comrade Pavel Sudoplatov be promoted to deputy chief of the Foreign Department and placed in charge of an operation that would marshal all necessary resources to eliminate Trotsky, the worst enemy of the people."

When Beria finished, both he and I looked at Sudoplatov, who, without moving, seemed to draw himself to attention. I could see that he was comfortable with the conversation, the logic, the tone. And I could see that he felt truly honored by the assignment.

Coming to a stop again and speaking in a way that precluded ambiguity, I said: "There are no important political figures in the Trotskyite movement except Trotsky himself. If Trotsky is finished, the threat will be eliminated."

The pain reduced to no more than a little crick, I sat back down at the table.

"If you are successful," I said to Sudoplatov, but in a way that included Beria as well, "you will be well honored and looked after, and so will every member of your family."

Sudoplatov nodded appreciatively, but then added, in a way that seemed more an honest admission than an attempt to disqualify himself, "I'm not totally fit for the assignment in Mexico," he said. "I don't speak any Spanish."

"You'll be reporting directly to Beria, who will be reporting directly to me. Don't worry, neither of us speaks Spanish either."

Sudoplatov said: "Request permission to draw on veterans of guerrilla operations in the Spanish Civil War for the mission."

"It's your job," I said, "and Party duty to find and select suitable and reliable personnel to carry out the assignment. You will be provided with whatever assistance and support you need. You should personally make arrangements to dispatch a task force to Mexico from Europe and report on it only in your own handwriting."

I paused to see if Sudoplatov would make any further efforts to evade the assignment. Taking it on was dangerous, but so was shirking it. I was glad to see that Sudoplatov was smart enough to see that.

I didn't have to tell Beria that I wanted any reports from Sudoplatov immediately, but I wanted Sudoplatov to hear it.

"I wish you success," I said, meaning, Don't fail.

I rose, we shook hands, and they left, the door held open for them by Poskryobyshev, his pale, doughy face impassive yet radiant because, after all these years, it was at last official.

"Air out the room," I said, "it stinks of cologne."

22

Once I had received Lenin's nod to proceed with the bank robbery, I saw to every detail myself. I left nothing to chance, because I knew so much would be left to chance—when you start hurling bombs at horses and Cossacks on a public square, anything can happen. The point is to create chaos, but not so much you can't take advantage of it. That's a fine line when people are screaming and bleeding.

We knew that a major shipment of money was scheduled to arrive at the Imperial Bank on Erevan Square in Tiflis on June 12, 1907. The money would be vulnerable three times.

First, the train could be attacked while on its way to Tiflis, but that gave the least chance for success. Train schedules were sometimes shifted at the last moment when such important cargo was involved. The car would be armored and heavily guarded. Casualties would definitely be taken and the risk of utter failure was high.

Second, the money would have to be transferred from the train to the post office on Pushkin Square. It was more vulnerable at that point, but the area around the post office was not conducive to loitering and large numbers of our people would have to be involved—bomb throwers, fighters armed with revolvers, those assigned to go directly for the money itself, those who would have to be waiting nearby with horses. Also, the money would be transferred from the train under the Imperial Guard, who were better trained than the men who would transport the money from the post office to the bank by horse-drawn coach.

So, the third choice—intercept the money between the post office and the Imperial Bank on Erevan Square—was the obvious one. But where along that route?

After many long walks through the streets of Tiflis, I decided that the holdup should take place right on Erevan Square itself. The bank was located on the square, which would be full of people at that time of day. That would make it easier to pass unnoticed. As the coach entered the square, it would have to slow down, because of all the other vehicles, horses, crowds of people. And the more people, the more panic.

There was also a revolutionary motive. Grabbing the money in the midst of the city's busiest square would make an impression on the populace. They would see that the authorities cannot even protect their own money, they would see just how determined the revolutionaries are, how hard and brazen.

I checked every detail from the initial information to the fuse length on the bombs.

How reliable was the information that a major shipment of money would arrive at the Imperial Bank on the morning of June 12? They had sources of information within our organization and we had sources within theirs. But it was also true that both sides fed the other false information. To smoke you out, to throw you off. Everything depended on the reliability of that initial point of information.

Yet we had good backup on that point. First, through contacts among railroad workers whose ranks we had been infiltrating for years, we would know that a special train was indeed arriving on that day because special signaling and switching instructions had to be issued well in advance. Second, the transfer of money from the train to the post office could simply be observed by a small number of persons. If it didn't take place, we could just call the whole thing off.

I visited the basement laboratory of the bomb maker, Vitya, who loved his work. Though great serenity is as much a part of a bomb maker's makeup as boldness is part of a bomb thrower's, there was still something otherworldly about Vitya's calm. It made me nervous. And of course there was no chance of smoking in his workshop.

Vitya's wire-frame spectacles always seemed to be cutting into the skin at the side of his head. When he took them off there was always a welt along the side of his face and across the bridge of his nose.

"Vitya, have you tested any yet?" I asked.

Vitya didn't answer. Frowning, he was bent over his worktable, which was dirty but neat, his pliers fastened on something that wouldn't give. Now his face broke into a grimace as the metal continued to resist. His forehead was only inches from the bomb.

"There she goes," said Vitya with a smile, rising back up. "What did you ask? Tests? Yes, yes, two have been tested. Both worked fine. And, more important, identically fine."

"Which means?"

"Which means that they produced a good flash of flame, considerable heavy black smoke, and threw enough shrapnel to kill a horse and five people, to take a number. And yet—here's the nicest part—they're light enough to hurl a good distance, if you've got the arm for it. And the nerve. I couldn't do it, could you?"

"I'd rather throw one than make one."

"*Making* them is nothing. *Not making mistakes* is what counts. Other than that, it's like fixing a stove."

"I'll take your word on that. How long will the fuses be?"

"I'm thinking twenty seconds—light it, throw it high enough to get some distance, and with several going off at the same time, even if people run from one, they'll be running into another."

"Sounds smart to me."

"If you have no objection, I'd like to be present on the square to witness the operation," said Vitya, taking off his glasses for a second and rubbing his watery eyes. "I can learn a lot from watching the actual functioning of the mechanisms."

"No objection."

He nodded thanks. Then for a second he just looked at me to see if there was anything else. He wanted to get back to work. And I wanted him to get back to work.

"Let me hold one," I said.

Vitya smiled, glad that his handiwork was to be appreciated not only by sight but by feel.

Though light, it still had a nice heft to it and would take a good arm to hurl it far enough so that no shrapnel would come flying your way.

As I weighed the bomb in my hand, I weighed a decision as well. I was tempted to hurl one myself, a last detail that I could control, and also just to know what it would feel like. But there were plenty of good reasons not to. My skills were better utilized in organizing than in on-the-spot action for which expendable candidates could always be found.

And another good reason not to hurl one was the inevitable foul-up factor. Lenin's brother had been hanged after being stopped by the police, who found a bomb concealed in a hollowed-out dictionary. If it could happen to him, it could happen to me. And who's to say that one piece of the shrapnel from the bomb I threw might not catch me just right by chance?

I told myself that the most important thing was that the whole operation go off like clockwork and that I bring Lenin a fortune. Everything else was an indulgence. But thinking about Lenin made me remember Trotsky spoiling the moment in London, brushing up against me as he walked away. In fact it was there in Vitya's workshop that the specific desire to kill Trotsky flashed in me for the first time. Until then I had felt only smarting insult and anger. Now the long, long fuse was lit.

I was about to hand the bomb back to Vitya when my mind made a sudden, dizzying ninety-degree turn. I was thinking ground-level, horizontal. It didn't have to be that way at all, it could be vertical, top to bottom. I had already located one building on the square where I could watch the action from a rooftop. I could always toss a bomb from up there, especially if it had been delivered earlier, relieving me of the need to walk through the town with it. And, from rooftop height, the danger of being hit by shrapnel was essentially nil.

"Make one extra for good measure," I said to Vitya, handing him back the bomb.

Then I checked with Kamo one last time. Kamo, an Armenian, was from my hometown of Gori and a few years younger than me. I had once been hired to be his tutor. Years later I would instruct him in Marxism. Loving danger and hating injustice, he had been easy to convert. I have met few people with simpler minds and often wondered if the reason Kamo never lost his head was because he scarcely knew he had one.

Kamo couldn't sit still. Which I didn't like. I wanted him more collected, solid, calm.

For a second I didn't say anything, but just watched the way he moved. Frightening physical vitality; you wouldn't want him coming at you. Hair, eyebrows, mustache—all jet-black. Simple eyes, childish eyes. The tops of his ears were turned away from his head, as if listening for footsteps.

But I knew how to control him; with the right words, the right tone of voice, Kamo would do as you said. The reason was simple. Kamo liked to act and hated to think. In fact, he was always grateful to be told what to do, for it saved him from something he wasn't good at.

"Sit down, Kamo, we need to talk," I said.

Kamo sat down.

Then I had him recount his role in the operation—disguised as a Tsarist army officer, he would dash into the square on horseback, snatch up the money once it had been grabbed from the coach, and then deliver it to other horsemen. I wanted to be certain his mind was clear on every point, or at least as clear as Kamo's could be.

Kamo was famous for not getting things 100 percent right. Even his nickname had been given him for the way he mangled the Russian word "kamoo," meaning "who to?" I teased him a little on that point to keep his attention: bombs—who to? The money—who to?

But he knew all the answers just as he had in the old days when I had tutored him. The only question was whether he'd remember them after he walked out the door. But the one thing I could be sure of was that the thicker the action got, the better he'd do. That was how he was put together. At the door I thumped his back as a sign of my confidence in him.

Finally, word came through—the money had arrived, been transferred to the post office, and would be transported by coach the following day at ten o'clock in the morning. At eight o'clock that morning, I walked across Erevan Square in the dirty clothes of a workman, carrying the sort of pitch pot and brush that is used for repairing chimneys. The bomb was waiting for me on the roof, wrapped in a rag, jammed in a drainpipe.

From the roof I could see the outlines of the mountains rising above the town in the clear June sky. But I kept my eyes on the square, watching for signs of anything unusual. Everything seemed normal—just people going about their business, mothers and children, officials in uniform, street vendors, a slow horse pulling a wagon of melons. From that height people were only shapes.

In a short while some of them would be dead or mutilated, losing an arm while on the way to the store for thread. Others would be spared; getting in to see an official unexpectedly early, they'd be on their way with the paper they needed, their pockets a few rubles lighter for the official fee and the bribe.

Except for the bomb, I was not armed. All I had in my pockets was a watch, a box of matches, and a work order to patch a chimney at that address. Every so often, for the sake of form, I daubed some pitch on the chimney, which in fact had cracked and needed a little sealing. Otherwise, I lay on the gravel roof, which was specked with white bird shit. Propped on my elbows, I waited and watched.

That skinny old woman with the bread under her arm who had stopped to gossip better not have too many tales to tell. That boy bouncing the red ball against a wall should hope to be called away by a playmate soon. The street vendors weren't going anywhere and some of them were as good as dead, though which ones was always the question.

By nine-thirty, all my attention was strained for the wave of sound and excitement that would precede the carriage's arrival on the square.

But by ten, still nothing. Had the route changed? The schedule? Had the signal system, which I always suspected was a little too intricate, broken down? Had one of the thousand things that can go wrong gone wrong—accident, panic, arrest?

I felt a moment of despair and self-hatred. I told myself that all my hopes of rising in the Party, being the trusted comrade-in-arms of Lenin himself, were nothing but the pathetic fantasies of a hick. I had no chance of being anything more than what I already was—a small-time organizer, a petty thief who had only gotten Lenin's attention for lack of anyone better from my neck of the woods. The robbery would never come off. In Europe, Lenin and Trotsky would snort with contempt.

But then I saw our signalman Bachua strolling through the square, opening and closing his newspaper, which caught the bright midmorning light. That meant everything had gone right. The entire series of signals—from the first sent by the woman on Pushkin Square to the bombers waiting in a nearby restaurant—had flashed like an impulse down a healthy nerve.

Then suddenly, as if bursting through the backdrop of a stage set, the armored postal coach came clattering into the square surrounded by dust and Cossacks. As we had anticipated, the dense crowds slowed the coach's progress almost to a crawl. The Cossacks, shouting and brandishing their whips, moved away from the coach to clear a path. That left the coach and the horses drawing it exposed. Three bombs were hurled—at those horses, those Cossacks, and one at random into the crowd to create chaos. Just as Vitya had said, the flash of flame was terrifyingly bright, followed immediately by thick waves of black smoke. Horses reared and toppled on people attempting to flee, their screams softened by the height from which I heard them.

But the bomb lobbed at the horses pulling the coach had exploded off to one side, only killing the coachman. Panicked, the horses had now burst through the cordon of Cossacks and were dashing madly toward the center of the square. As the smoke and dust cleared, I could see the Cossacks wheeling around to chase the coach.

From where I stood, the best I could do was hurl my bomb in their direction. I had to turn my back to the action to get away from the wind, which blew out my first match. I felt a touch of panic, but then regained my calm, and the second match set the fuse hissing. I waited three seconds, then wound up and hurled the bomb underarm with all I could muster in the direction of the Cossacks. It didn't hit them, but it frightened their horses, which bolted and reared.

Other bombs were now hurled from ground level. A child's red ball flew directly up through the smoke, hovered a second, then fell back down.

I could see Bachua running to cut off the coach. He caught up to it at the far end of the square, easy to see for everyone was fleeing in the other direction. Bachua threw a bomb right under the horses' legs. The blast killed them at once and threw him to the ground. But another of our men on the ground had seen what was happening and arrived on the spot a few seconds later. Now the Cossacks were again in control of their horses and racing across the square. Another bomb sliced their charge in two. Our man was already running with the money bag as fast as he could, which from my vantage didn't seem fast enough. But then in full Tsarist military regalia, Kamo came racing from a side street on horseback. Firing a revolver with one hand, he snatched the money bag up with the other and had galloped from the square before the regrouped Cossacks even had their sabres in the air.

It was ours, all 375,500 rubles of it. And ours, unfortunately, it remained. All the 751 five-hundred-ruble notes bore consecutive serial numbers—AM62900 to AM63650—that made them for all purposes "marked," as Kamo and others discovered when they attempted to cash them later in Europe and were arrested. I could not help but feel that Trotsky's shadow fell across the whole thing, jinxing it start to finish.

23

No sooner was the operation to eliminate Trotsky launched than it ran into a snafu.

None of it was Sudoplatov's fault. All his initial steps were quite intelligent. After establishing himself in Office 735 in Lubyanka, Sudoplatov immediately recruited Leonid Eitington to run the actual field operations. A better choice could hardly be imagined. Sudoplatov's first move had been to remedy his own lack of connections and experience in the Spanish-speaking world. During the Spanish Civil War, Eitington ran successful guerrilla operations under the alias of General Kotov; for a daredevil like Eitington, fighting the enemy on the front lines wasn't interesting enough, he had to be in the most dangerous position of all—behind enemy lines.

I know Eitington and like him. A man of great energy, always joking, even or especially when carrying out the riskiest of missions. He organized the abduction of an emigré general off the streets of Paris in broad daylight, shocking all Europe in 1930. He also served in China, Shanghai, and Harbin, and for a time was in charge of Guy Burgess, a member of our spy ring in Cambridge, England.

According to the dossier on him, Eitington drinks very little. His hobby is hunting, but he does not kill the animals. His pleasure is in the tracking of them. No interest in money whatsoever.

Born 1899 in Belorussia to a poor family. Real name Naum Isakovich Eitington. Fought in the Revolution. At age nineteen transferred to security police. Changed name to conceal Jewish origins.

The picture of him in his dossier carried the note that his shock of black hair and piercing gray-green eyes made him popular with the ladies. Always involved in romantic complications. Has two or three wives plus mistresses, girlfriends. But a good papa; all his children adore him.

Eitington has given the operation to eliminate Trotsky its name, "Operation Duck." I approve. The expression "the ducks are flying" means disinformation's in the air and there is something ducklike about the back of Trotsky's gray hair.

I don't care that Eitington is a Jew, but I am worried about all the erotic entanglements, especially since that's what has already thrown the first monkey wrench into the operation. Mixing high jinks and politics only makes trouble.

The Mexican artist Frida Kahlo was part of the greeting committee that came out to Trotsky's ship when he arrived in Tampico Bay in January 1937. Trotsky's wife, Natasha, was frightened of landing in Mexico, where the Stalinists control the powerful Mexican communist party. But Trotsky's wife was calmed by the sight of familiar faces among those on the boat who had come to ferry them in. Jauntily dressed in tweed knickerbockers, carrying a briefcase and a walking stick, Trotsky himself had no qualms about landing, and greeted the press photographers like a conquering hero.

Frida Kahlo is married to another Mexican artist, Diego Rivera, whom I met in Moscow once, in 1928. With his skinny legs, big belly, and bulging eyes, he looked like a frog. I saw him sketching me during the meeting and afterward I went over and looked through his drawings. Choosing the one I liked most, I signed it: "Greetings to the Mexican revolutionaries. Stalin."

Diego Rivera and Frida Kahlo were to be Trotsky's hosts in Mexico; they were giving the Trotskys one of their homes. Judging by the decent interval that he waited, Trotsky must have considered it bad form to sleep with his host's wife right at the start.

Frida may have been initially attracted by Trotsky's legend and energy, then Diego gave her cause for revenge by sleeping with her sister. With women you can understand the parts, but never the way they stitch them together.

In any case, Trotsky and Frida had a romance, a little exile tango. Sad in a way, shabby. The old goat. The same age as me, pushing sixty, and running after it like a young man who doesn't know what it is.

They go horseback riding in the desert, climb Mayan ruins. Trotsky's wife knows or suspects and is unhappy. Trotsky reassures her of his devotion but will not deny himself the pleasure of these rendezvous. For a while at least, Frida must have confined her vengeance to the act itself, because Rivera has not taken any steps that would indicate otherwise and he's known for firing his six-shooter at the slightest provocation.

Trotsky and Rivera are having other problems. Rivera, a fat Mexican painter who screws his wife's sister, would find in Trotsky the same thing any kinto would, a snob, a stiff. He'd bore and irritate Rivera before long. And Trotsky would be bored and irritated by Rivera too, finding him a fat colorful clown who preached revolution and blasted holes in the ceiling with his six-gun. Trotsky wouldn't stay long at the circus for that act.

It came to a head on the Mexican holiday of the Day of the Dead, which apparently the Mexicans celebrate by eating candy skeletons. And so, in keeping with national tradition, Rivera brings Trotsky a purple candy skull with the word STALIN written across it.

Rivera thought it was hilarious, Trotsky was insulted. The Mexicans love to laugh at death, their own included; nothing could be more Mexican than that—you'd think Trotsky would have learned that from his señorita. But his own true nature came out at that moment. His humorlessness. Of course Stalin was going to kill him, any fat Mexican painter knew that. The question was, could you laugh at it, could you take it in your mouth as sweet candy?

Who knows, this may have been the most important moment in Trotsky's life: his chance to free himself from death by laughing in its face.

Whatever it might have meant for Trotsky personally, in his relationship with Rivera it definitely marked a breaking point, of which there would be a few more.

The remaining clashes were political, public. Trotsky called a candidate Rivera was supporting "bourgeois" and Rivera called Trotsky's organization, the Fourth International, "a vainglorious dream" and resigned from it. A few days later, on January 11, 1939, Trotsky told the Mexican press that he no longer felt "moral solidarity" with Rivera.

Of course, if Rivera found Trotsky a dud, what could a fireball like Kahlo have found? We know on good authority that on more than one occasion she said, "I'm very tired of the old man." On Trotsky's birthday, Frida Kahlo gave him a self-portrait as a present, probably as a "something to remember me by," a way of tidying it all up with art. By an odd coincidence, Trotsky's birthday and the anniversary of the Russian Revolution fall on the same day. Another year older, a new love dead, and, salt in the wound, not him but Stalin on top of Lenin's tomb, waving to the roaring masses and the tanks.

So Trotsky too must have been negative and edgy as 1939 opened, which is why he and Rivera were clashing in the public press by then. Their break had taken a political cast, which in those circles meant that it was final, at least for a good while, because nothing is ever final in politics.

Trotsky had ample reasons for a break with Rivera: To be free of that crazy man who brings you a purple skull with the name of the man who is going to kill you written in white sugar. To be free of that man who breaks with the Fourth International, calling your organization a "vainglorious dream," which, politically speaking, meant he was going over to your enemy, the Stalinists. To be free of that man who, if he learns you slept with his wife, will want to avenge his honor with his gun.

All that matters is that in early April 1939, Trotsky no longer felt comfortable with the hospitality of Diego Rivera and Frida Kahlo in their house on Avenida Londres and so rented himself a house of his own on Avenida Viena.

Though the new place is within walking distance of the old, it still sets our surveillance operation back to stage one. Some of the lost time can be made up quickly—photographing exteriors and recalibrating attack and escape routes because of the changed access to streets are easy enough. But the real problems will be with the layout of the interior of the house and the changes in routine, especially security routine. In addition, construction has already begun around the new villa and can only involve fortifications.

Weeks will be lost, months. The only good of it is that all the commotion of packing and moving and reorganizing will also distract Trotsky from the task at hand—ransacking Stalin's life in search of a hangable offense.

24

As if to spite me, Trotsky is continuing to work, even under the disruptive conditions of moving his household and archives. His focus is still on the Erevan Square bank robbery. But I am glad to see that, once again, Trotsky's vanity is causing him to overlook important clues. When Lenin learned of the Erevan Square robbery, he called me a "splendid Georgian." This apparently nettles Trotsky's pride. He does not want to think me bound to Lenin, especially by crime. And this causes him to discount my role in the robbery, concluding that Stalin "was not in direct contact with the members of the detachments, did not instruct them, consequently was not the organizer of the act in the real sense of the word, let alone a direct participant."

He does not seem to notice that this contradicts what he wrote earlier about my visiting Lenin in Berlin and London for the express purpose of discussing the expropriation. Fine by me.

Now Trotsky will have to trace me through a maze of prisons and, unless he's very lucky, he won't find much of use to him there. In the ten years between the bank robbery in 1907 and the Revolution in 1917, I was arrested five times and five times exiled to Siberia, the last time to the Arctic Circle. I don't remember much of it myself. One prison blurs into another, and snow is snow.

In a city you are always surrounded by strangers, but in a city you are always running into people as well. Same in prison.

I ran into Benno the counterfeiter from my first cell, the one who had shoved Sasha to the floor and given him a few good kicks. We fell right in with each other as if the six or seven years had never passed.

"So tell me," he said, "Erevan Square, yours or not?"

"Even the police can't figure that out."

"Too bad about the serial numbers, though."

"A shame."

"And talk about bad luck, look at this," said Benno, holding up the heavily scarred index finger of his right hand.

"What happened?"

"Don't ask."

"I'm asking."

"I'll never know just how I did it, but I was engraving and spilled acid."

"I remember a bomb maker telling me his real job was not making mistakes."

"Well, I made mine. Now I couldn't forge a bus ticket."

"So how do you make a living?" I asked.

"The finger still bends," said Benno, snapping his index finger back and forth as if squeezing a trigger.

"Banks?"

"Banks. Stores. Citizens."

"There was the Goldenhof jewelry store . . ."

"The police are still trying to figure that one out."

We both laughed.

Benno and I met several times before I was sent off to exile. Now he treated me with more respect, even deference. Now he knew that revolutionaries were not just talkers, but could do something he knew from experience was no easy task. And he gave me more respect when I told him about traveling to London and Berlin to meet Lenin, who I said was the man who would one day knock the Tsar off his throne. He still wasn't buying it. "A bank is one thing, the Tsar is another."

Benno might have gained respect for revolutionaries in general and for me in particular, but he wasn't interested in our ideas and didn't think we had a chance anyway. What I think Benno was really doing was looking for work. As far as he was concerned, we were both in the same business. And we had the record for the biggest bank robbery ever. If we did one, we'd be doing more. You never know, there might be times when we could use a trustworthy pro. In any case, he made certain to let me know how he could be found in St. Petersburg, Moscow, and Tiflis. And was smart enough not to ask the same of me.

Not long after my meeting with Benno, I was transferred to a different prison where I was summoned to see another old acquaintance, Major Antonov.

"I'm looking through the list of new prisoners and what do I see, Dzhugashvili, Joseph V."

"Just like that?"

"It's my job."

"We all have our work."

"According to our files, you've given up poetry and switched over to journalism."

"It pays better."

"Not as well as holdups."

"I'm not in for that."

Antonov smiled. "We've worked together before and so we can get right down to business. The information you gave me about the whereabouts of the clandestine press did wonders for my career. In fact, the paperwork has already gone in for my permanent transfer back to St. Petersburg and I can't tell you how happy I am to be getting out of all this sticky sand and heat. But I've worked in this bureaucracy too long not to know that nothing's final till it's final. There are always other candidates, other sponsors. Plus, you know, it's Russia. What ever works right here?"

I grinned. "And that's the real reason the revolutionaries will win."

"Maybe," said Antonov. "Maybe not. Some things still work quite well. For example, us. Right here I have reports on you in London in 1907, was it?, Yes, here it is, 1907. And meeting beforehand with Lenin in Berlin. You do move in higher circles now."

"You always predicted I'd do well."

"You know, there's a story about Napoleon. After winning some battle in Italy, he suddenly realizes it all could be his. All. Whatever *all* means."

"All," I said, more to taste the word than to say anything.

"And what is your *all* now?"

"Good question."

"A good question deserves a good answer."

"Sorry. I can't tell you. Even my fantasies are illegal."

"Well, we do know from certain of your conversations and even, quite careless on your part I must say, from some of your letters, that you now believe there should be a sort of Central Committee here in Russia, of which you should be definitely a part, if not the outright leader."

"I said that?"

"Even if you didn't, you must agree it's a nice idea."

"Not bad."

"So, if this nice idea were true, there would also be a very nice symmetry between our positions. Both of us could well be on the verge of attaining something important to us. If I could break a nice case, it would probably speed up the paperwork in St. Petersburg."

"And in exchange?"

"What would help you?"

"A free hand."

"That's asking a lot. After all, you're our sworn enemy. I mean, you are on their side, aren't you?"

"I know whose side I'm on."

"I do too. The side of Dzhugashvili, Joseph V."

"You know what I want. A Central Committee here in Russia."

"That can only be decided in Petersburg. Help get me there."

"You hate the south so much, you might just put the whole thing out of mind when you get back to Petersburg."

"I'm not that sort."

"And I'm not the sort to buy pigs in a poke."

"You trusted me the last time."

"The last time I didn't want anything. This time I do, and I have to wait too long on it. So I guess we can't do business."

"Don't be in such a hurry. Let me give you something to think about. Perhaps it isn't that we just *know* you were in London in 1907 and that you met with Lenin in Berlin not long before the Erevan Square bank robbery; perhaps it's that we *let* you go to London and *let* you go to Berlin."

"And what would make you so generous?"

"Perhaps we've decided that you are always a divisive element. Perhaps we've decided that it serves our interests that our enemies be divided. Perhaps that's the reason we let you travel, because we saw you as an active agent of division."

"Easy to say you *let* a person do something, when that's all in the past and there's no way of checking."

"There are documents."

"You can always write up any papers you want."

"I don't mean just our official documents. Here, look at this newspaper clipping from the *Daily Express* of London for May 10, 1907. It even identifies our agent who stood outside the Brotherhood Church—"The tireless watcher was M. Sevrieff, one of Russia's secret police . . ."

"Must not have been the best agent if the newspapers found out his name."

"Maybe there was a reason for that too. The point is we knew who went in and out of that church. And everyone who was there from Russia was there because we wanted them all to be under one roof where we could observe them—and if you don't think we had people inside the church as well, you don't know how good we are."

"Every cell has its squealer."

"Now do you believe me?"

"No, because if you let everyone go, you weren't doing me any special favors."

I had him and for a second he didn't say anything. I had thwarted him. And fairly. Which made it worse. Besides, what did he care about "fairly"? All he wanted was to get back to Petersburg.

But then he smiled. "You're right. I can't prove it. Except in the negative. I can't show that we were cutting you slack, but we can definitely remove every inch of that slack. The rope can get pretty tight."

"Antonov, I did you a favor, you did me one back. We're even."

"People are never even."

"So this time it comes down to—either help Antonov get to Petersburg or . . ."

"Or rot away in the land of the polar bears while some other hotshot like Sverdlov or Trotsky rises to Lenin's side. So which is it, Dzhugashvili?"

I have never quite understood why I didn't hesitate a second but looked right at him, and past him, as I said: "Exile."

And exile it was. In September 1908, not long after speaking with Antonov, I was exiled to Solvychegodsk. In the summer of 1909 I escaped and was at liberty until April 1910, when I was picked up in Baku and sent back to Solvychegodsk to finish out my sentence. In September 1911 I was arrested again, this time in St. Petersburg. By December they'd exiled me to Vologda. Three arrests, three exiles; they were keeping their eye on me.

But I didn't quite get the game. Was it Antonov on my back? Or had he handed me over to somebody else? And why did they pick me up so fast sometimes while other times they'd let nearly a year go by? Were they giving me some play or was I giving them the slip?

* * *

Exile either kills or it cures.

There is an automatic panic that sets in when a cell door is slammed behind you; every dog hates a chain. But the panic of exile is different. It's a feeling that life is happening elsewhere and you are missing it. All that's left is the huge Siberian sky that squeezes you to the ground like a louse between a peasant's thumb and forefinger.

Some exiles succumb to despair and madness. But most combat it with furiously purposeful activities—writing the systematic analysis of Marx they'd never gotten around to or some ethnographic study of the locals.

The government supplied a few rubles to board you and a few other exiles in the hut of some Siberian fisherman, but if you didn't hunt and fish yourself, you could easily die of starvation or diseases brought on by malnutrition. Number one in Siberia: Survive the day.

I spent hundreds of hours ice-fishing and setting traps in the woods. I wasn't bad. You could live off a good fish for three days, and if you had enough traps, one of them would snag a rabbit or, if you were lucky, a fox or some other animal whose pelt was worth a few rubles. Not that there was always something to buy, even if you had the money.

In the hut where I boarded, there was another exile, a bearded Jew who always wanted to talk. Talking was how he kept from going mad. I was going a little mad myself, but I fought my madness with silence. So I would pretend to read, sipping watery tea and smoking pine-needle cigarettes, better than nothing. Sighing, offended, the other exile would keep on talking even as he washed his feet. If there is one thing you take with you from exile, it is the stink of feet.

In 1911, around the time of my thirty-second birthday, I came close to taking my own life. My wife had died of typhus when I was last at liberty. Trotsky quotes a childhood friend who describes how, when the funeral procession reached the entrance to the cemetery, I stopped and placed my hand over my heart and said: "This creature softened my heart of stone. . . . With her died my last warm feelings for human beings. It is all so incredibly desolate here inside."

I was always given to eloquence at funerals, but this seems a bit much to me. Not that I didn't say something of the sort, not that I didn't mean it.

Later on, I realized that even in dying Ekaterina had done me a favor. If she had lived longer and we had more children—in the year before her death, she had given me a son, Yakov—I could never have risen higher than Commissar of Nationalities, which was in fact the first post I was appointed to by Lenin after the Revolution. I'd never have been more than a mustached foreigner in the back row of newspaper pictures of the Politburo.

Still, at the time I was in despair. Solitude, Siberia, and grief were an overwhelming combination. I was fishing through a hole in the ice. The last gray light was about to make the sudden plunge into Siberian darkness. I had just gutted a fish by my ice hole, the guts bright red on the ice. I looked at the outside of the fish, the scales silvery, perfectly patterned, so different from the insides. My own body was the same—red guts and brown organs I could not see kept me alive. The knife I had was a good one, Finnish, with a serrated edge. I took off my gloves and rubbed my thumb along the blade, so cold my skin froze to it at once. I did the calculations. One quick gash at the wrist, then a minute or two at most before consciousness drained away with the blood. They might be horrible minutes, but they would be only that, minutes.

I touched the point of the knife to the veins at my wrist. The flesh shied away. The body did not want to die. The body was a dog. It had desires of its own, independent of my will. And so the only question was: To what was my will attached, my flesh or the knife in my hand?

And then all of a sudden in the endless Siberian ice and twilight, I burst out laughing. I was so idiotic, so literal. I did not want to die in the least, just to be rid of that weak, grieving creature by the ice hole.

I needed a new self, a new name. Once before I had transformed myself by taking the name of Koba, slowly but surely growing into it. By the time of that exile, I had had a dozen aliases, some simple like Ivanovich, others more elaborate like Oganess Vartanovich Totomyants. But none of them was right.

I'd have to invent the new name myself, not take it from literature this time. My own last name, Dzhugashvili, was from the ancient Georgian word *dzhuga*, meaning *iron.* I considered Dzhugin, but it sounded too much like my old name and not Russian enough. But red heat transforms iron into steel. In Russian, *steel* is *stal.* Just add *-in*, echoing Lenin and Darwin. Stalin.

And then, as in some Russian fairy tale, no sooner does the hero discover his own true name than everything magically changes for the better. In January 1912, word reached me that Lenin had formed a party of his own with the same name as his faction, the Bolsheviks, and had co-opted me onto the Central Committee. The Erevan Square bank job had not gone unrewarded. I was elated. My only concern was that somehow Major Antonov had had a hand in this, wishing to place me, a "divisive element," in the heart of the Party. But I didn't let that eat away at me. As a member of the Central Committee, I considered it my duty to escape at once.

After the sleet and logs and stinking feet of Siberia, St. Petersburg was dizzying. The city smelled of coffee and manure, sleighs skimmed by with laughing young ladies bundled in furs; I even imagined their cunts were like sable pelts. In the highest of spirits, I stayed with a family of revolutionary workers, the Alliluyevs. They fussed over me, fed me hot soup, gave me a clean bed of my own where I would fall asleep to the sound of children's voices from the next room. I would marry one of the daughters, Nadya, at that time an eleven-year-old schoolgirl with a ribbon in her hair but already gazing at me with hero-worshipping eyes.

I had been assigned an important task by Lenin—setting up a legal newspaper, *Pravda,* in St. Petersburg. After years of oppression and stagnation, it was a time of renewed energy. The gold miners on the Lena River in Siberia had gone on strike and fought with the police. More than a hundred were shot dead at once. The bloodshed was exhilarating. We knew the Tsar was always ready to kill a hundred workers, but it had been a long time since a hundred workers were ready to die.

I was arrested the first day *Pravda* came out in April 1912. Exiled again, I escaped again and was back on the streets of Petersburg by early October. I threw myself into work on *Pravda* but all too soon justified Antonov's description of me as a "divisive element." I somehow couldn't help taking editorial positions that infuriated Lenin, somehow was always slow in sending him the money due for his articles. He didn't mince words in his letters. So I was nervous when he summoned me to a meeting of the Central Committee in Krakow.

Supplied with good forged documents by the Party member in charge of such things, whom we jocularly called the "Minister of Foreign Affairs," I encountered no trouble with the border guards en route. The only problem came in a restaurant in a Polish train station where I had to change trains. I was hungry as a wolf. The waiters in soiled double-breasted white jackets seemed more interested in gossiping in their hissing language than in waiting on customers. Finally, after much waving, I got one to my table and, after pointing to the clock, I repeated the Russian word for soup, hoping he'd understand. He pretended not to, then pretended he finally had: "*Ah, zupa, zupa.*" He disappeared in back. I could hear the rattle of cutlery, the hiss of steam and their unpleasant language. He came out with cutlets for one table, cabbage rolls for another. Now he pretended to be terribly busy, never letting me catch his eye. How long does it take to ladle out a bowl of soup? Exactly as long as it takes for the connecting train to arrive. Suddenly, all the customers were jumping to their feet, grabbing one last bite on the run, slapping their money down on the table. No sooner did the warning bell sound than the waiter came out from the kitchen, tenderly carrying a bowl of barley soup with a beautiful dollop of sour cream floating on it.

With a look of feigned horror that was really happiness, he watched as I hurled the bowl to the floor, yelling, "Fuck you, fuck Poland, and fuck the soup!"

Lenin couldn't stop laughing when I told him the story. "Never," he said, his eyes moist, his voice breaking with laughter, "never order in Russian in a Polish restaurant. Just point."

Yet now my luck was running so good that the unpleasant incident not only proved useful, but doubly useful. It broke the ice with Lenin and gave him a natural way of broaching the new assignment he had for me.

"Look," he said, "all the empires are multinational, the British, the Austro-Hungarian, the Russian. In one of my articles I even called Russia the 'prison house of nations.' I want you to go to Vienna and write a paper on what's going to happen to all those nations, Latvians, Armenians, Georgians, Uzbeks, Jews, and so on, when we liberate them from that prison house."

That's what I liked most about Lenin: he assumed victory.

I was honored by the assignment, but I wasn't stupid. I knew it was also Lenin's way of getting me off *Pravda.*

At the meetings of the Central Committee, I said little and just watched Lenin run the room. Once again I saw that every organization is run by a few men in a room. In the right room, you could run all Russia.

Oddly enough, of all my fellow Central Committee members, the one I liked best was a Pole, Roman Malinovsky, who had done time for burglary and had proved himself as a brilliant labor organizer. There were allegations, which later proved true, that Malinovsky was a police spy, but at the time Lenin was adamant in refuting them. Referring to a comrade named Lubov who was famous for ineptitude, Lenin said, "Isn't it interesting that there are never any such allegations about comrades like Lubov, but only about the most able and useful men?"

It was in Vienna that I saw Trotsky for the second time. Out of tea, I entered a neighbor's apartment in the socialist workers' building where I was staying. I was surprised to see Trotsky, whom I had attacked in print a few weeks before as a "noisy champion with fake muscles." I didn't know if he had read the article or not, but he did recoil at the sight of me. Trotsky says he has no recollection of our first meeting in London, but does recall Vienna and my "hostile yellow eyes." Five years had passed since the desire to kill Trotsky had first flared in me while at Vitya's bomb lab, but seeing Trotsky again rekindled it.

After finishing the article on minorities, which ran some forty pages, I returned to St. Petersburg just as *Pravda* was about to hold a fund-raising concert and reception to celebrate its first anniversary. I asked Malinovsky if he thought it was safe for me to attend. Yes, but be very careful, he said.

Malinovsky drew me a quick sketch of the reception hall, marking the main exits as well as the side doors that led out to the street.

I decided to risk it; my luck was still running good. I skipped the concert, arriving at the reception only when it was in full swing. It was while sitting at a small table in one corner with my back to the room, drinking with some comrades, that I was arrested.

"Dzhugashvili, come with us."

"I'm not Dzhugashvili, I'm Stalin."

"Tell it to your grandmother."

One image haunted me all the way to Siberia—a silhouette backlit by a gas light, glimpsed as the police hustled me out of the hall. I couldn't be entirely sure, but something about the slope of the shoulders told me that Major Antonov had realized his old dream of returning to St. Petersburg and was on the spot, personally supervising the removal of all slack from his former charge, Dzhugashvili, Joseph V.

25

EITINGTON HAS PROVED ME WRONG—EROTIC HIGH JINKS AND politics do sometimes mix nicely. During the Spanish Civil War, Eitington found time for a love affair with a woman named Caridad Mercader, whom he recruited even before Operation Duck was officially launched.

According to her dossier, Caridad was born March 31, 1892, in Cuba, of wealthy aristocratic parents. Educated in Catholic schools in France and Barcelona, she showed an early attraction to devotion, mysticism. Briefly served a novitiate as a sister in the Order of the Carmelite Descalzas (the shoeless). Married off at age nineteen to a conservative man, she gave birth to three sons.

In her early thirties, Caridad, a woman of fantastic vitality, bored with her life as wife, mother, and society matron, takes up painting, drifts into a bohemian world. Art leads to sex, sex leads to radical politics. Breakup of marriage, two suicide attempts.

Joins Communist Party and in 1936 tours Mexico. Tall, striking, with prematurely gray hair, wearing a militia uniform of blue coveralls, she makes a great impression addressing huge crowds in the Mexican Chamber of Deputies and on the main square of Mexico City. She stresses that the world must choose between communism and fascism; the international communist movement must come to the aid of the Spanish Republic. She builds up a vast network of connections in Mexico ideal for Eitington to now exploit.

Caridad goes to Spain to fight in the Civil War. She leads a successful attack on a machine-gun nest in Barcelona and personally executes several Trotskyites. All three of her sons follow their mother to Spain and fight there as well.

Basically, I am pleased. Sudoplatov did well in selecting Eitington, who already had Caridad Mercader in place. Though no medals are given for this sort of heroics, Eitington resumed his love affair with her, even though she is now in her late forties. But what Eitington really wanted, and got, was Caridad to recruit her son Ramón, who is as smooth and handsome as a movie star. Ramón speaks Spanish, French, English. Trained as a sous chef at the Ritz, Barcelona's best hotel. Knows food, wine, an expert carver. Also fought well during the Spanish Civil War. When his brother Pablo, also a combatant, broke the rules by executing Trotskyites in broad daylight and not in secret, and was punished by being sent to the front lines, the equivalent of a death sentence, neither Ramón nor his mother protested in the slightest.

Eitington, who has an eye for these things, observed that many of the young women who worked for Trotsky as secretaries, couriers, researchers, were single and not the best looking. But, pretty or not, still these girls are human and want love. It's one thing to serve a heroic old man like Trotsky, another to be swept off your feet by a dashing young man like Ramón Mercader, who had the fine features of an aristocrat and perfect hair, glossy, always in place. But his mouth is weak.

A subject was finally selected, Sylvia Agelof, an American Jew from Brooklyn, New York, who visited Trotsky in Mexico and served him as a courier. At twenty-eight, she was three years older than Ramón. Plain, thick glasses, frumpy hair. An old maid in waiting.

It took months of machinations to set up a "chance" meeting between Sylvia and Ramón—in Paris, of course. She had traveled there in June 1938 to attend a conference of Trotsky's Fourth International. Part of Ramón's appeal was that he was apolitical. What he cared about, and knew about, was where to eat, what to order, and where to go after to make it a splendid night. Naturally, in the beginning she must have asked herself, What does he see in me? But then again of course why should a woman think so badly of herself? Were looks all that counted? And besides, there is no arguing with dizzying happiness in Paris, in the springtime, to complete the cliché.

She was hooked.

Thanks to Eitington's foresight, we already have someone in Trotsky's entourage who, though not with us in the strict sense, is unwittingly connected to our network. This is now more important than ever.

Not only has Trotsky recently moved, but, with the exception of the cleaning woman, we now no longer have any trained personnel inside the compound reporting to us. Our last trained person, Maria de la Sierra (code named Africa), a secretary, has been pulled. Her security was compromised by the sudden defection of our former head of security operations in Spain, Alexander Orlov.

Like Eitington, Orlov had performed brilliantly behind enemy lines in Spain, and had led terrorist attacks on Trotskyites. Orlov was also in charge of security in the shipping of more than $500 million in Republican gold to Moscow. Like Eitington, Orlov has a complicated love life—a young woman, herself a member of the security forces, shot herself to death in front of Lubyanka when Orlov left her.

And, like Eitington, Orlov is a Jew, real name Feldbein. How do so many Jews manage to slip in everywhere? Rivera and Kahlo, each half Jewish, Eitington, Orlov, Agelof, not to mention Trotsky himself. If suddenly there were Estonians everywhere you looked, wouldn't people ask where the hell they all came from?

In any case, afraid (wrongly) that he was about to be purged, Orlov defected. He wrote me a long letter, threatening to reveal, among other things, the fact that Soviet Russia had not aided Spain disinterestedly as proclaimed, but had grabbed half a billion in gold when all was lost. All the relevant materials were in a Swiss bank, set to be made public in the event anything happens to him or his family. Nothing has and nothing will.

It wasn't clear exactly how much Orlov knew about the operation to eliminate Trotsky. He knew enough to warn Trotsky against Etienne, though not by name. Trotsky just laughed that off as a provocation. And enough to warn Trotsky that Spanish connections would be used to get at him. Orlov probably knew about Maria de la Sierra, which was why she had to be pulled.

Eitington has set up a two-pronged operation. Ramón's task is to infiltrate Trotsky's entourage through his romance with Sylvia Agelof and obtain information about life inside Trotsky's compound.

A second group will lead the actual attack. The raiding party will be headed up by David Siqueiros, artist, Stalinist, leader of the Mexican Mine Workers' Union, and veteran of the Spanish Civil War, who is personally known to me. Siqueiros is bold in that madcap Mexican way, which is not so different from the Russian style, all balls and bravado.

In June 1939 Sudoplatov and Eitington traveled Moscow-Odessa-Athens-Marseilles-Paris, where they met with both groups separately. Neither group is aware of the other's existence, standard procedure.

Sudoplatov decided that Eitington should train Caridad and Ramón Mercader for one month in basic spycraft—operational methods, recognizing surveillance, changing appearance. Ramón was also subjected to a battery of tests in which he performed brilliantly. He has a photographic memory, excellent reaction time, keen hearing. Placed at the start of a chalk line, then blindfolded, he can stay on that line for six meters. Able to detect, by eye, variation in levels as slight as 3/10 mm and, by hand, 3/100. Psychologically dependent on mother, whom he resembles physically.

Testing and training are all to the good, but they take time. And time is short. All the powers are making last-minute overtures to one another. According to intercepted cables, the French ambassador to Germany, Coulondre, told Hitler that a long war could result in chaos and unexpected results: "You are thinking of youselves as victors . . . but have you thought of another possibility, that the victor might be Trotsky?" Hitler jumped from his chair "as if he had been hit in the pit of his stomach, and screamed."

I know how he feels.

26

According to our latest information, Trotsky has established an especially vigorous and unvarying schedule for himself in his new residence.

He rises at 7:15 and spends one hour tending his rabbits and chickens.

After breakfast he writes and dictates until lunch, which he consumes quickly, without pleasure, only to refuel. After lunch, thirty minutes of rest. Then he receives visitors, works more, does some gardening until dinnertime. After dinner he returns immediately to work.

Except for occasional visits to the dentist and a few outings to collect cactus plants, Trotsky confines himself to the compound, whose fortifications are being constantly upgraded. Trotsky is most vulnerable during the hours when he is outside in his garden or feeding his rabbits. But the Mexican police have set up a command post right by his house that makes any assault during daylight hours impossible.

Besides, Trotsky's work keeps him indoors nearly all the time. He keeps up a correspondence in several languages, issues statements to the world press about the impending war, writes articles to generate income, and devotes precious hours to speaking with Trotskyites from various countries who have made a pilgrimage to see the great man.

He complains to them that lately he doesn't have enough time to work on his biography of Stalin. But now he has started back to work again, Etienne having shipped him new material about my last four-year exile in the Arctic Circle, including the memoirs of a fellow exile who says of me: "Stalin . . . withdrew inside himself. Preoccupied with hunting and fishing, he lived in almost complete solitude. . . . He had practically no need for contact with people."

The description of my behavior is accurate, but the explanation is not. I still had need of people and was purposefully working to starve it in myself.

Siberia was a great university of boredom. The days huge, identical, empty. No color, no variety, nearly no motion. It is only human to hate boredom. And for that reason I taught myself to love it. And not only for that reason. I had already noticed how boring committee work and meetings were, how interminable. Many people could not take it. They would succuumb, agree, only to get on with it. The ability to tolerate ever greater doses of boredom is the great secret of my success. After the Revolution, I assumed all dullest positions, like head of personnel, the Organization Bureau, Orgburo for short. For people like Trotsky such work was deadening. Who wants to sit in a cold, brown room sorting through index cards? I did. Because I knew that every promotion won me an ally, a vote down the line. And I made it a point to promote the new people, the crude, ambitious, vengeful young people who could not have been more different from all the bookish, bearded old Bolsheviks. Trotsky could not bear their uncultured company. He even admitted it himself. When asked how it was possible that he, Leon Trotsky, genius, warrior, orator, had lost power to someone like Joseph Stalin, he replied that it was because he could not bear to associate with the new ruling elite: "I hated to inflict such boredom on myself."

For centuries to come, historians will write weighty tomes analyzing why Trotsky lost the power struggle to Stalin after Lenin's death. They will find dozens, hundreds of reasons, but really there was only one—Trotsky hated boredom and Stalin loved it.

In exile, people combat boredom by writing, congregating, talking, drinking tea, arguing, anything but the even greater boredom of solitude. I chose solitude because, like a monk, I wanted to scour myself of the last shreds of attachment, the last vestiges of feeling for anything but my new ideal of freedom, my new name. Stalin was my way of not being human.

But it was not all boredom and solitude. There was Katya.

Everything about Katya—the way she walked, the way she spoke, the way she looked at you—it was all to remind you that, no matter what, she had the one thing you wanted. I'd heard that her husband had been drafted into the Tsar's army, which meant that he'd be home in ten years if he was lucky. Like all sluts, Katya was lazy. She always found someone to live off—a lonely exile, a fisherman who'd lost his wife, a hunter passing through for the season. She got by.

Judging by her looks, she was of mixed blood; generations back some blond Cossack must have tumbled some local Asiatic, which gave Katya a flat, broad face, slanted gray-blue eyes, and thick dirty blond hair.

We had passed each other a few times on the street, which was no street at all, just the space between the two rows of huts. It was late December when we spoke.

"Getting cold," I said.

"I know a warm place," she said, smiling.

"Where's that?"

"Come to my house and I'll show you."

"All right," I said, "let's see in the New Year together."

"What can you bring?"

"What do you want?"

"Vodka, meat, bread."

But when I appeared at her door, she seemed a little surprised, as if she'd forgotten she'd invited me, though that was probably just part of her coquetry. Her eyes went from mine directly to the bundle in my hand, then she stood aside to let me in. A wooden table and two chairs, a sleeping space on the tile stove, some trapping gear on the wall. She took the bundle from me and placed it on the table, where she undid it. A pound of bread, a decent hunk of meat, and a liter of greenish home brew in a bottle with a rag stopper. She nodded. It was enough.

She fried the meat and sliced the bread. I poured the vodka into tin cups.

"May 1914 be the best of years for you," I said.

"And for you," she said, holding her cup up for me to clink.

Over the top of my cup I watched her toss her drink back. Good sign.

For a while neither of us said anything so that we could feel the first effects of the vodka, the scorch in the gullet, the electric leap up the spinal column.

"Why are you here?" she asked.

"Bad luck. You?"

"The same."

We ate the meat, wrapped in bread, after each slug. We must have gotten six or seven each from the bottle, which I slipped into my coat pocket when it was empty. I'd paid a small deposit on it. She noticed and smiled, liking the gesture because it was so unromantic.

We had saved a large drink for the last and it hit me hard, shaking my shoulders with a pleasant convulsion.

"Cold?" she asked.

"A little," I said.

"I'll show you the warm place."

She walked over to the tile stove and sat down on the bedding. Knees up, she hoisted her skirts as matter-of-factly as she had opened my bundle. She looked over at me. I nodded. It was enough.

I got through the winter with her. Then spring came to Siberia, late as always, the ice on the river cracking with a sound like howitzers. The ground thawed to muck, the insects arrived. I stopped going by Katya's. The weather wasn't right for it. Besides, by then I knew all her sounds and moves. And I hated to need.

But our New Year's toast proved prophetic—1914 was a good year after all. Stupid Tsar Nickie had done it again: in August he stumbled into another war, this time with Germany. The last war against Japan had led to the '05 Revolution. If he lost this war, a bigger one, it could lead to a bigger revolution. Now there was something to hope for, to live for. For me every Russian victory was a defeat and every defeat a victory.

But the worst of hope is the waiting for it to come true. Siberia was now twice a prison.

But I persevered. And the news was better all the time. Two million Russians killed in battle, another three million wounded or taken prisoner. Weapons, munitions in drastically short supply. Soldiers now sent into combat unarmed and instructed to take rifles from the dead. The Tsar under his wife's thumb and she under the spell of Rasputin, the Siberian "holy man" who could cure the Tsarevich's hemophilia. Now it was only a matter of time.

By late 1916, things had reached such a pass that it was decreed that all able-bodied men report for induction even if "they are under investigation, being tried, or serving a sentence for a crime." And so it was that I received a notice to report to the military board in the city of Krasnoyarsk. Tsar Nickie was in such trouble that he even needed Joseph Stalin for his army.

I looked forward to fomenting sedition in the ranks, but was rejected as physically unfit because of my withered left arm. I'd always wondered what it was for, what good it would do me. Now I knew. I soon heard of other revolutionaries dying stupid deaths in the army—run over by a truck, mashed by artillery, shredded by shrapnel.

I was not sent back to the Arctic Circle but to Achinsk, a village of some size near the Trans-Siberian railroad line. It was there in Achinsk in the month of February 1917 that I read six words, all familiar, all ordinary, but never before arranged in that particular order: REVOLUTION IN PETERSBURG. TSAR ABDICATES THRONE.

Lenin was in Switzerland, Trotsky in New York. I could be the first one on the spot.

27

I HATE REVOLUTIONS. I HAD FORGOTTEN JUST HOW MUCH, IN THE twelve years between 1905 and 1917, but it didn't take long for me to remember. Revolutions are public events and I am not a public man. It all came back to me on the train ride from Siberia to St. Petersburg. At every station there were crowds, flowers, speeches, ovations. Kisses for the heroes returning from exile. I spoke once or twice but I could feel the crowds politely waiting for someone who could set them on fire.

St. Petersburg was a strange mixture of everyday life and utter chaos. Children went to school, people attended the ballet, the trams ran. At the same time, the city was "one vast mass meeting," to steal a line from Trotsky's book on me. Soldiers deserting by the thousands sold their weapons—to the revolutionaries or to the criminals who flooded the city after the so-called Provisional Government opened the gates of all the city's prisons. Drunken mobs looted palaces. Revolutionaries were held up at gunpoint on their way home from meetings. Whores in furs waltzed into the gambling casinos that had sprung up everywhere. Fortunes were lost with a laugh at the roulette wheel, whose colors were the red of communism and the black of anarchy. And I myself wasn't 100 percent sure on which to stake my own bet. And so I made my first mistake. Seizing control of *Pravda* again, I printed articles calling for cooperation with the bourgeois democratic Provisional Government. My mistake was in heeding Marx over Darwin. Marx said that backward peasant Russia would be the last place on earth a successful proletarian revolution would ever occur. But Lenin proved a better Darwinist than a Marxist. He made his triumphant return to the Finland Station in a sealed train graciously provided by the German government, who were firing Lenin like a bullet into Russia's brain. Lenin knew that now it was survival of the fittest, a struggle to the death. Organized violence would decide the issue, not theories, parliaments, palaver. There were searchlights and red banners and crowds singing the Marseillaise at the Finland Station to welcome Lenin. He made a speech from on top of an armored car. I wasn't there.

I had good reasons for not attending. Now that Lenin was back, I wouldn't be the number-one man on the spot any more. And I wasn't quite ready to face his wrath for taking the wrong line in *Pravda.* But, most important, I was busy looking for two old friends, Major Antonov and Benno.

When I'd last run into Benno in prison, he'd given me a list of places where he could be contacted. If he was alive and at liberty, he'd be in Petersburg; the pickings were best there. But I couldn't find hide or hair of him. Either no one knew anything or people weren't talking. Finally, I took a chance and left the address of where I was staying—as usual, with the Alliluyevs. They had welcomed me as a hero, a comrade, a member of the family. The children loved my imitation of the bombastic speechifiers along the rail line—"at last our dear, holy, long-awaited revolution has come to pass." Nadya, now fifteen, still looked at me with worshipful eyes, but was now also assessing me more evenly, with the frank gaze of a young woman.

The Alliluyevs' new apartment was cozy yet roomy. Lenin stayed there sometimes too. At first he was brusque with me. But I knew how to fix things—vote with him on every point. As Lenin himself was fond of saying, it wasn't errors that mattered but persisting in error. Some of the comrades, Zinoviev, Kamenev, persisted in opposing Lenin, but then they of course were encumbered with principles.

By July 1917 Lenin was openly calling for the seizure of power. The Provisional Government issued a warrant for his arrest. Lenin wavered—should he use the trial as a public forum to amplify his call for revolution or should he flee, go into hiding, and risk losing his moment? Lenin, famous for saying "make your yes a yes and your no a no," could not make up his mind. He was besieged with advice from every side.

I saved the day. Lenin, on the run, had come to spend the night at the Alliluyevs, where he felt both safe and at home. The children peeked in the kitchen door to watch a god eat soup. With a smile I shooed them away. Lenin never noticed.

When we were drinking tea, I lit a cigarette and said, "Listen, I'll support any decision you make, you're the leader, but there's one thing I know better than you, one area where my expertise is greater than yours."

Lenin looked amused, interested. "What's that?"

"Jail."

"No argument there."

"You can't make up your mind whether to use the trial as a public forum or go into hiding, is that right?"

A little embarrassed to admit he was having trouble making up his mind, Lenin nodded brusquely. "That's right."

"The problem is," I said, leaning closer, "that's not the real choice. You'll never see the inside of a courtroom. Right now someone on the government side, some police official, is thinking like this: If Lenin allows himself to be taken into custody, we'll have a few days when he's entirely in our power. In times like these, anything can happen. Lenin could try to escape and be shot down by the guards. A fellow inmate could knife him in the prison yard. Or he might 'hang himself' in his cell. Or his heart might give out under the strain. Nothing unusual about any of that, happens all the time. And by the time the mess gets straightened out, the people responsible will be on some beach on the French Riviera or God knows where. And even if we track them down, so what? They'll have gotten what they wanted, you, dead. And who's going to take your place? Trotsky? The Russians aren't ready to accept a Jew as a leader, they're not that internationalist yet. The Revolution will die with you. To the government you're the enemy and there's only one thing to do with your enemy—kill him as fast as you can. If I can think that, so can they."

Lenin sat back in his chair and, tilting his head, gave me a quizzical, searching look, then laughed, saying: "I'm glad you're on our side."

"With you alive it's the winning side."

"What do you suggest?"

I looked at him the way a border guard does when checking papers. "Get rid of the beard," I said.

Lenin and I walked into the front room where the Alliluyev family was drinking tea while letting us deliberate in private. The children looked up from their schoolbooks.

"Stalin is right," said Lenin in a voice free of doubt. "I must leave St. Petersburg at once. Stalin says the beard must go. Could I trouble you for some shaving cream and a razor?"

Nadya hadn't been able to take her eyes off me from the moment Lenin said, "Stalin is right."

"Nadya," I said, "I need your help."

She jumped to her feet. I gave her the address of the "Minister of Foreign Affairs" and told her we'd need a photographer and the best passport he had on hand.

Then I shaved Lenin in the kitchen. Very gently under the throat. I could not help but be aware how little flesh separated the razor and Lenin's veins, and, if there was any one moment when I realized that politics was murder in the proper context, that was it.

There's a bright and startling moment when you first see a man without his beard. Suddenly, Lenin seemed less foxy, focused, intense. His face spread, the cheekbones broadened. He looked like a Russian sailor just arriving in port.

Lenin himself looked a little startled when he held up the hand mirror. But the man did not have an ounce of vanity. He was only interested in seeing how his new face looked so that he could act accordingly as he made his escape to Finland, which, though under Russian domination, was glad to help the enemies of the regime.

Lenin shook my hand. "Good work."

Then he was all business, gathering his clothes and papers, impatient for the photographer to arrive.

I did not accompany Lenin to Finland, but went there a few times to carry out tasks on his personal request. Trotsky is aware of that, but his suspicions are pricked by my disappearances. Fortunately, his explanation is more that of the amateur psychologist than the seasoned detective: Stalin, he says, "was absent six times from the twenty-four sessions of the Central Committee for August, September, and the first week of October. . . . In a number of cases his absence was undoubtedly explained by hurt feelings and irritation: whenever he cannot carry his point he is inclined to sulk in hiding and dream of revenge."

By then I had been elected a member of the Central Committee. By then I was fully aware that each passing day increased our chances for seizing power in Russia. And I had already long understood the key principle that there is always a room from which all power emanates. But I was too busy to attend meetings. I was turning Petersburg inside out for Major Antonov, the only man in the world with the power to deprive me of my place in the room that would run all Russia.

Obviously, I could seek no help from my fellow revolutionaries. If I could find Benno, I could at least double my chances of finding Antonov. But I did not want to involve any more of the criminal element in the hunt for Antonov; accomplices can prove dangerous down the line. Benno and I went way back, and I knew how he operated. Of course, if I found Antonov myself, that would be best of all. In any case, I carried two revolvers and a large sum of money with me in the event that I found Benno first. He'd get one of the guns and some good money down.

I spent the days and evenings looking for Antonov, and the nights looking for Benno.

Information was spotty. I learned that some of the gendarmerie had fled the country, others had switched loyalty to the new government, yet others were lying low, waiting to see who'd come out on top. I figured Antonov would be one of those—too much a Petersburger to flee the country, too smart to side with a shaky government that couldn't even control its own capital. But what if he'd gone to the countryside to stay with relatives and wait for things to sort themselves out?

Petersburg is a huge city, but I had narrowed the possible neighborhoods where Antonov might live, based on his income and his love for the city's look, "stately and severe." He wouldn't be living in any of the palaces that line the canals, and the vast slums and industrial areas could also be ruled out.

A detective once told me that most cases are solved because of luck or stupidity—a break for the police, a mistake by the fugitive. I got a break.

In a small restaurant I struck up a conversation with a postman who was complaining that he hadn't been able to do his work for weeks because of the mobs of soldiers, revolutionaries, and hoodlums who controlled the streets. I asked him if he happened to have any Antonovs on his route. He told me there'd been three and gave me their addresses. I bought him a vodka and told him not to worry, he'd be delivering mail again soon.

The second address was the right one. The building was better than I'd expected. I rang the bell, pounded on the door.

An older woman with a blue umbrella under one arm came up the stairs and stopped. She looked frightened by the sight of me—I was dressed shabbily so that I could merge with the masses on the streets.

"I'm looking for Boris Filippovich Antonov," I said. "I'm a colleague of his."

She stood stock-still like an animal waiting for a danger to pass.

"We work together," I repeated.

"He's gone," she said, her voice pitched one note from hysteria.

"Gone? Gone where?"

"Wherever people go these days. No, wait, now I remember. His wife and children went to the Crimea, but he moved to another apartment after they hanged someone from a lamppost right outside our building, can you imagine?"

Then she looked at me and saw that I could imagine and scurried past.

I found the superintendent, who for a few rubles let me into the apartment. Signs of a hasty departure—bureau drawers open, tea in a glass, papers strewn on the floor, desk, sofa. I skimmed through the papers, looking for any that pertained to me or for anything that might indicate where Antonov might have gone. Nothing on either score.

Before leaving I checked Antonov's desk one more time. Lifting a glass of tea, I saw in a tea-stained circle a few words scrawled on his blotter, "Vanya the Stick, nine o'clock."

I went out into the street. A drunken mob was carrying a whore in a gilded chair past a burning building. It was night. Time to look for Benno.

I went to the Swan's Wing, a basement bar. Entering a place like that with a wad of cash and two revolvers put me in a high state of alertness. Half the people would kill you just for the guns, forget the money. But I knew how to enter, how to order, how to sit. A few heads turned, a few greasy eyes took my measure, then turned back to their beers.

"Benno told me to look for him here," I said to the barman, who I could tell at a glance had done time.

"Is that right?" he said.

"That's right," I said. "We used to be roommates."

He smiled at the euphemism. "He's been coming in."

"How about Vanya the Stick?"

"Why, you need an apartment?"

"I might."

"If he comes in, I'll send him over."

I drank red wine mixed with vodka, and waited. A good tip to the barman bought me some talk. I learned that Vanya the Stick's business was providing apartments to people in trouble with the law, but since the prisons had been emptied his business was way off.

Vanya never showed, but Benno did, late, around two. I saw the barman indicate me with a movement of his head, and Benno grinned across the room at me. I was at a little table in the corner.

We pounded each other's backs.

"Son of a bitch," he said, "you guys were right."

"I told you."

"And I didn't listen."

"So, listen now. We took the bank in Tiflis and in a little while, we're taking the whole thing, you follow?"

"I follow."

"There's a Central Committee, a dozen guys who run the whole show. I'm one of them."

"I'm not surprised."

"People who help us now when it counts are going to be in very good shape when we take over."

"How can I help?"

"You know Vanya the Stick?"

"I see him around."

"Number one is to find him. You need money?"

"I could use a few rubles."

I slipped him some money and a revolver under the table.

"We killing Vanya?"

"No. We just need to talk to him. You find him. I'll come here every night. Twelve on the dot."

"Vanya's a bad one."

"How's that?"

"People say he was playing both sides of the street. He'd rent apartments to guys on the run but somehow the police would find them there, some of them anyway."

"Nobody's perfect."

"I could never figure you. Anyway, I'm buying you a beer," said Benno, flush with my money.

October came. Lenin was back in Petersburg. Cold winds began blowing in from the Gulf of Finland. The first chilly rains. Days passed. I couldn't find Antonov and Benno couldn't find Vanya the Stick.

Finally, some luck. "Vanya's coming tomorrow night," said Benno at the bar.

"Why not tonight?"

"He's nervous."

"Who isn't?"

A meeting of the Central Committee was called to plan the insurrection. No conflict there. The Revolution could happen without me, finding Antonov couldn't.

Vanya the Stick was late. It was almost two in the morning before he showed. He was tall, thin, sallow.

We sat at a table. Happy to have made me a present of Vanya, Benno ordered beers and sausage.

For a long minute no one said anything, Benno because it was his place to remain silent, Vanya because he was waiting to hear what it was all about, and me to show I was in charge.

"Benno told you I was all right?"

Vanya nodded. His eyes were milky blue and his face blank as a card player's.

"Here's what I hear," I said. "People are looking for you. People are angry at you. I don't care what you've done. I can make sure you have no problems. In a few days, we'll be running things, we're running things already, but in a few days it'll be official, you follow?"

Vanya nodded.

"You want a passport to get out of the country, you got it. You want money, you want a safe place to stay, they're yours. What do you want?"

Vanya took a second to think. "All three."

Benno and I laughed. Even Vanya smiled.

"You got it," I said. "Money I got with me. For the rest I'll give you the address of the safe apartment where we'll meet tomorrow."

"Three thousand," said Vanya. "Four."

"Three five."

"What do you want?"

"Boris Filippovich Antonov. Major Antonov."

Vanya stuck out his lower lip. "Easy enough."

"Maybe not so easy. You take us there. We find him there. Then, and only then, it's a deal."

"All right."

"A thousand tonight for good faith, the rest with the passport."

"Fair enough."

"But that good-faith thousand comes with one condition."

"Let's hear it."

"Benno stays with you until then. I don't want you disappearing."

"Done."

It wasn't easy getting the blank passport. In my absence the Central Committee had decided to storm the Winter Palace that same night. Everyone was running around like crazy; you couldn't find anyone. Still, by nine that evening, the agreed-on hour, the money, passport, and keys were on the table in the safe apartment when Benno and Vanya arrived.

"The city's going crazy," said Benno.

"Tonight's the night," I said.

Vanya held the banknotes up against the light, checked the passport and the apartment. He was satisfied.

I held up the keys to the apartment, rattled them to get his attention, then slipped them into my pocket along with the passport and the cash.

"Let's finish up," I said.

Armored cars sped through the drizzle. Sporadic light-arms fire. Bonfires at intersections. A dead horse on the sidewalk.

Vanya led us through winding streets—it seemed like we'd crossed the same canal three times—past the Hay Market and into the slums. No one talked. Finally, he came to a stop in front of an archway, through which we could see a dark blue building, white plaster showing where the paint had peeled.

"This is it," said Vanya. "Third floor. Apartment thirty-seven. That window," he pointed.

"Remember," I said, "we've only got a deal if he's here."

"He stays in at night, like everybody else."

"You wait here. Benno and I will go up. If he's there, we'll signal you through the window. Then you come up," I said, patting my pocket, "and this is all yours."

On the way up the cement stairs that smelled of fresh piss, I told Benno to knock and say Vanya sent him. "Have your gun out, push your way in."

Antonov was in his undershirt, his suspenders hanging down, as he opened the door. The shock on his face turned to relief as he saw me over Benno's shoulder. It wasn't a holdup, but something he might be able to deal with. There was nothing in the room but a chair, table, and a sofa made up as a bed.

Now I took out my own pistol. "Antonov, sit down on the chair and not a word out of you." To Benno I said: "Open the window and give Vanya the signal to come up."

I took the money out of my pocket and placed it on the table.

"What about the passport and the key?" asked Benno.

"The money's for you. Kill Vanya on the stairs."

"But I thought . . ."

"Don't think."

Benno shrugged and went out to the landing.

"You've come a long way, Poet," said Antonov.

"You too," I said with a look at the room's dirty yellow wallpaper.

"Here's my offer," said Antonov. "The way I figure, there are about six people between you and Lenin—Trotsky, Malinovsky, Sverdlov, Bukharin, Kamenev, Zinoviev. One of them was with us. I ran him personally."

"The papers to prove it in your apartment?"

"No. Not here and not there. You can do Lenin a great service and move one step closer to the top."

"In exchange for?"

"Just my life."

"Why'd you stay in the city?"

"A woman."

"A woman?"

The concrete stairwell magnified the reverberations of the shots, three of them, followed after a short pause by a fourth. Benno opened the door and stepped in over the body of Vanya the Stick.

Benno must have waited on the stairs above the landing until Vanya was at the door, then shot him three times in the back. The last shot, to the head, had been at close range and had splashed blood on the cuffs of Benno's pants. I could see that he was worked up but had not lost his self-control.

Antonov almost leaped up from his chair. He looked directly into my eyes, trying not to plead.

Keeping my revolver leveled at Antonov, I took a few steps back, saying to Benno, "One in the heart, one in the head."

"You'll never—," screamed Antonov as the first shot knocked him off his chair. He thrashed like a man trying to swim across the floor.

Benno ran over and went down on one knee but at first could not get his aim on Antonov's head because he was still flailing too much.

"Take your time," I said, moving behind Benno. "I'm here for backup."

In the long moment of silence I could hear the roar of distant crowds and what sounded like the flat thunder of artillery.

Now Antonov was only twitching like a fish on a dock. Benno positioned the muzzle of his revolver at Antonov's temple. As soon as he pulled the trigger, I opened fire at the back of Benno's head. He was, strictly speaking, the last man I ever killed.

PART

IV

28

But the killing of Major Antonov, its motive, is not the crime I worry Trotsky will discover. Bad as it is, it still isn't *that.*

From time to time, Tsarist secret police documents linking me with their organization surface both in Russia and abroad, but they are easy to dismiss as forgeries. And even if Major Antonov had had the foresight to get out of Russia in 1917 and had somehow miraculously survived and suddenly showed up in Mexico in the summer of 1939 and revealed all to Trotsky, even that would not have been that great a problem. Why would anybody believe him? Why had he waited so long to say anything? No, Antonov could have ruined me only in the immediate aftermath of the Revolution.

As the summer of 1939 drew to a close, two things had to be clear to Trotsky—war was only weeks away, and with the coming of war Stalin would want him dead as soon as possible. So it was time for Trotsky to make his move, now or never.

In all his public statements, Trotsky, of course, spoke out against fascism and for Soviet communism. But in his heart of hearts he had to know he had only one chance to save his life, his career, and the cause of communism as he sees it. That chance was to side with the Germans against me. But his pride stood in the way. Siding with the Germans would not only disgust him in and of itself, but would prove that all the charges hurled at him by Stalin were not slanders, but a true reading of Trotsky's secret intentions.

In fact, the Germans and Trotsky have a great deal in common.

The problem with the Germans is not that they think they're better than everyone else.

The problem is that the Germans *are* better than everyone else.

The Germans are scientific and must base their conclusions on something. They're not like the Russians, who will get excited if you say the right words—vodka, *Pravda,* Russia. But the Germans must have evidence, proof, logic.

So the Germans look around and see plenty of proof that everything they do is better—their trains are better, their planes are better, their brains are better. Who could blame them for drawing the proper and obvious conclusion?

The real flaw in the Germans' logic is that they think because they are better they must triumph. Nothing could be further from the truth. The good is the last thing to triumph in this world, not to mention the better.

So the Germans and Trotsky shared the mistaken belief that the superior must prevail.

Objectively, Trotsky *should* ally himself with the Nazis because they alone have the power to give him what he wants—Russia, the Kremlin. The Americans may have the power, but they have no interest in returning Trotsky to Russia. They couldn't give a shit about Trotsky, Russia, the whole thing. But the Germans, that's another story. The Germans are always interested in what's going on in Russia; it's right next door. And, after all, who was it beside the Germans who sent Lenin speeding back to Russia in a sealed train? Who's to say they might not want to send Trotsky back in another one?

Trotsky knows his history; he couldn't help but make the connection. War, German train, new leader for Russia: it isn't complicated.

Now, from Stalin's point of view, this could not be considered a good possibility. Trotsky and the Nazis, I couldn't think of a worse combination.

Since this is the worst possible combination from Stalin's point of view, Stalin was obliged—if only from the normal, healthy instinct of survival—to make sure that this worst of all possibilities never becomes the worst of all actual realities.

Eliminating the Nazis *and* Trotsky would of course be ideal. Nothing could be better than having all that's worst for you gone in a stroke. But we live in the real world. A world in which there are a great many Nazis.

Consequently, I found a way to make it absolutely impossible for Trotsky to join forces with the Nazis. On August 29, 1939, the world learned that I concluded a Non-Aggression Pact with Germany.

And besides, the whole business about Trotsky and the Nazis may have been nonsense anyway. What was Hitler going to do with that fucking Jew?

Still, you never know. If I could betray Russia, why couldn't Hitler betray Germany?

But by September 1, 1939, that was moot. Hitler invaded Poland and, according to the secret clauses of our agreement, we moved into eastern Poland on September 17. Now the lines were clear. France and England against Germany, with Russia and America sitting it out.

But the outbreak of war screwed up Operation Duck.

In midsummer Eitington had traveled to Paris to train Ramón and Caridad in espionage techniques. Mother and son sailed for New York from Le Havre in late August. But Eitington was still in Paris when the war broke out. He was using a Polish passport, which was bad for three reasons. One, it was forged. Two, it had expired. And three, by identifying him as a Polish national, it meant that he must now either serve in the French army, since France and Poland were allies, or else be interned as a suspicious foreign element. Eitington went into hiding.

I was furious. The war was supposed to free my hand against Trotsky, not block it. I summoned Beria and Sudoplatov to inform them that I did not want Eitington wasting his time in Paris when he should be heading up the operation to eliminate Trotsky. They swore they would get Eitington out of France as fast as humanly possible.

Connections with the French police in the Seventh Arrondissement are very good, but it still took a month for Eitington to receive the necessary papers that would allow him to leave France for the United States. That wasn't the problem. The problem was getting him an American entry visa.

In the meantime, Eitington was placed in a mental hospital and supplied with the forged French identity card of a Syrian Jew suffering from mental illness. This made him unfit for military service, eliminating one worry. But he could still be picked up and expelled as an undesirable alien.

An agent was dispatched to Lausanne, Switzerland, to make contact with Maxim Steinberg, a businessman who has good relations with the U.S. consulate. Steinberg is also an agent of ours, but has of late become quite skittish. Last year he was recalled to Moscow and refused to come, fearing he might be purged. He resisted meeting the agent we dispatched to Lausanne. Finally Steinberg agreed to a meeting, but, afraid he was going to be assassinated, he pulled a gun on our agent, who deserves a medal for talking Steinberg down and making him realize that he was in no danger. In the end, Steinberg agreed to cooperate in obtaining a U.S. entry visa for the Syrian Jew in question. That took another week. Almost a month and a half was lost. Finally, in October 1939, Eitington sailed to New York City. In Brooklyn, Eitington established an import–export company that is to serve as a communications center for Operation Duck and which also provides a cover profession for Ramón, who has now been issued a forged Canadian passport. We're back in business.

29

Apart from accomplishing many other useful political ends, my deal with Hitler just about checkmates Trotsky. In a way, that's good; in a way, that's bad. Good because now Trotsky is only one move away from total defeat. Bad because the only counterattack that can save him is the one that destroys me in a single move, and he's getting closer to *that* all the time. Having covered the Revolution, he's on to the Civil War.

Missing the Revolution, I missed nothing. Even Lenin himself said that it was "easier than lifting a feather." Only six people were killed in the storming of the Winter Palace in Petersburg, although casualties did run higher in Moscow. But in 1918 all hell broke loose. Civil war erupted between the Reds and Whites. And now for the first time the clash between Stalin and Trotsky was played out on the big stage. The Civil War lasted a little more than two years. The war between Stalin and Trotsky had a longer run.

In power, Lenin was brilliant, indomitable, ruthless. Nothing was going to stop him now. Certainly not a parliament elected by the rules of bourgeois democracy in which we Bolsheviks had not received a majority. He closed it down after its first session in January 1918. Russia needed unified action, not talk. Enemies were coming at us from every side. The Germans were still attacking, threatening to take St. Petersburg, forcing Lenin to shift the capital to Moscow. The Whites had large armies everywhere from the outskirts of Moscow to the ends of Siberia. Every fucking country in the world was invading us. The Americans moved into Siberia, the French landed in Odessa. Churchill was screaming for Bolshevism to be strangled in its cradle and sent the Whites advisors and a new weapon of war, tanks—light "Whippets" and the heavier Mark V's. A large Czech army was fighting its way east across the country. Bands of anarchists and robbers were marauding everywhere. Cities would change hands three times in a week.

The only thing that mattered was to kill your enemies before they killed you. Again I was of use to Lenin. As Trotsky says, "I soon noticed that Lenin was 'advancing' Stalin, valuing in him his firmness, grit, stubbornness, and to a certain extent his slyness, as attributes necessary in the struggle. . . . Lenin had great need of Stalin. . . . The ability to 'exert pressure' was what Lenin prized so highly in Stalin."

Our strength was in the cities. The workers were for communism. But the stingy, thick-headed peasants were in no hurry to feed the cities. In the spring of 1918 Lenin assigned me to grain-rich southern Russia to exert a little pressure. I promised him "my hand would not tremble."

By then I was Commissar of Nationalities and had employed Nadya Alliluyeva as a typist. She still saw me as a hero but she was not a schoolgirl with a ribbon in her hair anymore. Nadya had grown into a good-looking young woman. There was something Gypsy-like about her dark eyes, dark eyebrows, and swarthy skin, though she did have a little turned-up Russian nose. She had also become a fiery communist, willing to do whatever it took to win. I asked her to come south with me.

On June 3, 1918, I arrived in the Volga city of Tsaritsyn, which I later renamed Stalingrad, with a detachment of Red Guards, two armored trains, and as Trotsky correctly says, "unlimited power for provisioning the hungry political and industrial centers with grain."

That "unlimited power" allowed me both to get the job done and to fulfill an old childhood dream of mine, one that went back to my reading about Ivan the Terrible's scientific interest in human psychology as revealed in the laboratory conditions of torture: At what exact degree of pain does the instinct for self-preservation overcome all other loyalties? At what temperature does dignity melt?

We didn't have much time for torture in Tsaritsyn. We needed answers quick. Where was the grain? Who was against us? Either you answered or you died. Sometimes one man would be shot in front of others so they would realize we meant business. Still, I was curious and wanted to learn. So I designed a little "social experiment," a trick I had learned from Major Antonov. I ordered that from the prisoners awaiting execution, five be selected and placed in the same cell. Each of the five was to differ as much as possible socially from the others. We ended up with a Jew, a Cossack, a peasant, a priest, and an intellectual. For some reason we had no aristocrats behind bars at the time, and even though I was Commissar of Nationalities, I had no interest in including any of the minorities in my experiment.

Interrogate them individually or as a group? There were advantages both ways. In a group they could be played off against one another, but questioned individually they might show their true colors more. I decided to go that route.

I went to their cell and, without entering, said: "Sometimes in a firing squad one man is given blanks so no one can ever be absolutely sure if he was the killer. This is something of that sort but with a little difference. All of you have been sentenced to die. I'll give each of you ten minutes to tell me why you should live. The one who does best will live to see tomorrow; the rest of you die tonight."

"Why should we believe you?" snapped the intellectual.

"Why shouldn't you?"

No one else said anything. I said to the intellectual, "You first."

"I refuse to play your ugly, barbaric little game."

"Fine," I said, shifting my attention to the others. "Your odds just improved 20 percent. Who's next?"

The Jew rose heavily to his feet. Balding, fleshy, he looked fond of the table, a paterfamilias, full of jokes at a wedding.

In the interrogation room, I glanced at my watch to let him know the clock was running, and said: "I'm listening."

"My name is Yakov Binder and I have three sons and three daughters. I am no enemy of your revolution—"

"The fact that you say 'your revolution' proves that you are."

"I was neither for it nor against it."

"Who is not with us is against us."

He sighed heavily, conceding the point. "As soon as the war with the Germans broke out, I saw trouble coming. Other people in my family emigrated to America and tried to convince me to come. No, I said, this too will blow over, everything blows over. But, to be on the safe side, I'll bury some gold. Gold gets you through anything. That's what my father taught me."

"So you want to buy your way out?"

"I know you're short of guns and ammunition. I know there's talk about buying rifles from the American company Winchester. And the Americans aren't going to take IOUs. A thousand rifles to point at your enemies so that one rifle is not pointed at this Jew."

"Would you get down on your knees and beg for your life?"

"If it would help."

"No need. Your offer makes sense in itself."

I called for the Cossack next. Waiting for him to be brought, I thought of the mounted Cossack I had shot through the mouth years back during the May Day demonstration. But unlike that blond-bearded, burly man, this one was small, dark, sympatico.

"What's your name?" I asked.

"Bogdan."

"All right then, what landed you in here, Bogdan?"

"The war started; everyone in the village said, Let's fight the Reds, they'll take our land. So I got on my horse and rode out with everyone else. Next thing I know I'm in here."

"And would you fight for us now?"

"To the death."

"Why?"

"Because . . . because now I've seen that the people are with the Reds and it's only the masters who are tricking us into fighting for them again."

"The Jew that was just in here says he's got enough buried gold to buy a thousand rifles for the Revolution. You don't even have a rifle and who knows who you'll fight for once you walk out the door. Why should I take you over him?"

Bogdan fell silent. A furrow like the wings of a bird appeared in his forehead.

"Why . . . why should you take me over him? Because he's a fucking Jew!"

I laughed out loud. "Excellent argument. And would you beg on your knees for your life?"

His face darkened. "A Cossack does not beg on his knees."

Catching the look of displeasure on my face, Bogdan was quick to add: "And you don't want anyone fighting for you who would even think of begging for his life."

"You're smart for a Cossack."

"Still, I'm here."

"Yes."

Then it was a choice between the peasant and the priest. Peasants I didn't like and wanted it over fast.

The peasant didn't have to be asked; he fell right to his knees as soon as he entered the room.

"Your Lordship, spare my life. Yes, I was greedy, yes, I hid my grain and my cattle, but now I'll give you every last kernel, every cow, every steer. Let me live, Your Excellency, and my family and I will eat bark and grass, just let me live. I don't believe in heaven. I don't want to die. I'm only forty. I've got children, eleven children, I'll bring them up to be good farmers for you and teach them to give their grain to the state and never hide any. Now I've learned. Let me live so that we can help feed the cities and the workers."

"Oh, you got smart in a hurry too, Timofei Timofeiyevich, is that your name?"

"Let it be my name, Your Lordship."

"So, you're hiding behind a false name, is that it?"

"No, no, Your Excellency, my real name is Ivan Fyodorovich Nikolaev."

I paused for a moment, then asked: "Have you shit your pants, Ivan Fyodorovich?"

"Yes, Your Excellency, but out of respect."

"Respect. And how many head of cattle have you hidden away?"

"Thirty, Your Lordship."

"Thirty?"

"Thirty and not one more."

"And would you personally request to be shot on the spot if we discovered that there were thirty-one?"

"There could only be thirty-one if one of the cows has calved in the meantime."

"You may leave now. But hold on to your cuffs to keep your business in your pants, you understand?"

"Excellency, I understand."

I went out and smoked a pipe before calling the priest to give the stink time to disperse, though I did take it as a form of tribute. While smoking, I was informed that the intellectual had changed his mind and wanted to talk to me, but I just shook my head.

The priest was in his fifties, his long fluffy beard still black. His eyes looked tired, contemptuous, scared.

"According to your file, you preached against the 'godless Reds,' is that right?"

"Was I wrong? You're God-fearing men?"

"We're not afraid of anything."

"That's a mistake."

"Why?"

"Because we answer for our lives."

"After death you mean?"

"Before and after."

"So you believe there's a life after this one?"

"I do."

"So then death holds no fear for you?"

"My faith is strong, but I'm still a man. I fear pain, I fear death."

"Then what help is your God?"

"It is a help to remember that He created all the stars and worlds and not just this one, where men do evil in the name of justice."

"You haven't told me why I should let you live."

"There is no reason a man like you should let a man like me stay alive."

"I don't agree. Since the time of Peter the Great, the Church has been the willing slave of the state. You could offer your services to the new Russia, buy yourself some time."

"You mean inform on the people who make confession to me?"

"That's one idea."

"God would never forgive me for that."

"Then why doesn't your God help you now in your hour of true need?"

"I cannot know His reasons."

"You'll be dead in less than half an hour."

He seemed stunned, though I was not telling him anything he didn't already know. Maybe it was the shortness of the time left him that made him speechless.

"Think of everything you'll be leaving," I said. "The blueness of the sky, a nice fish for dinner, the sound of bells, people."

The sadness of his face inspired me. "The sound of brooks and choirs, reading the Bible, the taste of jam in your tea, birch trees with icicles on them, Russia, life."

Then very softly he said: "What is it you want of me?"

"Two things. One, that you cooperate in every way we ask—inform us who our secret enemies are, preach *for* us, not against us."

"And the other?"

"The other is that you get down on your knees and say that you renounce God, that the only God you now recognize is the man in this room with the power of life and death over you."

Slowly, he slid from the chair to the floor. He closed his eyes. I gave him a few moments to collect himself.

"Say it!"

"I want to, but my lips won't obey me."

After I had the priest removed from the room, I had some hard thinking to do. Of course, I had the power to have them all executed or none of them executed, but I wanted to stick by the strict rules I had set up. The priest and the intellectual were out. I liked Bogdan the Cossack and he would probably make a good soldier for the Revolution, but the struggle would be decided by the masses; one individual more or less would make no difference. That left the Jew and the peasant. I disliked them both, but that didn't matter any more than liking Bogdan. The Jew's offer was attractive: I'd look good in Moscow sending Lenin enough gold to buy a thousand rifles. But starving soldiers can't shoot straight, and Lenin's express orders to me had been to requisition grain. I could spare the Jew *and* the peasant, get the gold *and* the grain, have one or the other shot on the spot, and trust that the one who was set free would land back in trouble sooner or later.

That solution satisfied my reason but still somehow irritated me. What good was unlimited power if you had to obey the dictates of reason? I ordered all five prisoners brought out and lined up against the wall. Deciding at the very last moment appealed to me—I was torturing myself a little too.

They were brought to the motor-pool garage, which was often used for executions; the blood could run down the drains used for oil changes, and the trucks could be started up to cover the sound of gunfire. Not that the people of the city didn't know what the sound of truck motors in the night meant.

"Don't start the motors yet," I said to the man climbing into the cab of one of the trucks.

"I knew you were lying!" screamed the intellectual.

I waited until the squad had shouldered their rifles. My eyes went to each of the five. The intellectual was trying to summon a defiance he had already compromised, the Jew looked miserable, Bogdan held himself straight, the peasant looked ready to fall to his knees again, and the priest was trying to mumble himself back into God's good graces.

Until I said it, I had no idea what was going to come out of my mouth. "Bogdan, step out. Start the motors. Fire at will."

When I returned to the armored train where I was living, Nadya was drinking tea with one of the comrades.

"You look tired," she said. "Tea?"

"Some tea would be good," I said, interested that it was only my fatigue that showed.

But the Jew had been right about the lack of bullets. We didn't have enough to execute all the people we were arresting. I solved that problem by having a large number of prisoners placed on a huge barge in the middle of the Volga.

To test Nadya, I told her to type up an order—BARGE TO BE SUNK IMMEDIATELY BY ARTILLERY. She tapped it right out and pulled the paper smartly from the typewriter for me to sign. Her hand did not tremble either.

A short while later we learned that the Whites had come close to the city where Tsar Nickie and the royal family were being held under house arrest. It was like chess. If the Whites could liberate their king and queen, they'd be in a much stronger position. That could not be allowed. Logic dictated their execution. It was carried out on the night of July 16, 1918. Bullets bounced off the diamonds the princesses had sewn into their underclothes, which meant that the poor dears had to be bayoneted and clubbed to death with rifle butts.

I laughed when I heard about the diamonds. For the first time, Nadya scolded me. "Still," she said, "they were children."

"That's right," I said. "And when they grew up they'd have ordered the execution of our children."

Not that she was pregnant yet; our first child wouldn't be born until 1921.

It was there in Tsaritsyn that the trouble started with Trotsky. He was Commissar of War, and resented my interference in military matters, as if there were a clear distinction to be made in that bloody mess. Even Trotsky admits, "What happened to Stalin was what happened to many other Soviet officials, droves of them. They were sent to various provinces to mobilize the collection of grain surpluses. Once there, they ran into White insurrections. Whereupon their provisioning detachments turned into military detachments."

Trotsky didn't like the way I was running the show or maybe the fact that I was running the show. Anyway, he telegraphed Lenin: "I insist categorically on Stalin's recall. . . . We have a colossal superiority of forces, but there is utter anarchy at the top. I can put a stop to it in twenty-four hours, provided I have your firm and clear-cut support."

Trotsky beat me there. Or did he? Yes, I was recalled by Lenin, but Trotsky was winning too many brilliant victories on the field of battle. Lenin didn't want any Red Napoleons suddenly rising up against him and so began to use me as a counterweight to Trotsky, who at the time looked like the ambitious one. Especially in August 1918, when a woman revolutionary, Fanya Kaplan, angered by Lenin's closing of Parliament, shot him in the neck as he came out of a factory meeting. Trotsky immediately abandoned his military responsibilities and dashed off to Moscow, revealing to all his certainty that he was the heir apparent and needed to be in the capital to take charge of the country in the event Lenin died. But Lenin didn't die. And I had stayed at my post the whole time, surrounded by the men I had forged bonds with in Tsaritsyn and who now hated Trotsky nearly as much as I did. And those were the people I would use against Trotsky when the power struggle between us broke out in the open after Lenin's death in 1924. Dialectics is a tricky business. Trotsky's victories made Lenin suspicious of him. And my "defeat" by Trotsky provided me with key allies that would lead to his defeat. All you need is patience.

The Civil War was Trotsky's heyday. Judging by the latest packets of material I've received, Trotsky can't stop writing about those times, his glory, my "tragic pettiness." I couldn't be more pleased. There's nothing in this period that can help Trotsky build his indictment against me. I have no secrets from those days. Everything was out in the open. There were enemies on every side and we spent every waking hour in killing them.

And Trotsky made his own mistakes back then. He used too many Tsarist officers, neglected guerrilla tactics, and was altogether too haughty in the way he went about his business. One comrade wrote of "Trotsky's princely journeys along the front." And he kept forgetting he was a Jew and that Russians don't like to be sent to their death by Jews.

You could see an immediate change of expression on someone's face if you happened to mention that Trotsky's real name was Bronstein. Russians dislike Jews, and they have even more dislike for Jews who hide behind changed names. Not that the choice of Trotsky as an alias was all that brilliant either. "Trotsky" was supposedly the name of a guard at a prison he escaped from, and taking it as his own was a nervy move. But names ending in "-sky" have a foreign ring to a Russian ear, they sound Polish or Jewish. A good Russian name should end in "-ov" or "-in." Of course, there wasn't much time to think about that sort of thing in the middle of a war, but wars don't last forever either.

Once England, France, and America had defeated Germany, they lost half their reason for invading Russia, which was to keep us in the war. The other half, to strangle Bolshevism in its cradle, turned out to be of less interest, especially when it became clear that the Whites were not united, had little active support from the populace, and were probably going to lose. And nobody likes a loser.

In fact, it wouldn't be long before Paris was full of Russian counts driving taxicabs and waiting on tables. By the end of 1920 the whole thing was pretty much over except for the mopping up, a job I was good at and one Lenin constantly assigned to me. Lenin was still "advancing" me to counterbalance Trotsky. Sometimes when there were certain kinds of business that I was best at taking care of, Lenin would look at me hard. I wasn't sure whether he was retaking my measure or feeling a certain distaste at having to deal with people like me, who were all too good at doing the dirty work that comes with war and revolution. But our relations were still comradely, brusque but cordial. He praised me when I succeeded and let me have it when I screwed up. By then one thing was clear to me: Lenin would make the transition from war to peace without breaking stride, but Trotsky would feel cramped in the room that ran all Russia. He needed the roaring crowds, the steaming trains, the ramparts and trenches, history in all the more obvious senses of the word. He may have beaten me in war but I'd have his ass come peacetime.

And besides, I don't begrudge Trotsky all his brilliant victories during the Civil War. They secured the success of the Revolution. He was working for me.

30

What frightens me most about Trotsky's account of the Civil War is all the telegrams he quotes. Telegrams from me to Lenin, Lenin to Trotsky, Lenin to me. Not that there is anything particularly damaging in those telegrams, but it is the sheer quantity of them that disturbs me. When, with Etienne's help, we had stolen Trotsky's archives in Paris in 1936, I thought we'd gotten the bulk of the key material, but obviously Trotsky had other sources, other stashes. Who knows what else he has? That matters more than ever now, as Trotsky sits down to write about the twenties, the decade in which everything changed forever. In 1921, with the end of the Civil War, Lenin and Trotsky were the commanding figures and I was still operating behind the scenes, the little-known Commissar of Nationalities. By 1929 Lenin was five years dead, Trotsky had been exiled from the Soviet Union, and I was the undisputed master of the Kremlin.

Now, another ten years later, my position is even better. I turned sixty on December 21, 1939, and ten days later saw in a new year that looks nothing if not promising. The international situation has been stabilized—Hitler is busy warring with England and France, we've grabbed Eastern Poland, Lithuania, Estonia, and Latvia.

And Operation Duck is back on track. Ramón is now in Mexico City romancing Trotsky's courier and sometime secretary, Sylvia Agelof, who arrived there in January 1940. Ramón has made no effort to be invited inside Trotsky's compound yet, contenting himself to wait for Sylvia outside, where he chats up the guards. In the meantime, the painter Siqueiros is almost done assembling the group that will carry out the frontal assault on Trotsky's compound. With any luck, I should be rid of Trotsky by spring. In principle, I should be able to relax. But I can't. Lately something has been driving me to spend time in the section of Lubyanka devoted to Trotsky. It covers three floors. I go late at night, wander the stacks, pulling down files at will and at random.

At first I had a quite definite reason—to recheck the inventory of the archives stolen from Trotsky in Paris. I was shocked by some of the material he had assembled on me and grateful to Etienne for organizing its theft. The only question was, Did Trotsky have other copies of these same files elsewhere? If he did, he'd have to work quickly. At best he now had only months.

Then I flipped through other files—photos, documents, fading carbons. Coming across a picture of Trotsky boarding a train, I suddenly burst out laughing. I flipped the photo over. It was dated January 16, 1928. Yes, of course, it all came back to me. After gradually slicing away at Trotsky's power, removing him from one post after the other, always by democratic vote of the Central Committee of course, I finally felt strong enough in 1928 to exile Trotsky from Moscow. But he had been organizing demonstrations against me at that time and I did not want his expulsion from Moscow to turn into that sort of spontaneous street protest that can so easily get out of hand. We solved that problem handily. Trotsky was arrested, kicking and screaming, then taken by car to a railway station a good distance from Moscow where he was put on the Trans-Siberian train for his place of exile, Alma-Ata, in distant Kazakhstan. Meanwhile, the actor who had played Trotsky in any number of historical films about the Revolution meekly boarded the Trans-Siberian train in Moscow. Nobody could tell the difference. For nearly everyone, Trotsky was a figure at a podium, a picture in a magazine. That's why people are always surprised and disappointed when they meet some great figure in person—they always seem smaller, more ordinary. In any case, it worked like a charm. The actor waved resignedly and boarded the train. And maybe the actor's air of dejection was not only a triumph of craft; he had to be aware that his movie career playing the heroic Trotsky was over.

Suddenly I had to know if that actor was still alive and what he looked like now. As usual, Boss Two was downstairs, waiting to be sent back to the Kremlin ahead of me or to ride with me, as we sometimes did when it was late and I wasn't too worried about assassins. Boss Two was asleep in his chair with a newspaper on his chest when I entered the room. For a moment, I felt a flash of envy: though he still looked exactly like me, he was aging better, fewer wrinkles, his mustache more bristly. Of course, he had less to worry about. Still, it's strange how faces change—one of the other doubles, Boss Three or Four, I don't remember, all of a sudden, in a year's time, stopped looking like me at all. He was heartbroken. I knew that he traded on his looks to get women.

"Wake up, old man," I said. "We're done for the night."

Three nights later, an unheard-of event occurred—a tête-à-tête between Stalin and Trotsky in the Kremlin!

The actor who played Trotsky in the movies was alive and well, having aged more or less in parallel with the original. He was summoned to the Kremlin at midnight. Poskryobyshev came out of my office, leaving the door open enough for "Trotsky Two" to get a glimpse of Stalin on the telephone from the waiting room.

"Comrade Stalin is dealing with an emergency situation," said Poskryobyshev, "and apologizes for the delay. Can we bring you some little sandwiches, tea, fruit, anything in the meantime?"

Nervous, hopeful, unsure of the situation, the actor declined.

"It could take a little while," said Poskryobyshev. "Are you sure?"

"Well, a few sandwiches and tea might give me strength," said Trotsky Two.

"And fruit is good for the health."

"That's true too."

"I'll take care of it right away," said Poskryobyshev, returning to the office and closing the door discreetly behind him.

The actor jumped out of his chair five minutes later when another door to the waiting room opened and he saw something his mind could not grasp—Stalin carrying a tray of sandwiches, tea, and oranges.

"Comrade Stalin!" he cried.

"What Comrade Stalin? I'm a double like you. They gave me the tray on the way up."

"My heart almost stopped."

"Don't let yourself get too excited."

"Now that I take a closer look, I can see it's not him."

"The sandwiches are for both of us. The one thing I've learned in all my years as Boss Two—that's what they call me—is when they offer food, you take it. Where else are you going to get oranges in this country?"

"Don't say anything bad. They could be listening."

"The Boss doesn't mind a crack or two as long as it's not personal. You'll see, he's fine to work with."

"What does he want from us?"

"God only knows."

"The sandwiches are excellent; what wonderful sausage."

"You used to play Trotsky in the movies?"

"That's right. For a time it was a good living. But now . . . not only is there no work, but a few months ago I was walking down the street and some drunk comes over to me and says, Oh, so you came back, you treacherous kike—and punches me in the nose."

"Pardon me for laughing, but it is sort of funny."

"Maybe to you. Anyway, it's a problem you don't have."

"Not that the Boss doesn't have enemies. Sometimes I worry some Trotskyite will come out of nowhere and cut my throat, so it's no picnic either."

"I can see that. Where do you suppose these oranges are from?"

"I don't know. We used to get them from Spain. Ask the Boss, he knows every detail."

"So, what's he like?"

"Tough, of course, but with a good sense of humor. He'll probably call you Trotsky Two."

"Well, I'm glad he beat out Trotsky, except of course that it cost me my job."

"So what do you do for a living now?"

"Drama coach. I can barely make ends meet."

"I don't know what the Boss wants, but maybe there are a few rubles in it."

"He pays well?"

"Decent, though he's a little on the cheap side."

Poskryobyshev opened the door and said: "You may come in now, both of you."

They came in and sat down in the two chairs Poskryobyshev had placed before my desk.

"I apologize for keeping you both waiting. As you know, we're at war with Finland and somehow that little country is proving difficult to subdue. There was just a little crisis that required my personal attention and I'm afraid it's going to require some more. So let me come right to the point. Trotsky Two, I can see that you've made efforts to look as little like Trotsky as possible. I understand and I sympathize. But now that must change. Here's a batch of the latest photos of Trotsky from Mexico. Your assignment is to grow back your goatee and do whatever else it takes so that you resemble the Trotsky in these photographs. Understood?"

"Understood."

"And you'll need a white suit and a blue French peasant's jacket like Trotsky wears. On your way out, Poskryobyshev will give you an envelope with some money for expenses and to help you eat a little better. Trotsky himself has put on some weight in Mexico."

"Thank you, Comrade Stalin."

"I'll see you back here in about a month's time. I wish you good luck and good appetite. You may leave now. Boss Two, you stay, we still have some business."

No sooner did Trotsky Two leave the room than I said to Boss Two with a laugh, "Good work, but now get the fuck out from behind my desk."

31

Now my only hope is Trotsky's arrogance. As he investigates the period from 1921 to Lenin's death in 1924, he must face all the blunders he made in those years, which cost him everything he held dear. But he won't want to, who would? So his critical faculties will be dulled and he may fail to make the essential connections.

After the Civil War, the country was a wreck. Bombed factories, scorched fields, typhus, famine, cannibalism. Except for a loyal hard core of workers and politicos, nobody wanted us communists. We ruled by terror and by inflicting death; we had the guns now.

So, at the Tenth Party Congress in April 1921, Lenin made two smart moves. He introduced his New Economic Policy, which everyone was soon calling NEP. Lenin bit the bullet and allowed small-scale capitalism to flourish, knowing greed is always a good fuel. It worked well and it worked fast. Trotsky was against it. He wanted "labor armies," forced battalions of conscripts marched off to the factories and fields. But the heady romantic days of the Revolution and Civil War were over. It was a time of greasy compromise. My time.

Lenin's other smart move barely went noticed at the time. If there was one thing Lenin was afraid of, it was a split in the Party. Our hold on power was tenuous enough; one fracture and we were dead men. So he introduced a secret clause stating that any member of the Central Committee found guilty of creating an opposition could be expelled from the Party by a two-thirds vote. Everything was very democratic in those days.

Just how tenuous our hold on power was became apparent immediately. No sooner did we finish up our business at the Congress than the sailors on the island of Kronstadt off St. Petersburg revolted. Their slogan was "Soviets without communism," meaning without us. The problem was that the sailors were, as Trotsky put it, the "pride and glory of the Revolution," the reddest and bravest of them all. But Lenin had no illusions. You didn't give up power just because you'd lost an election and you didn't give up power because some sailors happened to be truer to your own principles than you were. He sent Trotsky to crush the rebellion. It was just the sort of thing Trotsky liked—cavalry charges across the frozen bay, hurrah, storm the fortress.

It was another greasy compromise, utterly necessary, but one some of the comrades never quite forgave Trotsky for. It just didn't smell right, a Jew killing our boys.

I kept low and kept busy, doing all the boring work that my long years in Siberia had prepared me for. I headed up the oversight committee known officially as the Workers' and Peasants' Inspectorate, and ran the Orgburo, which was in charge of personnel. Trotsky made seven-hour speeches and stormed fortresses; I sat in my office and studied index cards, promoting, demoting. My nickname at the time was even Comrade Cardfile. Slowly, slowly, I was stocking all the main organs of power with people who knew they owed their positions to me. I spent time with those people too, sharing a smoke, shooting the breeze. Most of them were young and hungry. For them the Revolution meant that a plumber's kid could run a town.

Aside from having a good nose, I had other ways of knowing what people really thought. I was in charge of the installation of a special closed telephone system for the exclusive use of people in the inner circle. Designed by a Czech engineer, the system originally had only eighty terminals. I prevailed on that engineer to create a special phone for me that allowed me to listen in to any other conversation. But, his work done, that unfortunate engineer was now in possession of dangerous knowledge. Though my act may not have been as grandiose as Ivan's blinding the architect of St. Basil's, I did have the engineer shot, the best you could do in modern times.

Trotsky made one of his worst mistakes at the Eleventh Party Congress in April 1922. Lenin had appointed me General Secretary of the Party, a post which carried no great weight at the time, but had offered Trotsky the position of Deputy Chairman of the Council of People's Commissars, the number two slot, the position you'd give the heir apparent. Trotsky had already shown that he thought of himself that way when he rushed back to Moscow when Lenin was shot. But now, when offered what he thought rightfully his, Trotsky refused.

Why? That was the main subject of discussion out in the corridors during a break. I went from group to group listening to what people said.

"He's too stiff-necked."

"He's worried there are already too many Jews on the Council."

"He doesn't want to be appointed, he wants to win it by popular acclaim."

"He's still ashamed that he rushed back to Moscow when Lenin was shot."

It was from listening in on phone conversations that I first learned of Lenin's medical problems. There were still two bullets in Lenin, left from the assassination attempt four years before. He'd been suffering terrible headaches and now, right after the Congress, it was decided to operate on him. There were various ideas—lead from the bullets was poisoning him; the bullets were dumdums dipped in curare. But maybe it was other things that were causing the headaches. Lenin was troubled by the rise of bureaucracy and the continued presence of enemies, Mensheviks and other revolutionaries who had not come over to our side. He had a solution for that—put them up against the wall and put some bullets into *them.*

The operation was a success, but a month later, in late May 1922, Lenin had a stroke. We received daily medical bulletins. Lenin was being kept on a strict regime. No politics, no newspapers, no work, no visitors. Sitting in the room from which all Russia was ruled, I took a piece of paper and did some simple math. Lenin was fifty-two. I was forty-two. If he came back from the stroke, he might have nine or ten good years left. That meant that if I played my cards right, I could be running the show by the time I was his age. That is, if Trotsky didn't have a sudden change of heart and decide it wasn't beneath him to take the number-two post he'd been offered.

I had to see how Lenin was doing and traveled out to Gorki, a village about an hour from Moscow. Lenin didn't look bad, though he had some trouble speaking. His humor was good, sly. With playful irony he said: "They won't let me read the newspapers. I'm not allowed to talk politics. So I carefully avoid even the smallest piece of paper lying on the table for fear it might be a newspaper. I must obey the doctors' orders."

Of course all he wanted to do was talk politics. I filled him in, always inserting some subtle jabs against Trotsky but not so many that it would stick out. Still, I could see that he didn't like that.

Yet on other visits I found him despondent. He spoke of suicide and even asked me to give him poison so that he could take his own life if it became obvious that he was turning into a vegetable. It was too horrible for him to consider living like that—a man who devoted his entire life to seizing and exercising power, nodding off in his chair, drooling. Lenin asked his wife and others as well for poison, and constantly spoke of the suicide of Marx's daughter. I assured him that he would always be my leader and that I would always obey him, but that it would never come to that.

"Think of it like a bad hangover," I said. "You swear you'll never drink again. But that vow is just part of the hangover. The doctors say you'll be back at work by the end of the summer."

And by late September he was. On October 31, 1922, he made his first public appearance, delivering a speech that, except for some slurred words, went over well. Still, he looked gaunt, frail, a little lost.

Maybe Lenin threw himself back into work with too much energy, for he suffered a second stroke on December 16. Now a medical/political committee was created to oversee Lenin's health and activities. I headed up that committee, which issued a ruling: Lenin "has the right to dictate every day for five to ten minutes. . . . It is forbidden for him to have any visitors. Neither friends nor those around him are allowed to convey to him any political news."

It was an odd feeling, ordering Lenin, forbidding Lenin, but of course it was all only for his own good.

Yet Lenin, who always believed that with the proper lever he could overturn anything, now began using those five or ten minutes as his lever to overturn me. In late December 1922 and January 1923, Lenin, obsessed by the feud between Trotsky and me, which threatened to split the Party, directed all his force against that "tragic eventuality," writing what became known as his Testament. Lenin kept one copy, gave three to his wife, and had a fifth placed in a secret file.

In his Testament, Lenin called Trotsky "perhaps the most able man on the present Central Committee," but did note his "excessive self-assurance."

But he saved his harshest words for me:

> Comrade Stalin, having become General Secretary, has concentrated immeasurable power in his hands, and I am not sure he always knows how to use that power with sufficient caution. . . .
>
> Stalin is too coarse, and this fault, though tolerable in dealings among us Communists, becomes unbearable in a General Secretary. Therefore I propose to the comrades to find some way of removing Stalin from his position and appointing somebody else who differs in all respects from Comrade Stalin.

Lenin had betrayed me. And betrayed himself. He was growing soft, childish, a weak forgiving smile playing on the lips that had ordered ten thousand executions. He was, of all things, apologizing. "I am, I believe, strongly guilty before the workers of Russia. . . ."

And he attacked not only my person but my power base as well, writing articles for *Pravda* calling for the committees I ran to be either reduced in size or flooded with so many new members that the majority I had so carefully built up would be diminished to a little, isolatable faction. Now I regretted not obtaining poison for him when he asked for it. At this rate, I wouldn't be the leader in ten years—I'd never be.

But then in March 1923, after breaking off all "comradely relations" with me, Lenin suffered a third stroke. "God voted for Stalin," quipped the journalist Karl Radek.

Having turned against me, and remembering that he had requested poison from me, Lenin now grew scared. He insisted on eating with everyone else in the household. But, as the saying goes, fear has big eyes. I myself was no longer worried about Lenin. I knew it was rare for anyone to recover from a third stroke. Lenin could barely walk, and his speech was reduced to a few monosyllabic words. He was finished. Trotsky was the one I was worried about now.

All my efforts went into forming a bloc against Trotsky. As usual, I took a moderate position, claiming that I wanted only to be part of the collective leadership as opposed to Trotsky, who by his very nature could not share the stage. By the end of the year, some of the comrades were accusing Trotsky of treason and calling for his arrest.

But then all of a sudden, against all expectations, in late 1923, Lenin seemed on the road to recovery. He'd never be able to run the whole show again, but he could use his renewed vigor to advance Trotsky against me. I knew I had to make my move at the Thirteenth Party Conference in January 1924, since neither Lenin nor Trotsky would attend. Trotsky had been sent to the south, to a health resort in Sukhum on the Black Sea, for rest and recuperation; his health too had begun to deteriorate after all the years of stress and strain.

I hammered away at Trotsky during the Conference: "He has elevated himself into a superman standing above the Central Committee, above its laws, and above its decisions, and in this way he has provided certain groups within the Party with a pretext for undermining confidence in the Central Committee." In other words, it was Trotsky who was guilty of the worst sin, splitting the Party; it was Trotsky who had indeed committed the very treason that Lenin feared and of which he had mistakenly accused me. Now it was only a matter of time before I could use Lenin's own weapon—the secret clause allowing for Oppositionists to be expelled by a two-thirds vote—against Trotsky.

The only question was what Lenin would do. But then God voted again. Five days later, Lenin died. The autopsy revealed advanced arteriosclerosis of the brain, which had so hardened that it gave off pings when touched, as if made of ceramics.

I moved fast. First, I played a nice trick on Trotsky. I telegraphed him, informing him of Lenin's death and saying that the funeral would be held on January 26. That would not allow him time to return, so he should continue on his way. Actually, the funeral was to be held a day later, which would have given Trotsky just enough time to return to Moscow. His greatest blunder was to believe me.

The day of the funeral was bitter cold, but millions attended. At precisely four o'clock, every factory siren, locomotive whistle, fog horn, and artillery piece in all Russia sounded for exactly three minutes.

People were shocked by Trotsky's absence, a final proof of his arrogance and disrespect. And people were moved by the funeral oration that I delivered, having also been one of the principal pallbearers. I decided to strike a religious note, using the rhetorical flourishes I had learned in the seminary.

"Leaving us, Comrade Lenin ordered us to hold high and keep pure the great calling of Member of the Party. We vow to thee, Comrade Lenin, that we will honor this, thy commandment." (Meaning that there is no power in Russia besides the power of the Party.)

"Leaving us, Comrade Lenin enjoined us to keep the unity of the Party like the apple of our eye. We vow to thee, Comrade Lenin, that we will with honor fulfill this, thy commandment." (Meaning that Trotsky's absence was a sign that he was breaking ranks.)

"Leaving us, Comrade Lenin enjoined us to keep and strengthen the dictatorship of the proletariat. We vow to thee, Comrade Lenin, that we will not spare our strength to fulfill with honor this, thy commandment." (Meaning that the power and unity of the Party can only be kept by closing ranks behind Lenin's successor, who is of course the person delivering the oration, not the conspicuously and contemptuously absent Trotsky.)

Finally, over the strenuous objections of Lenin's widow, Krupskaya, I ordered his body embalmed and launched a competition to design a mausoleum on Red Square. Krupskaya insisted that Lenin would never have wanted any of that. She was right. But I wanted it, and I told her that if she didn't shut up we'd find another widow for Lenin.

I expected Trotsky to treat this period in microscopic detail, and yet so far he has written very little about it. Is it only because it all reminds him of the series of colossal blunders he made—opposing NEP, crushing Kronstadt, missing Lenin's funeral? Or is there some other reason? In fact, according to our sources, as of late January and early February 1940, Trotsky has stopped working on my biography altogether. Why has he fallen silent? Has Trotsky finally broken the code of my life?

32

Maybe I worry too much. Now it appears that Trotsky was not distracted by stumbling onto *that* but by the drumbeat that precedes assassination. The Mexican communist press has been attacking him ceaselessly, mercilessly. In the first months of 1940, the papers under our control, *La Voz de Mexico, El Popular, Futuro*, have been blasting him with all the usual epithets—"traitor," "slippery fish," "cur," "the new pontiff, Leon XXX"—and making the usual references to the "thirty pieces of silver" paid to Judas Iscariot, which is in fact the code name assigned Trotsky in his file at Lubyanka.

Trotsky's response—"This is the way people write who are preparing to change the pen for the machine gun"—indicates that he is now less concerned with my crimes than with his own mortality. In fact, he has picked up his pen again, but this time to write his own Testament, bidding farewell to life and to his wife, Natasha:

> If I had to begin all over again, I would of course try to avoid this or that mistake, but the main course of my life would remain unchanged. I shall die a proletarian revolutionist, a Marxist, a dialectical materialist, and consequently an irreconcilable atheist. My faith in the communist future of mankind is not less ardent, indeed it is firmer today than it was in the days of my youth.

> Natasha has just come up to the window from the courtyard and opened it wider so that the air may enter more freely into my room. I can see the bright green strip of grass beneath the wall, and the clear blue sky above the wall, and sunlight everywhere. Life is beautiful. Let the future generations cleanse it of all evil, oppression, and violence and enjoy it to the full.

Very nice. But still I have to be concerned that the prospect of death might resharpen Trotsky's faculties. I remember the words of a cellmate of mine, from the old days in the Tsarist prisons, who was scheduled to be hanged in a day's time: "It's all so clear now, so clear. I was asleep my whole life, in a fog, only now is everything clear and real." So, even though the attacks by the Mexican press have distracted Trotsky, who has guessed what the fanfare is all about, he still has time for one great moment of clarity, like my friend in the cell.

According to the reports that flow from Eitington to Sudoplatov to Beria to me, this year's May Day demonstrations in Mexico City will include a group of at least twenty thousand communists calling for Trotsky's deportation. That should rattle him. And if all goes well, the actual attack on the fortress should take place no later than the end of May. Trotsky was prophetic when saying that the pen would be exchanged for the machine gun. Siqueiros, head of the assault group, has recently purchased a couple.

Meanwhile Ramón continues romancing Sylvia Agelof, who is often inside Trotsky's compound. Ramón, however, shows little interest in politics, Trotsky, or the villa. He pretends to be interested only in her and his business dealings, though he has recently allowed himself, under her influence, to take some passing interest in Trotsky's view of the world.

Eitington, who is still carrying on his own affair with Ramón's mother, Caridad, occasionally takes her to a restaurant where her son is dining with Sylvia Agelof. Though Eitington does not sit close enough to hear what they are saying—not that it matters, it's mostly nonsense and Ramón can in any case be debriefed later—he apparently enjoys observing the dumbshow of their gestures, how Ramón touches her hand, laughs at her little jokes, how she smiles to herself after he has excused himself from the table for a moment to use the men's room. On one occasion Eitington joined him there and, while they were pissing side by side, checked on his progress. Recently there was a little trouble.

"Tonight Sylvia told me that she doesn't want me ever to go with her into Trotsky's compound."

"Why not?"

"She did some checking up on me, went to my office. It's no big deal, but I think she's worried there's something fishy about my business and she doesn't want Trotsky embarrassed in any way. No more to it than that."

The budget for Operation Duck is already approaching the $500,000 mark, but some of that money was well spent indeed. Ramón, as part of his man-about-town image, purchased himself a big, beautiful Buick. Everybody likes riding in it and taking in the sights of Mexico. Among his recent passengers were the French Trotskyites Alfred and Marguerite Rosmer, who have just brought Trotsky's orphaned grandson to live with his grandfather. The Rosmers are staying inside the compound with Trotsky but from time to time go out for a drive or an evening's dinner with Sylvia and Ramón.

In March 1940 Sylvia has to return to New York and her job at the City Home Relief Bureau. Once again she makes Ramón promise to stay away from the compound. But then Alfred Rosmer falls ill. Someone is needed to ferry him back and forth from the hospital. Ramón does not so much volunteer as let himself be asked. Without ever laying eyes on Trotsky, Ramón now manages to enter the compound several times. He never stays long, just long enough to escort Rosmer, who, fortunately, moves slowly due to his illness. On some occasions Ramón makes use of his excellent visual memory and on others he is able to take photographs with a small concealed camera as he was trained to by Eitington in Paris. Foresight pays off.

We now have a much clearer idea of the layout of the villa, its defenses, weaknesses, routine, personnel, and so forth. A small mockup of the villa in the Trotsky section of Lubyanka is constantly updated as new information flows in. Ramón was also able to get a glimpse into Trotsky's study—the door open, the room empty. The furniture is the same as in the previous house: a writing table, a gooseneck lamp, Mexican chairs with thatched seats. And we know from Trotsky's own Testament what the view from the study is—green grass, white wall, blue sky.

On that basis I ordered our craftsmen at Lubyanka to create a life-size replica of Trotsky's study. I am basically satisfied with how it turned out, even though our own version of Trotsky's study still has a fresh sawdust smell, and the painting of a bright Mexican courtyard covering the window, which would otherwise reveal a grim Moscow winter, is on the crude side. Some nights I go there and sit at "Trotsky's desk" and read his latest pages about me, for now the old man has gone back to work, drumbeat or no drumbeat.

Yet the heart seems to have gone out of Trotsky. His writing has become fragmentary; he starts one thing, then switches to another. Maybe the prospect of imminent death has not sharpened his faculties but scattered them. Or maybe once again it's a matter of pride for him. The fatal blunders he made in the years between the Revolution and Lenin's death bore bitter fruit in the five years between Lenin's death and Trotsky's exile from the USSR in 1929.

I destroyed him a slice at a time. At least one major blow a year. In 1925 I had him removed from his post as Commissar of War and had his views identified as those of the dreaded Opposition. By 1926 I was able to have him expelled from the Politburo. "By 1927," says Trotsky, "the official sessions of the Central Committee became truly disgusting spectacles. No question was discussed on its merits. Everything was decided behind the scenes at a private session with

Stalin." Not wishing Trotsky to stay anyplace he did not feel welcome, by late 1927 my supporters voted him out of both the Central Committee and the Communist Party. A few months later, in January 1928, I had Trotsky exiled from Moscow to Alma-Ata in Kazakhstan, using the double at the railroad station in Moscow so Trotsky's departure would not result in speeches, protests, clashes with the police.

And recalling this reminded me that by now Trotsky Two should have had enough time to put on some weight and grow a goatee. On the eve of the 1940 May Day holidays, I summoned Trotsky Two to Lubyanka.

"Don't have a heart attack," I said as he entered the room pale as a ghost, having now realized that the Stalin who brought him the tea and sandwiches that night in the Kremlin was Stalin himself.

"And don't worry about our little conversation in the waiting room; you didn't say anything that could cost you your head," I said. "Nothing I can think of right now at least."

"I'm loyal."

"We'll see."

"What can I do for you tonight?"

"Sit at the writing table. Be Trotsky."

"Should I be doing anything? Reading, writing, thinking?"

"Good question. Sure, why not? Pick up a pen. There's paper there, isn't there? Good."

I lit a cigarette and began pacing the room. "I'll tell you what Trotsky's thinking. Can you take dictation?"

"If you don't go too fast."

"Don't be afraid to tell me if I'm going too fast. All right. Let me see. . . . Here goes Trotsky:

"Stalin exiled me to Alma-Ata in 1928. By then I was for all practical purposes out of the game. What I wrote before about Stalin arranging everything behind the scenes was not, strictly speaking, true. In the first place, politics are always arranged behind the scenes. And in the second place, Stalin did not have to arrange all that much either. His supporters needed only a word, a wink, or a nod to know what the Boss was thinking and what he wanted. And there was no question ever that what Stalin wanted was me, Leon Trotsky, out of the Party, out of the capital, and then finally, in 1929, out of the country.

"Nineteen twenty-nine was the greatest year in Stalin's life. He was the undisputed ruler of Soviet Russia, I had been exiled to Turkey, and the stock market had crashed in America. Except for one very short column, the entire issue of *Pravda* was devoted to Stalin on the occasion of his fiftieth birthday on December 21, 1929.

"History has proved that I, Leon Trotsky, could not have been more wrong in my doctrine of permanent revolution. Stalin was right—socialism could be built in one country at a time. Even Marx was wrong and only Stalin was right. The working class in the advanced industrial nations did not rise up in successful revolution after we showed the way in 1917. Socialism not only *could* be built in one country but *had to be.*

"After exiling me from the USSR, Stalin performed heroic labors in collectivizing agriculture and industrializing the nation. True, Stalin was forced to take certain harsh actions, but as in the Civil War, his 'hand did not tremble,' which is why he is so respected by the Russian people, who love strong drink, strong tobacco, strong leaders.

"But let us not forget that, despite all his strength, Stalin is a human being. Nowhere is this clearer than in his family life. In 1918 he married Nadya Alliluyeva. She was seventeen and he thirty-nine. Though she had always worshipped him, that did not in the least keep her from having her own opinions. She was a very modern woman. She even kept her own name when they married. She bore Stalin two children, Vassily and Svetlana, and also took good care of Yasha, Stalin's son from his first marriage. But Nadya clashed with Stalin, especially over the children. When Yasha tried to commit suicide by shooting himself in the chest, Stalin only laughed, saying, 'Hah! Missed! Can't even shoot straight.' Nadya took this as crudeness, but it wasn't. Stalin wanted his son to be a man, not a sensitive weakling who couldn't take the rigors of life. His joke was an effort to shame the lad back into his senses. With the contrariness typical of a woman, she also accused Stalin of being too soft on their own children, spoiling them with kisses and attention, playing little games with Svetlana where she was his 'boss' and ordered him around, to his immense amusement.

"Stalin was entirely faithful to her, but Nadya was not faithful to Stalin. Not in the conventional sense but in a much more important and deeper sense. Though she was a revolutionary and though she had fought by Stalin's side during the Civil War, Nadya could not accept some of the harshness that comes with being the leader of a country like Russia.

"Still, they had some very happy years together, especially in the beginning when the children were little. But really there must have been something faithless and unbalanced in her very nature, because in 1932, when Stalin was entertaining some friends at the table and said to her, 'Hey you, come have a drink,' meaning it in the most friendly, harmless way, she exploded, right there in front of the other men, his comrades. 'Don't you "hey you" me!' she yelled, and stormed out of the room. Later, back at their Kremlin apartment . . ."

"Later, back at their Kremlin apartment," repeated Trotsky Two, looking up from his labors after my pause had lengthened.

"I'm getting tired," I said. "That's enough for tonight. I just thought it might be amusing to see Trotsky writing the truth for a change."

Trotsky Two nodded.

There was no sense in finishing the sentence and saying that later, back in our Kremlin apartment, she committed the greatest of infidelities, suicide, especially since the official version was and remains that she died of a sudden illness. If I had run on and let Trotsky Two know something he had no need to know, he might begin fearing in earnest for his life and do something stupid. And I needed him hale and hearty.

"You look good in that white suit," I said, "but you're too pale. Take a two-week vacation down on the Black Sea and get some sun."

"Thank you very much. It would also be helpful to me to view some recent footage of Trotsky, to see how he moves, walks, gestures now. Is that possible?"

"Good idea. I'll see what I can do. Go home and get some sleep," I said, dismissing him abruptly.

Though the game with Trotsky Two had been amusing at first, it left me with a bitter taste in the end. It had brought back the final blowup with Nadya. It was over an engineer named Kovarsky, who had been awarded the Order of Lenin, then unmasked as a traitor and sentenced to death. Nadya was one of Kovarsky's admirers and became obsessed with the case. She began making inquiries. How could a patriot turn into a traitor overnight? Some other traitor apparently hinted to her that Kovarsky's real treason was not praising Stalin enough in his acceptance speech during the Order of Lenin award ceremonies.

She came to my office in the Kremlin and demanded to see me. "Why are you letting this happen?"

"I've told you a thousand times to keep out of these things."

"You know he's innocent. And you know the real reason he's been sentenced to die."

A long look passed between us. Finally, I said: "What do you want?"

"Do something about his sentence."

"All right, if you insist."

I picked up the phone and called Yagoda: "Kovarsky's sentence is to be carried out immediately."

Pale, trembling, Nadya said: "Now I see who you are, Joseph Stalin."

And that night, after I had tried to smooth things over by inviting her to join me and the comrades for a drink, she shot herself dead in our Kremlin apartment. And after all these years I still cannot understand how she could do that to our children, our family.

33

What a mess! Not only do those Mexican morons botch the assault on Trotsky's compound, but I have to learn about it from the press like everyone else because somehow the coded cables got screwed up en route. I go to bed thinking I'll wake up in a world in which my enemy and his archives have ceased to exist, only to find that their threat to me is greater than ever. Trotsky will be inspired to dig even deeper into my life, knowing that a botched attempt on his life can only mean that I will not allow the next attempt to fail. It's down to the wire now.

I did not summon either Beria or Sudoplatov immediately. Let them twitch, imagining my displeasure. And, until the cables finally arrived and were decoded, there was nothing to talk about. Not that what happened, or didn't happen, matters much anymore, except as a basis for not making the same mistakes twice.

Finally I summoned Beria and Sudoplatov to my dacha late in the evening. It was toward the end of May. France was about to fall.

Beria entered first, looking distressed, his expression intended to convey that he was taking this every bit as hard as I was. He smelled of his usual cheap cologne, but this time it was mixed with something acrid, urinous—fear. Sudoplatov looked downcast but determined.

We sat at a small table and drank red wine.

Looking at Beria, I said: "Perhaps I'm mistaken, but I always believed the function of Security was security. But the failure of the raid has put my life in jeopardy. If Trotsky is ever going to make his move on me, it has to be now that I've made mine on him. That's only logical, isn't it?"

"Yes, Comrade Stalin," said Beria, afraid to meet my eyes, and afraid not to.

Then, turning to Sudoplatov, I said: "And just exactly why did the raid fail?"

"The attempt failed because the assault team was composed of peasants, miners, artists—not professional assassins experienced in direct personal attack. Unfortunately, Eitington did not take part in the raid."

"Why not?"

"He wanted to keep it a purely Mexican affair, so that if any of the raiding party was caught, our network wouldn't be exposed."

"You have Eitington's report with you?"

"I do, Comrade Stalin," said Sudoplatov.

"Read it."

Sudoplatov cleared his throat and began: "The raiding party of twenty men assembled at a safe house on Cuba Street in the early hours of May 23, 1940. They were dressed in police and army uniforms, some of which had been stolen, some made by tailors. They traveled in four cars that also contained their weapons and equipment, two Thompson submachine guns, pistols, extra ammunition, a 1.5-kilo dynamite bomb, two incendiary bombs, an extension ladder, and rotary power saw. The cars were parked a few blocks from Trotsky's compound.

"In the meantime, two female comrades, Julia and Anita, who had rented an apartment in the vicinity, were giving a party. Julia and Anita had posed as whores and seduced some of the policemen, who were part of the permanent five-man post across the street from Trotsky's compound.

"The police had been 'softened up' by the whores' party and were easy to overpower and tie up. The group of twenty, now joined by a few others, proceeded to cut the phone lines to the house and the secret electric line to an alarm at police headquarters. The guard on gate duty at Trotsky's compound that night was Robert Sheldon Harte, twenty-three, son of a wealthy New York businessman, more an adventurous young man than a true Trotskyite. He had been won over to our side. At four A.M., he let the raiding party into the compound.

"Trotsky's house is T-shaped and single-storied, except for a two-story tower used for surveillance. The guards also sleep there. The raiding party broke into five groups as per plan. One group moved to a position outside the guard-tower doors. The other four groups took up positions on all four sides of Trotsky's bedroom, at the doors of the adjoining rooms and at the windows on either side. It was not possible to enter the bedroom itself because of a device that, once set, would open fire on anyone attempting to enter. At the same time, an incendiary bomb was placed in the yard and another by the archives in Trotsky's study. The dynamite bomb was also emplaced, but its timer was not yet set.

"On a signal from Siqueiros, the group by the guard-tower door opened fire, warning the guards that they would not be hurt unless they offered resistance. According to Harte, Trotsky had worked late that night on his biography of Comrade Stalin and had then taken sleeping powders. Still, hearing those first shots, he and his wife were able to wake and respond quickly, hiding under their bed. A second later the four groups surrounding Trotsky's bedroom opened fire with submachine guns and pistols, firing close to one hundred rounds in three to four minutes."

"Firing from all four sides! It's a miracle they didn't kill each other," I said.

"Continuing to fire, the group lit the incendiary bombs and set the timer on the dynamite bomb. Trotsky's two cars, which always have the keys in the ignition in case of emergency, were driven from the compound and abandoned a few blocks away to make pursuit impossible. It was necessary for the group to take with them Robert Sheldon Harte, who could identify the raiders, and to dispose of him later on.

"Neither of the incendiary bombs did any significant damage.

"Due to a technical defect, the dynamite bomb, which had the power to destroy the entire compound, failed to explode.

"The only injury caused by the raid was a slight flesh wound to the big toe of Trotsky's young grandson."

I laughed out loud. "All that planning and money and people and guns and cars and whores and power saws so that we could strike a blow where Trotsky is most vulnerable—his grandson's big toe!"

Both Beria and Sudoplatov listened attentively to the quality of my laughter, how much of its scorn was dangerous to them, how much of it forgiving. If they were listening well, their attention uncorrupted by fear, they would have heard that I had already kissed the whole mess good-bye and was ready to move on to the next phase. What still rankled me was the failure of the incendiary bomb placed by Trotsky's archives. If only that had worked, I could have written the whole thing off as a minor success. But not even a document was singed.

As a sign of my forgiveness, I ordered a light dinner for us, lamb in garlic sauce, potatoes, more wine. For a few minutes, we ate in silence, then I said: "What about lover boy?"

"Ramón?" said Sudoplatov.

"Yes, Ramón. He's been inside the compound now. He's won the trust of some of Trotsky's associates."

"His mission is still only to gather information," said Beria.

"Missions can change," I said, "especially when other missions fail."

"He did stab a sentry to death on a bridge during the Spanish Civil War," said Sudoplatov.

"And according to his file," I said, "he's a mountain climber and can smash a big block of ice with his Alpine ice axe."

"Physically, he's capable, no question," said Beria. "Psychologically, he needs to be prepared."

"Who has power over him?" I asked.

"His mother," said Beria.

"And who has power over her?"

"Eitington."

"They're still lovers?"

"Yes."

"Then it's clear how to proceed," I said. "This time Eitington stays involved right up to the end. No more Mexicans, no more painters."

"Yes, Comrade Stalin," said Beria and Sudoplatov almost in unison.

"I can see by your face you have a question," I said to Sudoplatov.

"Eitington's involvement could place our network of agents inside the Trotskyite movement in jeopardy and . . ."

I cut him off. "No Trotsky, no Trotskyites. The elimination of Trotsky will mean the total collapse of the Trotskyite movement."

"And our agents?" asked Sudoplatov.

"As I'm fond of saying," I said, looking at both of them at once, "no one is indispensable."

They both lowered their heads.

"Eitington is to be informed of the new tack. Inform him that my confidence in him remains undiminished. Eitington is to be personally responsible for Ramón's escape. However, in the event Ramón is unable to escape from Trotsky's compound, he must have in his possession a letter explaining his motives. We should play the love card—Trotsky opposed Ramón's marriage to Sylvia Agelof."

"And we could add that as a businessman with political leanings, Ramón had contributed money to the Trotskyite cause, but found out that it was being used for personal expenses by Trotsky and other members of his entourage," added Sudoplatov.

"Good," I said.

"And, number three," said Beria, warming to the task, "Trotsky was attempting to recruit Ramón into an international terrorist brigade whose mission was to assassinate Comrade Stalin."

"Bravo!" I said, letting Beria know his suggestion had won him some partial redemption.

As they were leaving, I took Beria by the sleeve and, looking into his owlish eyes, whispered: "Lavrenty, my dear, you have one hundred days."

34

Colonel Salazar, head of the Mexican secret police, in charge of investigating the attack on Trotsky's villa, asks the same question I did: How is it possible for more than twenty heavily armed men to fire hundreds of rounds and set off three bombs, with the only result being a flesh wound to the big toe of a boy? Salazar draws a wonderfully incorrect conclusion: The raid was actually staged by Trotsky to win sympathy for himself and his cause or to forestall an impending attack by Stalin's men. So Trotsky is now forced to waste valuable hours arguing with the police and defending himself in the press. Hours that could otherwise have been spent rummaging through his archives, which may well contain a bombshell of their own, if he knows where to look and how to see.

What I hate most of all about Operation Duck is how far away everything and everyone is. All the main players—Trotsky, Ramón, Caridad, Eitington—seem only like dark shapes, outlines, the way people looked to me from the roof of the building as I watched the bank robbery unfold on Erevan Square. Oddly enough, Kamo, my protégé who raced into the square on horseback disguised as a Tsarist officer and snatched up the money bag, turns out to be one of Ramón's heroes, a very good sign. Ramón too wants to perform acts of derring-do for the cause, only proving once again that history is made by cunning old men exploiting the stupidity of youth.

Ramón has not yet been informed that his assignment has changed from surveillance to assassination. His mother is balking at the idea. One of her sons has already given his life in the Spanish Civil War and, though she understands the importance of the assignment, she does not want to lose another.

But brilliant Eitington has ferreted out her fatal flaw. And what is it that this wild bohemian and flaming revolutionary wants and needs more than anything? Marriage. She's lonely, she's in love. Aside from the fact that Eitington already has two or three wives, he promises to marry Caridad, providing, of course, that she convinces Ramón to accept the honor of eliminating Trotsky.

Still unaware of what his assignment now is, Ramón, only four days after the failed attack, enters Trotsky's villa on May 28, 1940, on another of his banal and Buick-related errands. This time he has offered a ride to the Rosmers, who have to go to Vera Cruz, from where they will sail back to France.

He arrives at 7:58 in the morning. Trotsky is tending his rabbits and chickens. Ramón makes small talk with Trotsky, who complains that it is difficult to find the right scientific mixture of food for his rabbits. Ramón agrees, saying that without a properly balanced diet the rabbits' stomachs will become distended. With exquisite timing and as proof that he has no wish to impose himself on Trotsky, Ramón greets Trotsky's grandson, who has come out to the courtyard, hobbling a little because of the injury to his foot. Ramón has brought him a toy glider made of balsa wood as a present. He instructs the lad in how to make the plane dip and soar. The two of them take turns flying the plane about the courtyard, Ramón retrieving it when it gets stuck in one of the cactus plants that Trotsky cultivates in his garden.

Trotsky watches. Probably at that moment he is only a grandfather, happy in the morning sun.

As he cavorts with Trotsky's grandson, Ramón is taking photographs with a small, concealed camera. Construction has already begun in order to increase security at the villa. The barn door is being shut tight.

The good host, Trotsky invites the young man to breakfast, where Ramón takes a few more photographs. Trotsky looks older, shaken, indignant. As always, Trotsky talks too much. Confining himself mostly to the sort of pleasant chitchat at which he excels, Ramón does ask Trotsky how his work is going.

"There's never enough time," says Trotsky. "It looks as though France is about to fall to the Nazis and I'll have to write something about that too. And the police keep pestering me with questions. But today, France or no France, police or no police, I'm getting back to work on my book on Stalin."

"When can we see that in print?" asks Ramón.

"It won't be long; it's going well," says Trotsky. "And yet . . . you know how it is when you've just left on a trip and you have the feeling you've forgotten something but can't think what it is? That's the feeling I have with this book."

"Maybe it'll come to you yet."

"Maybe," says Trotsky, rising from the table as a sign it was time for him to go to work. Turning to his wife, he says with a rueful smile: "Another day, Natasha, courtesy of Stalin!"

We don't need anyone on the inside to know that fortifications on Trotsky's villa are now well underway. The walls are being made higher and strung with trip wires connected to alarm bells, which are occasionally set off by pigeons flying into them. New brick watchtowers are being erected, and there are now more guards to man them. Well-wishers have sent Trotsky a bulletproof vest and a siren as presents. The doors and windows of his bedroom are being fitted with steel plating. Trotsky hates the clang of steel. "This reminds me of the first jail I was in," he says. "The door makes the same sound."

On June 9, Ramón is ordered to report to New York in order to confer with Eitington. But the more important meeting will be the one between Ramón and his mother. On June 12, Ramón makes a very nice move. He visits Trotsky's compound very briefly, solely to leave his Buick there for the use of Trotsky's staff or of Trotsky himself, who still occasionally ventures out for trips to the dentist or the mountains. It's a nice move because it both further ingratiates him and gives him a perfectly humdrum reason to return to the compound—to retrieve his car.

Only two people know what really happened in that room in New York: Ramón and his mother, Caridad. Caridad recounted that conversation to Eitington as her superior and her lover, a mixture of report and pillow talk.

"Ramón," she said, "Comrade Stalin has personally selected you for this task. It is an enormous responsibility. You will go down in history."

"I don't want to do it."

"Why not?"

"Trotsky's harmless, and I've come to like him."

"He's not harmless. He's the one man Stalin fears. And whether you like him or not is of no importance. You might have liked the guard you stabbed to death on that bridge in Spain if you'd gotten to know him."

"That was war."

"So is this."

"But Trotsky's an old man."

"He's the same age as Stalin."

"But there's something dishonorable about it, drinking tea with him, playing with his grandson . . ."

"In Spain we killed Trotskyites. Now we kill Trotsky. And that's an honor."

"I just don't know if I can control myself."

"Are you my son?"

"Yes, mother."

"Then you can control yourself."

"But what am I really? Just a playboy; I like women and cars and good food. I'm in over my head."

"You're right, so far you've been little more than a playboy. Now's your chance to be a man, a real man, even a hero. Or do you want to stay a boy forever?"

"No, mother."

"So you'll do it then?"

"I can't."

"Listen to me, Ramón. Everything I've lived for depends on this. You know the little pistol I carry in my purse?"

"I do."

"If you don't accept this task, the shame will be too great for me. I'll blow my brains out, I swear it. So either you kill Trotsky or you kill your mother, because it'll be your finger on the trigger of that little pistol, understand, Ramón?"

"Yes, mother."

Ramón returns to Mexico City in July and in another nice move—or is it just reluctance to face the music?—he does not return to Trotsky's villa for a few weeks. It must be reluctance, because other reports of his behavior are not encouraging in the least. He holes up in his hotel room for days, either refusing to see Sylvia Agelof or arguing with her. Eitington reports that Ramón looks pale, nervous, ill.

Finally, on July 29, he summons up the nerve to retrieve his Buick, taking Sylvia along. He makes inappropriate remarks to the guards, saying all their new fortifications won't help, Stalin will use other methods next time. Fortunately, like everyone else at the compound, the guards treat him as a lightweight and pay little attention to his remarks, especially after he admits not having even paid a single visit to Trotskyite headquarters in New York. Since Ramón had displayed some interest in Trotsky's politics of late and had even made financial contributions to the cause (so that later he could say his funds were used for personal, not political ends), this lapse strikes the guards as especially frivolous. When informed of this, Trotsky says of

Ramón: "It is true, of course, that he is rather light-minded and will probably not become a strong member of the Fourth International. Nevertheless, he can be won over. In order to build the Party, we must have confidence that people can be changed."

And indeed Ramón seems to be changing. Now, during his more frequent visits to the compound with Sylvia, he takes part in some of the political conversations, at first confining himself to a modest, minor role. Sylvia is proud that she has succeeded in transforming her apolitical "husband" into something of a Trotskyite. Ramón is even able to hold his own in the latest dispute. A portion of the American Trotskyite party has now broken with Trotsky, who maintains that Stalin's Russia is still, at least in potential, a workers' state and thus must be defended no matter what. Sylvia takes the "American" position, contending that Stalin's Russia is not worth defending because it has degenerated into bureaucratic tyranny. Ramón backs Trotsky in the dispute. Could anything more delicious be imagined? Trotsky sides with Stalin and is supported by Ramón!

35

It had to happen. Trotsky knows. He's finally put all the pieces together. *That* is no longer a secret.

This morning, by coded cable, I received a part of the bombshell that Trotsky plans to rush into print as an article in an American magazine:

> Now I am about to adduce a few rather unusual facts, supplemented by certain thoughts and suspicions, from the story of how a provincial revolutionist became the dictator of a great country. These thoughts and suspicions have not come to me full-blown. They matured slowly, and whenever they occurred to me in the past, I brushed them aside as the product of an excessive mistrustfulness. But the Moscow trials—which revealed an infernal hive of intrigues, forgeries, falsifications, surreptitious poisonings, and murders backed by the Kremlin dictator—have cast a sinister light on the preceding years. I began to ask myself with growing insistency: What was Stalin's actual role at the time of Lenin's illness? Did not the disciple do something to expedite his master's death?
>
> I realize more than anyone the monstrosity of such suspicion. But that cannot be helped, when it follows from the circumstance, the facts, and Stalin's very character. In 1922, the ap-

prehensive Lenin had warned: "That cook will prepare nothing but peppery dishes." They proved to be not only peppery but poisoned. . . .

I should add that every fact I mention, every reference and quotation, can be substantiated either by official Soviet publications or by documents preserved in my archives.

During Lenin's second illness, toward the end of February 1923, at a meeting of the Politburo members Zinoviev, Kamenev, and the author of these lines, Stalin informed us, after the departure of the secretary, that Lenin had suddenly called him in and had asked him for poison. Lenin was again losing the faculty of speech, considered his situation hopeless, foresaw the approach of a new stroke, and did not trust his physicians, whom he had no difficulty catching in contradictions. His mind was perfectly clear and he suffered unendurably. I was able to follow the course of Lenin's illness day by day through the physician we had in common, Doctor Guetier, who was also a family friend of ours.

"Is it possible that this is the end?" my wife and I would ask the doctor time and again.

"That cannot be said at all. Lenin can get on his feet again. He has a powerful constitution."

"And his mental faculties?"

"Basically, they will remain untouched. Not every note, perhaps, will keep its former purity, but the virtuoso will remain a virtuoso."

We continued to hope. Yet here I was unexpectedly confronted with the disclosure that Lenin, who seemed the very incarnation of the will to live, was seeking poison for himself. What must have been his inward state!

I recall how extraordinary, enigmatic, and out of tune with the circumstances Stalin's face seemed to me. The request he was transmitting to us was tragic, yet a sickly smile was transfixed on his face, as on a mask. We were not unfamiliar with discrepancy between his facial expression and his speech. But this time it was utterly insufferable. The horror of it was enhanced by Stalin's failure to express any opinion about Lenin's request, as if he were waiting to see what others would say: Did he want to catch the overtones of our reaction to it without committing himself? Or did he have some hidden thoughts of his own? . . .

"Naturally, we cannot even consider carrying out this request!" I exclaimed. "Dr. Guetier has not lost hope. Lenin can still recover."

"I told him all that," Stalin replied, not without a touch of annoyance. "But he wouldn't listen to reason. The Old Man is suffering. He says he wants to have the poison at hand—he'll use it only when he is convinced that his condition is hopeless."

"Anyway, it's out of the question," I insisted—this time, I think, with Zinoviev's support. "He might succumb to a passing mood and take the irrevocable step."

"The Old Man is suffering," Stalin repeated, staring vaguely past us and, as before, saying nothing one way or the other. . . . No vote was taken, since this was not a formal conference, but we parted with the implicit understanding that we could not even consider sending poison to Lenin.

Here naturally arises the question: How and why did Lenin, who at the time was extremely suspicious of Stalin, turn to him with such a request, which on the face of it presupposed the highest degree of personal confidence? A mere month before he made this request of Stalin, Lenin had written his pitiless postscript to the Testament. Several days after making this request, he broke off all personal relations with him. Stalin himself could not have failed to ask himself the question: Why did Lenin turn to him, of all people? The answer is simple: Lenin saw in Stalin the only man who would grant his tragic request, since he was directly interested in doing so. With his faultless instinct, the sick man guessed what was going on in the Kremlin and outside its

> walls and how Stalin really felt about him. Lenin did not even have to review the list of his closest comrades in order to say to himself that no one except Stalin would do him this "favor." At the same time, it is possible that he wanted to test Stalin: just how eager would the chef of the peppery dishes be to take advantage of this opportunity?

Yes, Lenin may have wanted to test me. I thought of it at the time. Even though we were sitting indoors, Lenin was wearing his cap.

"That looks like the same cap you've been wearing for years," I said.

"Years."

"Cold?"

"No."

"Then why wear it indoors?"

"Brings me luck," he said with an ironic grin. Speech cost him effort. He chose short words. "Many years ago," he continued, after drawing on some inner dynamo, "an old peasant said I'd die of a stroke. 'Why do you say that?' I asked him. 'Because of your thick neck,' he said. At the time I laughed, but now look at me: the old peasant was right."

"No, he wasn't," I said. "You're still with us."

"Barely, barely. I'll tell you one thing: if I couldn't move around, couldn't talk, I would want it over. To just sit in a chair, staring like an idiot, no, not for me."

"I wouldn't want that either."

"For me or for yourself?"

"Both."

"Ask your friend Yagoda what he's got that's quick and painless—just in case."

"All right," I said, "just in case. Meanwhile, just keep wearing your lucky cap."

What's most maddening about the latest fragment of Trotsky's writing is that it suddenly breaks off without his having added any of the documentation from his archives. The accusation is bad enough; proofs would be fatal. But what exactly does he have in those archives?

I ordered a coded cable be sent at once to Eitington, instructing him: (1) ANYTHING TROTSKY WRITES TO BE CABLED TO ME IMMEDIATELY; (2) ACCELERATE SCHEDULE FOR RAMON'S INFILTRATION OF TROTSKY ENTOURAGE. DATE FOR DIRECT ACTION SHOULD BE CHOSEN, AND KEPT.

The latest reports about Ramón have been mixed. On the one hand, Trotsky's wife, Natasha, seems to have taken a liking to him. And now Ramón is courting her as well, the way you court old ladies, with flowers and chocolates, compliments and little favors. On the other hand, Ramón has been dangerously sloppy about his cover story. He tells some people he's involved in a road engineering project, others that he's dealing in coconut oil, and still others that he trades diamonds for sugar and oil. Word has also reached me that while taking a delegation of American Trotskyites for a tour in his Buick, Ramón almost drove the car over a precipice, but stopped himself just in time, saying, That would have put an end to the whole thing.

Erratic behavior. The tension must be getting to him. He could break. And that musn't happen, especially now that Trotsky is on the verge of broadcasting his discovery to the world. But even that would matter much less with Trotsky dead and unable to take my place.

And now would be an especially excellent time to bring Operation Duck to a close. Still distracted by the fall of France in June, the world is now absorbed in the Battle of Britain. London is burning; German and British planes are clashing every day in the skies over England. Churchill is extolling the RAF pilots. "Never in the field of human conflict was so much owed by so many to so few." America, England, and France have too much else on their minds to be much concerned about the death of one old communist in Mexico.

* * *

The latest batch is just in. Trotsky has now made the connection between the final Moscow trial and the death of Lenin. It was inevitable. Once he got the main idea, all the rest had to follow.

> More than ten years before the notorious Moscow trials, Stalin had confessed to some comrades over a bottle of wine one summer night on the balcony of a summer resort that his highest delight in life was to keep a keen eye on an enemy, prepare everything painstakingly, mercilessly revenge himself, and then go to sleep. Later he avenged himself on a whole generation of Bolsheviks! There is no reason here to return to the Moscow judicial frame-ups. The judgment they were accorded in their day was both authoritative and exhaustive. But in order to understand the real Stalin and the manner of his behavior during the days of Lenin's illness and death, it is necessary to shed light on certain episodes of the last big trial staged in March 1938.
>
> A special place in the prisoner's dock was occupied by Yagoda, who had worked in the security organs for sixteen years, at first as an assistant chief, later as the head, and all the time in close contact with General Secretary Stalin as his most trusted aide in the fight against the Opposition. The system of confessions to crimes that had never been committed is Yagoda's handiwork, if not his brainchild. In 1933 Stalin rewarded Yagoda with the Order of Lenin; in 1935 he elevated him to the rank of General Commissar of State Defense—that is, Marshal of the Political Police. . . . In Yagoda's person a nonentity was elevated, known as such to all and held in contempt by all. The old revolutionists must have exchanged looks of indignation. Even in the submissive Politburo an attempt was made to oppose this. But some secret bound Stalin to Yagoda—apparently forever. Yet the mysterious bond was mysteriously broken. During the great "purge," Stalin decided to liquidate at the same time his fellow culprit, who knew too much. In April 1937, Yagoda was ar-

rested. As always, Stalin thus achieved several supplementary advantages: for the promise of a pardon, Yagoda assumed at the trial personal guilt for crimes rumor had ascribed to Stalin. Of course, the promise was not kept: Yagoda was executed. . . .

But exceedingly illuminating testimony was made public at that trial. According to the testimony of his secretary and confidant, Yagoda had a special poison chest, from which, as the need arose, he would obtain precious vials and entrust them to his agents with appropriate instructions. The chief of the security organs, a former pharmacist, displayed exceptional interest in poisons. He had at his disposal several toxicologists for whom he organized a special laboratory, providing it with means without stint and without control.

At the 1938 trial, Stalin charged Bukharin, as if incidentally, with having prepared in 1918 an attempt on Lenin's life. The naive and ardent Bukharin venerated Lenin. . . . Bukharin, "soft as wax," to use Lenin's expression, did not have and could not have had personal ambitious designs. If in the old days anyone had predicted that the time would come when Bukharin would be accused of an attempt on Lenin's life, each of us, and above all Lenin, would have laughed and advised putting such a prophet in an insane asylum. Why then did Stalin resort to such a patently absurd accusation? Most likely this was his answer to Bukharin's suspicions, carelessly expressed, with reference to Stalin himself. Generally, all the accusations are cut to this pattern. The basic elements of Stalin's frame-ups are not the products of pure fantasy; they are derived from reality—for the most part, from either the deeds or the designs of the chef of the peppery dishes himself. . . .

Lenin asked for poison at the end of February 1923. In the beginning of March he was again paralyzed. The medical prognosis at the time was cautiously unfavorable. Feeling more sure of himself, Stalin began to act as if Lenin were already dead. But the sick man fooled him. His powerful organism, supported by

> his inflexible will, reasserted itself. Toward winter Lenin began to improve slowly, to move around more freely; he listened to reading and read himself; his faculty of speech began to come back to him. The findings of his physicians became increasingly more hopeful.
>
> For Stalin himself it was . . . a question of . . . his own fate: either he could manage at once, this very day, to become the boss of the political machine and hence of the Party and of the country, or he would be relegated to a third-rate role for the rest of his life. Stalin was after power, all of it, come what may. He already had a firm grip on it. His goal was near, but the danger emanating from Lenin was even nearer. At this time Stalin must have made up his mind that it was imperative to act without delay. Everywhere he had accomplices whose fate was completely bound to his. At his side was the pharmacist, Yagoda. . . . Stalin could not have waited passively when his fate hung by a thread and the decision depended on a small, very small motion of his hand.

But I couldn't make that small, very small motion of my hand just like that. If it had been anyone else but Lenin, my hand would not have hesitated. But Lenin! It was not only my admiration for the man, all the years we went back, what we'd been through together. It was also the danger of losing everything, power, my life. If any hint of my involvement in Lenin's death reached Trotsky or any of the rest of them, it'd be my turn for a bullet behind the ear. But if I didn't act, I would indeed be "relegated to a third-rate role" for the rest of my life.

I couldn't concentrate on anything. I smoked, I sat alone in my office for hours, staring at papers that had become meaningless.

Finally, late one night I went for a walk on Red Square, instructing my bodyguard to stay well behind me, not that there was much danger to fear in those days, at that time of night. I paused by the large circular stone where beheadings were performed in the old days and for a moment imagined the feel of the cool stone because, for all practical purposes, my head might soon well be on the block. Then I looked up to the floodlit cupolas of St. Basil's Church, but this time what I remembered was not the architect who Ivan the Terrible had blinded but the fact that Ivan had killed his own son, who he suspected of treason. And that had driven Ivan mad. Some crimes were more than the mind could stand. This time I could not take Ivan as my hero. Even Ivan failed me in my hour of need. I was without hope. I who had begun with such hope. I who had once even been the poet of hope. That train of thought must have sparked something in my mind, because a moment later my lips began to move slightly as one of those poems came back to me across the space of thirty years:

> Know this, he who fell to earth like ashes,
> and was so very long oppressed,
> will rise higher than great mountains
> on the wings of shining hope.

At first I brushed the memory aside. But then I looked deeper. This was, after all, my soul speaking. The hope of my youth. Was I really going to betray my youth, my dreams, myself, and let my life be turned to rags and shit?

I summoned Yagoda at once, Yagoda who thirteen years later I would personally interrogate, blinding his eyes with floodlights in a cell in Lubyanka.

We met in Lubyanka this time too, in one of his basement laboratories that smelled of burned alcohol and noxious chemicals.

"Welcome to my pharmacy," said Yagoda with a smile to break the tension. A late-night call meant a crisis of some sort, he knew. But smiles always seemed out of place on his hound-dog face with its postage-stamp mustache.

"And you were a pharmacist before the Revolution, weren't you?"

"I was."

"A Jewish profession."

"It is."

"But in the new Russia Jews can rise higher than that."

"And Georgians too."

"Yes, and Georgians too. Perhaps even a certain Jew and a certain Georgian could work together and rise very high."

"How high could that certain Jew rise?"

"That Jew could find himself not just employed in a building on Lubyanka Square but in charge of it."

"That high?"

"That high."

"And how high could that certain Georgian rise?"

"That Georgian could be in charge of another building, the one on Red Square."

"And so how could that Jew help that Georgian?"

"Whenever something very tough had to be done—say, robbing a bank—a certain Russian leader would always turn to that Georgian for help. At one point that Russian suffered a stroke and was afraid he'd lose the power of speech and movement and would rather die than see that happen. So he asked that Georgian to bring him poison to have at hand in case he felt himself slipping away into helplessness."

"And so that Georgian wants that Jew to supply that poison for that Russian?"

"Not exactly."

"Meaning?"

"The Russian should be supplied with that poison, but not quite in the way he desires."

"I see. I think I see."

"It's a small difference, really. His request should of course be honored, but in a way that best serves the interests of the cause he devoted his life to, which is what he himself would want."

"Of course."

"Now, since that Russian has become very particular about what he eats and always makes a point of eating with others, the question is: Is there any other way of granting his request?"

"Well," said Yagoda, "the body's largest organ is the skin. There are certain substances that can be absorbed through the skin, but they need time and repeated exposure."

"Would those substances work if they were applied to something like, say, the sweatband of a favorite cap?"

"Should. And I have also heard that that Russian leader is to be fitted for a special orthopedic shoe. But you should know that minute traces could still be detected by an autopsy."

"Let me worry about that."

"Anything else?"

"All the people who work in the house where that Russian is living—the gardeners, the cooks, the laundry women—those are all your people?"

"Of course."

"When it's all over, all those in any way involved should be convicted at once of capital crimes."

"As well they should."

I'm not afraid that the conversation was recorded or that Yagoda took notes on it and hid them away. If he had any such documentation, he would have used it as a bargaining chip when I interrogated him in Lubyanka. But, consumed with the power struggle after Lenin's death, I had trusted Yagoda to dispose of all the people involved. The lab people. Whoever brought the substance to the house where Lenin was living. Whoever was in charge of applying a daily dose to the sweatband of Lenin's cap or to the inside of his orthopedic shoe. Had they all in fact been executed? Did Yagoda overlook anyone, spare anyone? Where is that person now? Could he even be in Mexico?

According to the latest reports from Mexico, Trotsky has not received any unusual visitors recently. But that doesn't prove anything. Trotsky wouldn't want anyone who could testify about the death of

Lenin appearing at his compound in Mexico. Any witnesses or participants were probably safely in New York.

In fact, things are unusually quiet at Trotsky's residence—the old man is devoting himself full-steam to his article on my poisoning Lenin. The only recent visitor of note was Ramón, who brought Trotsky's wife a box of chocolates on July 31, then returned with Sylvia Agelof on August 8 for tea with the Trotskys, where once again politics were discussed. Now Ramón is supporting Trotsky even more ardently. Trotsky has taken a liking to Ramón, but his erratic behavior has also begun to raise some eyebrows in the compound.

If Ramón cracks now, heads will roll from Mexico to Moscow. I summon Beria.

"Lavrenty, what's today's date?" I ask.

"Today? August 9, 1940."

"And what day was the Siqueiros raid?"

"May 23."

"That's right. And how many days did I give you after that to finish up with Trotsky?"

"One hundred."

"So, how many left?"

"Three weeks and a day."

"Is Ramón losing his nerve?"

"He'll be all right."

"So you say."

"Eitington's keeping watch on him. And so's his mother."

"I have an idea. Actually, two. One I got from something Trotsky wrote on board ship while sailing to Mexico. He said, 'Stalin doesn't attack his opponent's ideas, he attacks his skull.'"

Beria snorts with appreciation.

"I agree," I say, "not a bad line. But that got me to thinking. We know that Trotsky is against visitors being searched. Ramón is a mountain climber. Why couldn't he conceal an ice axe under a coat or in a briefcase?"

"It's an idea," says Beria. "Still, it calls for a lot of . . . direct physical involvement. The nice thing about a pistol is that you just pull a little piece of metal with one finger and, bam! the person's dead."

"So let him bring a pistol too."

"And Ramón could only use the ice axe if they were alone. The pistol he could pull out anywhere."

"True," I say. "But that's where my other idea comes in. What does Trotsky like more than anything in the world? More than anything in the world, Trotsky likes to instruct. He even said that he was interested in recruiting Ramón for his organization, even though he considers Ramón light-minded."

"Yes?"

"Trotsky already thinks that Ramón has been politicized by his association with him. So let Ramón try his hand at writing something, I don't know, about the fall of France to Germany. Trotsky may even do him the honor of inviting him into his study to discuss the article. Once they're alone, I don't give a shit how Ramón does it—axe, bullet, knife—I just want it over. You've seen the latest slander Trotsky's cooked up."

"I have. Disgusting."

"And dangerous. Lavrenty, even before your time, the organs used the code name of 'Judas' for Trotsky. Let's shuffle things around a little. Let Trotsky be Jesus and let Ramón play Judas for a while."

"Your mother always said you should have been a priest."

I smile. "Three weeks and a day."

Instructions are immediately cabled to Eitington concerning Ramón. Ramón is to "write" an article on the division among the Trotskyites in France, good enough to interest Trotsky but with enough lapses and errors to rouse Trotsky's instinct to instruct.

Now things are moving. Trotsky took the bait. On August 17, Ramón arrives for an appointment to show his article to Trotsky. After the usual small talk by the rabbit hutch, the two of them go into Trotsky's study, where Trotsky sits down at his desk.

It should have happened then and there. I understand the need for preparation, dress rehearsal. But some opportunities only come once. Lately Ramón has been making indiscreet remarks that have put the Trotskys on their guard. He offered to invest money for the Trotskyite movement, which did not appeal at all to Trotsky. And he also made the mistake of sitting on the edge of Trotsky's desk while Trotsky read the manuscript, which he later said he found boring and confused. Why couldn't our people have written something a little better? And Trotsky didn't like the disrespect implied by Ramón's sitting on his desk, though he was too polite to mention it. But I understand. Ramón has his own needs. Some things you do for the soul. The important thing is that Ramón has arranged to see Trotsky one more time, on August 20, to show him the manuscript after Trotsky's suggestions have been incorporated. That Trotsky won't be able to resist.

Ramón will bring his ice axe concealed by his raincoat, and will carry a pistol, either to shoot Trotsky or to shoot his way out of the compound. Two cars will be waiting for Ramón, his mother in one, Eitington in the other. If everything goes according to plan, Ramón will kill Trotsky with the axe before Trotsky has the chance to grab the loaded pistol he keeps on his desk or even to press the alarm buzzer. Ramón will be able to calmly walk out the gate and drive away in his Buick, then switch to one of the two waiting cars, which will drive him to the airport where a private plane and a new passport will be waiting for him. But when does everything go according to plan?

Of course I prefer that Ramón escapes intact, but all that matters is that he kills Trotsky, who has now jiggled in the last key piece of the puzzle.

Trotsky has now realized that the telegram I sent him that made him miss Lenin's funeral was not only intended to disgrace him politically.

In the latest part of his article to reach me, Trotsky quotes that telegram: THE FUNERAL WILL TAKE PLACE ON SATURDAY. YOU WILL NOT

BE ABLE TO RETURN ON TIME. THE POLITBURO THINKS THAT BECAUSE OF THE STATE OF YOUR HEALTH YOU MUST PROCEED TO THE SANATORIUM IN SUKHUM. STALIN.

It took him sixteen years, but Trotsky has finally fathomed both why he was kept away from the funeral and the real reason Lenin was immediately embalmed:

> Stalin . . . might have feared that I would connect Lenin's death with the conversation about poison, would ask the doctors whether poisoning was involved and demand a special autopsy. It was, therefore, safer in all respects to keep me away until after the body had been embalmed and the viscera cremated, so a postmortem examination inspired by such suspicions would no longer be feasible.

Yes.

36

Politely, but with a slight frown of irritation, Trotsky shows Ramón into his study. Trotsky has on the blue French peasant's jacket he favors for gardening. Wearing a rakish hat, Ramón holds a typed article in one hand and has a tan raincoat draped over his other arm.

Trotsky sits down at his desk. On that desk is a large blotter, an ivory paper cutter, a gooseneck lamp, stacks of books and papers, a Dictaphone, and a .25-caliber automatic. Trotsky clears away some of the books and pushes the pistol to one side. As he does, he looks up at Ramón, a look of suspicion sharpening his gaze for a moment, but then he shakes it off.

Ramón smiles deferentially and hands Trotsky the article. Ramón moves behind Trotsky, to his left, as if to look over his shoulder as he reads, but really to prevent him from reaching the alarm switch. Ramón places his raincoat on the table, at the same time sliding out the ice axe by its sawn-off handle.

Trotsky adjusts his glasses and begins reading, scowling slightly. Waiting until Trotsky is fully absorbed, Ramón raises the axe above his own head with both hands and drives it into the back of Trotsky's skull.

Blood sprays everywhere as Trotsky howls in agony and outrage. The scream paralyzes Ramón, axe still in hand.

Trotsky jumps to his feet and begins hurling books at Ramón, inkwells, the Dictaphone. His flailing arms send blood-spattered papers flying from the desk.

Trotsky snatches the axe away from Ramón, then like a mad animal sinks his teeth into Ramón's hand. Ramón screams, which snaps him out of his paralysis. He shoves Trotsky, who staggers away, blinded by blood.

Trotsky almost collides with Natasha as she runs in. "What happened?" she cries, looking up at the ceiling for a second to see if something fell.

But then Trotsky points to Ramón.

She grasps Trotsky by the arm, looking back with terrified hatred at Ramón. His hand, reaching for his pistol in his coat, comes to a halt.

Natasha guides Trotsky for a few steps. Ramón stands and stares at what he has made happen, as if watching that were a greater responsibility than escaping.

Trotsky slumps to the floor. "Natasha, I love you."

She places a cushion under his head and begins swabbing the blood off his forehead and cheeks.

"Look what they've done to you," says Natasha.

"This is the end, Natasha," says Trotsky.

Weeping, she begins kissing his face.

Two big guards run in. They beat Ramón with their revolver butts. He offers no resistance. "Kill me," he says.

"Tell the boys not to kill him," says Trotsky weakly. "No, no, he must not be killed—he must be made to talk."

"They made me do it," pleads Ramón. "They've got my mother. Sylvia had nothing to do with it. . . . I'm not Stalin's agent. . . . It was just me."

Natasha covers Trotsky's chest and legs with a white shawl. She holds his bleeding head in both her hands and sobs inconsolably.

Laughing, applauding, springing up from my chair, I call out: "Bravo! Bravo!"

Trotsky Two rises to his feet and takes a little professional bow. The others, who are not actors but employees of Lubyanka, simply come to a stop and stand in expectation of orders.

"The axe?" I ask Trotsky Two.

"Rubber."

"And the blood's the same kind they use in the movies?" I ask.

"It is," says Trotsky Two.

Shaking my head in appreciation, I say: "Art is great."

The last few spattered pages are just fluttering to the floor like feathers after a pogrom.

* * *

It is late when I return to the Kremlin and undress for bed.

When I went to bed on the night Trotsky was killed and when I woke the next morning, I did not feel any of my famous "highest delight." I did not feel triumph, or relief, not even the satisfactions of a tidy conclusion. And that was more than a week ago.

Maybe, I thought, I feel nothing because the whole business happened so far away. Coded cables, newspaper photos, all just paper.

First, I considered doing a filmed reenactment, but there's so much equipment and they're always starting and stopping. So I decided a play would be better, the action live, continuous. The script was based exclusively on police and press accounts.

I pull the blanket up to my chin and turn off the light. The room is so dark I don't even know if my eyes are open or closed.

Still no surge of joy in my blood, no glow in the pit of my stomach.

Why do I still feel nothing? I should at least feel a twinge of regret—after all, I can never look forward to killing Trotsky again.

Or is this Trotsky's final attempt to destroy me, his death gutting my life of its meaning and drive?

No, that's not it either.

It's simple.

I feel nothing because nothing is all there is to feel.

The same nothing into which everyone goes, my father, my mother, my wives. My Trotsky. My Lenin.

The nothing in which I have always believed.

In the dark I can smell my tobacco-stained mustache as it rises in a smile.

Now I know what my name really means: Stalin is the strength to bear a world in which there is only nothing and yourself.

At last I have defeated God at loneliness.